RIPPED TO SHREDS

KINGDOM OF WOLVES

KATIE MAY

EXPRESSO PUBLISHING, LLC

To my dad, who I still don't let read my books. Hahaha. Never going to happen. Please stop asking. I don't wanna have to move to a foreign country and change my name.

FOREWORD

This is a shifter mafia/MC reverse harem romance and is not suitable for anyone under the age of 18. It contains strong language, sexual situations, and psychotic males. You must read Torn to Bits before Ripped to Shreds.

This is a part of the Kingdom of Wolves shared world. However, you do not need to read the other books in the series to enjoy this one. Each author has put her own twist on the wolves and the world, so please keep that in mind while reading. There will be differences from one book to the next, based on the author's interpretation of the world.

Enjoy!

The main character, Blair, is an assassin and spy for the bitten wolves. During a mission, she unwittingly captures the attention of Vincent and Valentina Davenport, the leaders of the supernatural mafia and a rivaling pack.

During the annual summit, where the four wolf packs meet up to discuss peace, Valentina offers a trade: Blair for peace between the Davenports and the bitten pack.

The other two packs—the Bloody Skulls and the Totemic Tribe—decide to throw their hats into the ring as well, mainly to screw with Valentina. Blair will date each prince for thirty days, and at the end of the ninety day period, she will be forced to choose one man to marry, thus creating an alliance with the pack she chooses.

She spends her first thirty days with Vincent and Valentina Davenport, who she becomes close to.

At the end of her thirty days with Vincent, she discovers a few shocking secrets.

One, his father was the man who murdered her entire family.

Two, the Bloody Skulls and Totemic Tribe want to ally and eradicate all bitten and lycan wolves.

And finally, Vincent Davenport is her fated mate.

Book one ends with Blair traveling to the Bloody Skulls' Clubhouse to spend her next thirty days with the VP, Mason.

<u>Wolf Types:</u>

Totemic: A ritual is performed to allow a wolf spirit to enter them, which means the wolf and human are two separate entities inside of one vessel. These shifters are capable of transforming into timber wolves at will.

Fenrir: They take on aggressive, wolf-like behavior but don't transform. Only their eyes change.

Lycan: Transformation decided by the moon. Traditional werewolves.

Bitten: Can change at will into wolves once bitten.

<u>PACKS:</u>

Totemic Tribe: Controls the North. Run by Sarai, the alpha. Made up of totemic wolves.

Bloody Skulls: Controls the West. Run by Grim, the president of the motorcycle club. Hates humans and bitten wolves. Made up primarily of fenrir wolves.

Davenports: Controls the East. Run by Vincent. Made up of lycan wolves.

Bittens: Controls the South. Run by Papa Gray. Members live in poverty. Made up of bitten wolves.

<u>CHARACTERS:</u>

Blair: Spy and assassin for the bitten wolves. Orphan. Recently discovered her mate is Vincent Davenport. Alpha.

Vincent: Leader of the Davenports and family head. Twin brother of Valentina. Recently discovered his mate is Blair Windsor. Alpha.

Mason: Vice president of the Bloody Skulls and son of Grim. Best friends with Grunt. Recently discovered his mate is Blair Windsor. Alpha.

Tai: Prince of the Totemic Tribe and son of Sarai. Fights every day to unseat his father but is overwhelmed by his four evil brothers. Recently discovered his mate is Blair Windsor. Alpha.

Valentina: Twin sister of Vincent. Prefers to use sharp words over sharp knives. Best friends with Blair. Beta.

Grunt: Bitten wolf and a part of the Bloody Skulls motorcycle club. Best friends with Mason. Had his vocal cords destroyed when he was a child, making him mute. Alpha.

Sarai: Leader of the Totemic Tribe and Tai's father. Abusive. Alpha.

Grim: President of the Bloody Skulls and Mason's father. Alpha.

Papa Gray: Leader of the bitten wolves. Blair's adoptive father. In a relationship with the head of security, Johnson. Alpha

Annabelle: Vincent and Valentina's kind mother and matriarch of the Davenport household. Omega.

Paco: Tai's best friend, a member of the Totemic Tribe, and one of Sarai's confidants. Beta.

PROLOGUE

VINCENT

There's something that happens to a man when his world is irrevocably altered. When his surroundings freeze, his mind shuts down, and he goes through life as if on autopilot.

He knows when to smile, when to laugh, when to nod, but inside, he is empty. Nothing but a vessel with organs struggling to function properly and clotted blood rushing through his veins.

I'm sure there's a word for such a state of being, but whatever that word is eludes me. I know nothing but the numbness that encases me in a block of ice. I know my heart is racing, my lungs are taking in air, and my chest is rising and falling steadily…but that's all I'm aware of. Everything else is nothing but a buzz—a pesky insect flying around my head too fast for me to squish.

Blair…

Her name plays on repeat in my head, an endless loop of "what now" and "what if." Questions that I know I won't get answers to.

My mate…is gone. Taken to my enemy's territory.

Worry for her cascades through me, nearly over-powering the numbness I've grown accustomed to. Along with that worry is an almost incandescent, white-hot fear that something will happen to her, something I won't be able to protect her from.

And then there's the jealousy.

So much jealousy, I fear I'll go blind from it. I want nothing more than to shoot that prick Mason between the eyes, the same way I did that slimy weapons dealer. I want him to pay for taking my girl.

When I close my eyes, I can see her straddling the back of his bike, her thin arms wrapped around his waist.

An angry growl escapes me before I can contain it, and my nails dig into my palms hard enough to draw blood.

I've heard about the things that go down at the Bloody Skulls' Clubhouse. They're a ruthless MC who see women as commodities and bitten wolves as nothing more than slaves. They only partook in this ridiculous competition to fuck with me and my sister.

But beneath the jealousy and fear and anguish… is something else. Something I don't care to name.

Because Blair will be away from me for sixty days, passed between Mason, the playboy from the Bloody Skulls, and Tai, the ruthless alpha's son from the Totemic Tribe. Because Blair will be forced to choose a man to marry after the allocated time.

Because I fear the man she chooses won't be me.

She's my fated mate—her wolf calling to my own, her soul caressing mine—yet I believe a part of her hates me, even if she doesn't want to admit it to herself. My face resembles the man who murdered her family, and my name represents everything she hates in this fucked up world. Privilege, speciesism, prosperity.

Vincent Davenport.

Heir to the Davenport empire.

My heart threatens to cleave in two as I stare out the living room window. All around me, staff hurry about to complete their tasks for the day, but the mansion has never felt emptier. Even in the presence of hundreds of people, I'm left in a crippling isolation that only grows more and more pronounced. Pain squeezes down on my heart like an iron vise as I keep my gaze fixed on the curving driveway that B disappeared down with that fuckwad Mason.

Blair…

"Vincent." My sister's haughty voice isn't enough to pull me out of my fog. Her manicured hand rests on my shoulder, and for a moment, she doesn't speak. Out of my periphery, I see her eyes glued to the window as well, a frown pulling at her lips. "I miss her too," she says at last.

A growl rumbles through my chest before I can stop it. "It's not the fucking same."

My twin drops her hand from my shoulder and gives me a glare, one that would cause lesser men to fall to their knees. She taps one high heel against the polished flooring and places her hands on her hips.

"Are you going to sit here and mope like a little bitch-baby?" she demands, a scowl still twisting her features. "Or are you going to do something about it?"

"What the fuck can I do, Val?" I demand, finally ripping my gaze from the window to give her my complete attention. Irritation splays itself across her face, and she gives me a look like I'm the stupidest fool to ever walk this earth.

And then, she smiles.

It's not a nice one.

"Why, my darling brother, I thought it would be obvious." She claps her hands together gleefully, that smile still firmly in place. But her eyes? Her eyes promise violence and pain. "We've already decided that the Bloody Skulls and Totemic Tribe are in need of new leadership…" She trails off, allowing me to put the remaining pieces of the puzzle together.

My eyes narrow. "Are you suggesting…?" I can barely believe it. It's too ludicrous, even for my sister. Blair must've weaseled her way into Valentina's cold, black heart to make her even suggest such a thing.

"I think it's about time we put this war into gear, don't you think, brother?"

THE BLOODY SKULLS

1

———

BLAIR

DAY 1

I wrap my arms even tighter around Mason's waist as around me, the scenery changes from highly congested trees to industrial warehouses and rickety homes. The wind blows the loose strands of my brown hair back as a heady sense of exhilaration bombards me.

I never would've suspected that I would *like* riding on the back of a motorcycle, but here I am.

Mason handles the bike with expert ease as he turns into the parking lot of a familiar, dilapidated bar—the Bloody Skulls' clubhouse. Skid marks join the ones already present on the asphalt as he twists us sharply to the side, directly in front of the main entrance.

"Home sweet home," Mason calls over the purr of the bike as he switches off the ignition.

I'm much slower than him getting off the metal machine, my legs clumsy and wobbly. When he reaches out a hand to steady me, I back away before I can stop myself. Something dark flashes in his eyes for the briefest of seconds before he smiles chipperly, throwing his bike keys into the air and catching them.

"You look skittish," he points out as I remove the helmet from my head, shaking out my brown hair. The strands have become tangled together, and I just know they'll be a bitch to get out.

"Probably because I'm at the home of my enemy," I retort.

His eyes dance with mirth. "You didn't seem to consider me an enemy when you put on that show at Wolves Den."

I don't get embarrassed by his words, despite knowing that was his intended reaction. If anything, I push my chest out even further and walk with a sway to my hips, as if my body has a mind of its own and it's reminding him of what he'll never have.

Especially if I'm to believe Vincent.

My mate.

That single word momentarily freezes my limbs, my heart racing in tandem to the blood rushing inside my head.

I'm Vincent Davenport's *fated mate*.

How can he be my mate? A man who's a self-professed serial killer? A man who's part of the underground, supernatural mafia? A man whose father murdered my entire family, making me an orphan and bitten shifter before I even knew my multiplication tables?

Almost absently, I touch the spot on my neck where he bit me. The wound has long since healed, but I swear I can feel the phantom pressure of his lips on my skin. It's almost like I can sense his very presence through that menial contact, like a sliver of wood in my soul that I don't want to remove but know I have to.

Unlike in movies and television shows, mating marks don't remain on the wolf's skin for long. Our natural healing tendencies kick in, which is a godsend, if you truly think about it. What woman wants to walk around with a giant hickey on her neck for the rest of her life? Not this one, that's for damn sure.

I felt the bond between us the night we had sex,

the silver cord that connected my soul to his, but…it has to be fake, right? After everything that has happened between us, everything that has happened to *me*, the world really isn't so cruel as to make him my fated mate and then rip me away from him, right? Right? It's not as if I don't care about him, because I do, but I can't afford to be tied to one man when the fate of my pack is on the line. And especially not when I feel a strange bond with the other two princes as well.

I can't afford to fall in love with any of these men, yet I fear I already have. The mere thought terrifies me unlike anything else I've ever experienced before.

And unfortunately for both Vincent and me, I can't act on these foreign sensations. I can't afford to even think about them, not when I know that there's a particular role I have to play in order to maintain the peace between all of our packs.

Every muscle in my body locks together, seizing as if they've been shocked repeatedly, and I don't relax until Mason places a hand on my shoulder, startling me out of my thoughts.

His blond brows furrow as he stares at me in concern. "You okay?"

"Fine," I snap briskly, shaking him off of me and stalking toward the entrance. Mason—or Bullseye, as he's known by the club—rushes to keep pace with me, a bright smile plastered on his angelic face.

Everything about Mason's appearance screams innocent and sweet. From his shoulder-length blond hair, piercing green eyes, and chiseled features, he could be ripped straight from the cover of a magazine or even a stained-glass window in church.

But there's a darkness in his eyes, a darkness that not even his ethereal beauty can hide, that warns you to run in the opposite direction, screaming and crying.

"Are you dumb, baby girl?" he practically purrs, grabbing my hand and forcing me to a stop.

I bristle at the insult. "What the fuck?"

"The fenrirs will eat you alive." He rolls his eyes as if my reaction both amuses and exasperates him in equal measure. "You can't just walk into the lion's den looking like a tasty, perfect bunny."

I bare my teeth but don't refute him—after all, he only speaks the truth.

I'm a bitten wolf, turned by a lycan many years ago. As such, the other shifters see me as somehow "lesser" than them.

The Davenports—one of the last lycan packs in the city—live in a mansion, controlling one-third of the town with a fist of pure ice. It's where I stayed the last thirty days, after Valentina Davenport, the stone-cold heiress, proposed a trade—me, for her pack's protection. In all actuality, she was just trying to win me for her brother. Or steal me, whichever word you prefer. As such, the wolf packs decided to trade me around like a piece of meat, like property, for thirty days each. After ninety days, I'll be forced to choose a husband from the three heirs.

Vincent, heir to the Davenport empire. Stony, impassive, sophisticated, and apparently, my fated mate.

Mason, the VP of the Bloody Skulls, a local motorcycle club who controls the west side of the town. A total flirt, a closeted psychopath, and the biggest prick I've ever met.

And finally, Tai, the alpha's son from the Totemic Tribe to the north of us. Arrogant, hot-headed, and sexy as hell.

All three of these tribes own the city and everyone in it, including my pack—the bitten wolves.

I'm nothing but a pawn for these packs to utilize and discard, a plaything for the princes. They claim that our "marriage" will spark an alliance between the bitten pack and whatever group I marry into, but I see this for what it is—a power play. A way to assert dominance over another section of the city and gather more warriors for the coming war.

When Mason intertwines our fingers and begins to swing our combined hands, I release a growl and try to pull myself free. He simply laughs and holds me tighter, completely unperturbed by my ire.

Before I can think better of it, I grab Mason's arm and tug it behind his back, applying just enough pressure for him to grunt in pain.

"Don't touch me," I hiss in his ear, and his body begins to shake. At first, I believe he's shaking in rage, but when I twist him around to face me, I realize it's in laughter. Tears actually stream down his face as he grips his stomach, keeling over.

"Fuck, that was hot," he praises around gasping chuckles.

I growl. "Mason, stop it."

"Mason, stop it," he mocks in an over-exaggerated imitation of my voice. When I simply cross my arms over my chest and glare at him, he throws his hands up in exasperation. "Fine! You're so sensitive today." He winks at me before striding toward the front door of the sleazy-looking bar.

I hurry to keep pace with him, refusing to be out by myself for longer than I need to. I tell myself it's because this place is disgusting and I don't want to attract a sexually transmitted disease, but I know that it's deeper than that. I'm…terrified. I'm in the heart of the enemy's stronghold, in unfamiliar terrain, and I'm drowning in waters too deep. I can try to swim, try to beat the current, but I know it'll only pull me under in a whirlpool I can't escape.

With Vincent and Valentina Davenport, I thought I knew what I could expect.

With Grim, Mason, and the rest of the Bloody Skulls? I have no fucking idea, and that concept is terrifying.

"Are you coming or what?" Mason calls from where he stands in the entrance of the clubhouse, that indecipherable expression I saw earlier reappearing on his face.

I glance around the parking lot mindlessly, struggling to get myself together, before clenching my jaw and stalking forward.

When I shoulder past Mason, he surprises the shit out of me by slapping my ass. I jump, startled, and a flare of heat I have no right feeling rushes through me. Instead of allowing that to show, however, I simply level him with a fierce glare over my shoulder. He holds up his hands unrepentantly and offers me that cocksure smile of his.

"My hand slipped," he says innocently in response to my look.

I snort. "Sure it did."

I venture a few steps in front of him, allowing my eyes to travel across the desolate, graffiti-covered bar with a heavy sense of trepidation and disgust.

The roughly hewn brick walls are covered in bright red, orange, and yellow spray paint. It appears as if someone tried to scrub some of the lewder comments away before eventually giving up. I see the upper half of a penis and a dim outline of a ball-sack below it.

Rickety wooden tables take up every square inch of flooring, each surrounded by mismatched chairs and stools. Numerous beer cans and poker chips rest beside platters of greasy burgers and half-eaten chicken tenders. A pool table sits opposite the bar, the green felt faded with age and use.

As I step inside the room, all eyes turn to look at me intently. I count twenty-two men—no, twenty-two *fenrir wolves*—present. Most of them are shirt-less besides their leather cuts, their tattoos displayed proudly on their arms and upper torsos. Every person I see has the same tattoo I saw on Mason once before—a white skull with blood cascading down its hollow cheeks.

An uneasy sensation—almost like an army of angry fire ants—erupts inside me at being the sole focus of all of their gazes.

Some of them stare at me with stark hunger, while others glare at me in disgust and pure, utter hatred.

Mason growls low in his throat and moves to stand beside me, slinging an arm over my shoulder and pulling me closer to him.

I don't push him away.

"Who's the bitch?" someone calls from the opposite end of the bar where he sits in a booth alongside three other men. He's a large, bearded man with a scar down his right cheek.

Mason's growl grows even louder, the noise nearly deafening.

"It's that bitten slut. From the summit," someone else exclaims. This one has a mop of red and orange hair and a lean, almost stringy physique. He reclines in his chair near the center of the room as a blonde bombshell in tight leather pants sucks his cock—right in plain view of the entire bar.

The man, noting the direction of my gaze, smirks devilishly and grabs the girl's hair, roughly pulling her to her feet. I'm about to insert myself, a growl of my own escaping my lips at his rough treatment of her, when I see the girl's lust-filled eyes and salacious grin. Without preamble, the man pulls her tight pants down, baring her pussy for everyone to see, and drops her on his cock. She releases a moan of her own, reaching for the ties of her corset to free her heavy breasts. The man's hand snakes around her body to pluck at one of her nipples as she kneads the flesh of her other tit.

But she barely seems to notice the man pounding into her—her gaze is intent on Mason.

Another growl threatens to escape me as I watch her hooded eyes lock on the man beside me, the lust in them plain to see. There's also a *familiarity* that has a red sheen distorting my vision, almost as if she's imagining his cock inside of her.

Where the fuck is this reaction coming from? I barely know Mason, and to be perfectly honest, I hate his guts.

Her breasts bounce wildly as the man ruts into her like a fucking demon, but she doesn't remove her gaze from Mason. For some odd reason, I can't bring myself to look back at him. Is he watching her? Is there lust in his gaze?

I knew when I first offered myself to the three packs that I wouldn't marry for love, and a part of me accepted that, but...

But something white-hot and searing—something akin to jealousy—threatens to strangle my airways. I want nothing more than to leap across the room and rip out the hussy's throat.

"Mason." Her husky voice is laced with desire as she blinks at him coyishly.

"Emerald," Mason greets from behind me, his tone expressionless.

I don't even realize I'm growling until Mason is directly behind me, one of his hands going to my throat in a hold that borders that precarious line between possessive and protective. His hard cock rubs against my ass, and something inside of me tightens.

But then his words penetrate the green haze consuming me. "I love it when you get jealous, baby girl. Watching your face turn bright red with anger and your eyes flash with fire. Watching your chest heave." His other hand moves to my shirt, a ghost of a touch over my breasts. "Fuck, you have the best fucking tits."

"You're so...crude," I murmur, trying to ignore my body's instinctive reaction to his presence. In front of me, the girl must've forgotten about trying to win over Mason...or she's too consumed by pleasure to really care that he doesn't seem to be into her. The bearded man I noted earlier is sucking on one of her tits, his tongue flicking around her nipple, while a third man is on his hands and knees, licking at her pussy. He doesn't seem to care when his tongue comes into contact with the other man's cock either.

The blonde throws her head back with a groan.

"You like this, don't you?" Mason whispers in my ear. "Who would've thought you would be such a kinky little shit?"

"I'm not turned on, if that's what you mean," I snap, though I can't peel my eyes away. It's not as if I'm getting turned on by them specifically, but the thought of three men touching me, worshipping me…

The bearded man removes his cock from his jeans as the girl pushes her breasts together, allowing him a place to enter. As he begins to fuck her tits, his hand reaches for the third man's cock, freeing it from its confines and then wrapping his thick hand around it.

All four of them groan in unison, and I feel myself grow wet.

"What turns you on, baby girl?" Mason continues to whisper in my ear, his hand sneaking beneath my top to cup my breast through the fabric of my bra. I should push him away, I should tell him to stop, but I remain silent, watching. I don't even stop him when his fingers creep beneath the fabric of my bra and squeeze my hard nipple, twisting to the point of pain. When I glance to the side, I see his gaze intent on me, almost as if he can't bring himself to look away.

In front of me, the man with red hair has fallen off the chair and onto the ground, dragging the girl with him so she's riding his cock. The entire bar has gone silent, watching the show with rapt fascination. I see more than one cock held in a fist.

"Does this type of thing happen a lot?" I pant out as the bearded man calls for someone named "Crystal."

A beautiful brunette with bronze skin and bright green eyes crawls out from underneath one of the tables—where she must've been pleasing one of the men—and moves to join the rapidly growing orgy pile. She's completely naked, her toned body instantly making me feel self-conscious.

"We're a ruthless MC gang, Blair." Mason nips at my ear. "If there's not at least one public orgy, then we're not fucking doing it right."

"Have you ever partaken in these…um…orgies?" The words leave my mouth before I can stop them—

before I can take them back. I want to retract my statement, but I know if I do, it'll only add fuel to the fire. I can't let him know how much he gets under my skin.

Crystal moves to her hands and knees, and the bearded man waits no time before thrusting into her from behind. The movement pushes the brunette forward, and she takes Emerald's breast into her mouth, her teeth biting down on the other woman's nipple.

"Fuck!" Emerald curses, bouncing erratically on the man's cock.

Mason squeezes my own breast before removing his hand from my shirt.

"I never would've expected you to be into watching," he muses instead of answering, taking a step away from me. I instantly feel bereft—which is ridiculous—and try to hide the uneasiness that permeates my system with a scowl.

"I'm not."

I spin to face him, ignoring the cries and grunts that echo behind me.

Mason narrows his eyes curiously, his blond head cocked to the side. I find great satisfaction that his eyes don't stray once to the show behind us.

"It's not the orgy that's turning you on, is it?" His

brows rise with amusement, something dark flashing in his beautiful green eyes.

"Fuck off." I move to push past him and go…I have no idea where…when he spins me back around.

"You like the idea of having multiple people touching your sweet body, don't you?" He takes a step closer until all I can feel is his body heat setting my skin ablaze. "You like the thought of three cocks entering your sweet holes—"

"Enough!" I throw my hands up in the air, giving him an exasperated eye roll. "It doesn't even matter if what you just said is true."

"Why is that?" He grabs my elbow and guides me toward a hallway. I can't help but glance back behind me one last time.

The bearded man is now fucking Emerald from behind as she licks at the brunette's—Crystal's— pussy. Crystal's mouth is open as the red-haired man guides his dick into it. His own mouth is occupied by the dick of the third and final man.

Screw massage trains—this is a fucking orgasm train, and one I would happily be a passenger on.

Mason fake coughs into his fist. "Kinky."

"Shut up!" I hiss. I try for flippant as I move to walk in front of him, putting an extra swing to my hips as I pass. I know his eyes are glued to my ass when I say, "You're right. I do think it'd be sexy as hell to be in a threesome…or foursome. Or even a fucking fivesome. But you want to know why this doesn't concern you?" I don't wait for him to respond. "Because one of those guys is *never* going to be you."

Before I even realize what's happening, my back is against the wall of the hallway and Mason's hand is around my throat once more. I know that if he applied even the slightest bit of pressure, he'd squeeze my windpipe, but he doesn't. If anything, his touch feels…erotic.

I shove the thought aside, drowning it in a wave of guilt.

How can I be feeling any lust toward Mason if Vincent is my fated mate?

But at the same time…how can Vincent be my fated mate if I'm feeling lust toward Mason?

Confusion joins the toxic cocktail of emotions currently swirling inside of me, though I push those thoughts aside to focus on Mason's growly words.

"You know what, baby girl? I'm willing to make a bet with you."

"A bet." I try to laugh, but when he presses down slightly on my throat, the noise comes out as a husky rasp. "What is up with you guys and betting?"

He ignores my quip and focuses his emerald orbs on me with laser-like intensity. "At the end of these thirty days, I bet that you'll fall madly and helplessly in love with me."

I snort before I can stop myself. "As if."

He doesn't appear amused, his eyes heating with twin fires that draw out all of the oxygen in the room.

"Blair…" he warns, his voice a low and predatory growl.

"Fine." I grab his wrist and throw it away from my throat, watching his eyes darken with surprise and then heat with lust. "You can believe that, but I know the truth." I take a step toward him until it's *his* back against the wall, *his* eyes dropping to my parted lips before flashing back up to meet my eyes. "At the end of the thirty days, *you'll* fall in love with *me*. Madly and helplessly."

"I don't believe in love," he whispers, once again staring at my lips.

"You say that now, but I—"

Movement to the left of Mason has me freezing, my head snapping up in alarm.

A large man stands at the end of the hall, his black, curly hair falling in front of his face and obscuring his features from view. But I'd know those eyes anywhere, even with the white scar pulling down the corner of his lips.

Time freezes. The world goes still. Everything stops.

All I can hear is the drum-shattering sound of blood sluicing in my ears as I turn to face the newcomer fully. Mason growls sharply, the noise laced with irritation, and grunts out, "What the fuck?"

"Oh my god," I whisper, tears filling my eyes. "How is this possible?"

2

MASON

DAY 1

Jealousy consumes me as I watch my mate run into the arms of my best friend. Hugging him. Touching him. Repeating his real name in both awe and reverence.

Grunt's face is slack in shock as he stares at her with wide, unreadable eyes.

A growl breaks free from my chest before I can stop it, the sound low and threatening. What the fuck does he think he's doing? Why is he *touching* her? I watch as he automatically wraps his arms around her waist, his face ashen, and she releases a strangled sob, burying her nose in his neck as she fucking inhales his scent.

What. The. *Fuck.*

I consider myself a reasonable man—most of the time—but I can't remember ever feeling such...such *rage* before. Such blinding, incandescent rage that burns a hole in my stomach like a corrosive acid.

Another growl escapes me before I can think better of it, and I take a step closer. My claws have elongated, breaking free of my fingertips, and I want nothing more than to stab them into my best friend's neck. The force of my jealousy and anger takes me by surprise...but only for a second. The rest of me understands that my reaction is normal. Well, as normal as it can be, considering I'm a psychopath.

A man is touching my mate. Crying into her hair. Hugging her.

Best friend or not, he can't be allowed to live.

"Mason," Blair gasps out, and her sweet voice momentarily pulls me out of my murderous resolve.

Fuck, what am I thinking? I can't just go around murdering my best friend for touching my mate in the middle of the hallway.

I'll need an alibi first. And a way to dispose of the body without anyone knowing.

Shaking my head once to clear my rapidly swirling thoughts, I try to keep the growl out of my voice as I answer. "Yes?" That one word is low and thunderous, and there's no doubt in my mind that both Blair and Grunt can hear the threat in it.

Grunt goes ramrod straight and stiffens almost imperceptibly, his eyes sharpening on my face as he carefully tries to detangle himself from Blair.

But she doesn't let him go.

If anything, she hugs him even tighter, looking almost petite and vulnerable up against his massive form.

I'm fucking livid. I literally see red in the corners of my vision, and my wolf struggles against the restraints in my mind, wanting nothing more than to break free and rip them apart. I want the walls to be painted red in Grunt's blood. I want the world to know what will happen if someone tries to take Blair from me. I want—

"Mason," Blair chokes out a second time, her sweet voice diverting my attention back to her. Still in Grunt's arms. Still clinging to him like her life depends on it. I'm gonna kill him. I'm gonna fucking maim him and— "This is my brother."

Her...?

Oh my god.

Well, shit. Look at me, jumping to conclusions. Preemptively planning a murder.

Whoops.

Her words calm my raging wolf enough for me to speak. "Your brother?"

My research told me that Blair was an orphan, that her entire family had been murdered when she was changed into a bitten wolf many years ago.

Apparently, that's not the full story.

Now that I'm not blinded by my jealousy, I can see distinct similarities between the two of them—heart-shaped faces, similar jawlines, dimples. But while Blair has brown wavy hair streaked with sunlit gold, Grunt has pitch-black hair that accentuates the scars on his face. Blair's eyes are a bright Caribbean blue, while Grunt's are dark brown, almost as black as his hair.

Something akin to wonderment explodes inside of me as I stare at the two of them together. I never knew what happened to my best friend's family—he'd been reluctant to speak of it—but I always assumed it was horrible. Why else would shadows enter his eyes whenever I brought it up? And Blair…

All I have ever wanted was for her to be happy. And now, she has her brother back.

I don't want to toot my own horn—toot fucking toot—but I think I can give myself a clap on the back for reuniting the two of them, even if it was unintentional.

"I'm happy for you both," I manage to say at last, though those words feel wrong in my mouth. Too... tame. They don't even begin to encapsulate all that I'm feeling. When Blair glances back up at her brother, wearing a radiant smile, I feel my own lips twitch upward instinctively. It's almost as if her happiness radiates off of her in palpable waves, affecting everyone in the immediate vicinity. How can I not be happy when she smiles like that?

Fuck, what is happening to me? For the first time in my life, I care about another person more than myself.

And Grunt...

He's been my best friend for years, despite my eccentricities, and I'm so fucking happy for him that I want to cry, something I haven't done in many, many years.

Blair's eyebrows scrunch together abruptly, and something dark flashes to life in her bright blue gaze. "What happened to you, Brett?" she demands, using a name I haven't heard in fucking years. Brett. When did we start calling him Grunt? I can't remember off the top of my head, but a sliver of unease embeds itself in my heart regardless. A name is crucial to a man's identity, and I can't help but feel that I rid Grunt's—Brett's—of his.

Grunt glances at me helplessly, lifting his hands up in the air, and I clear my throat to draw Blair's attention back to me.

"He can't answer you," I tell her. "When he was brought here many years ago, he…um…" Fuck, why is this so hard? "His vocal cords are damaged irreparably."

I watch Blair's face gradually drain of all color until she's as pale as a sheet. She takes a step backward, away from us both, until she's flush against the wall.

"His vocal cords…?" Horror infuses her words as she stares between me and her brother. Tears prick at her eyes, and I want nothing more than to breach the distance between us, pull her into my arms, and kiss her senseless until she forgets about this sadness she's feeling. But I can't do that. Not when this moment isn't about me and what I want—it's about her and the discovery that her older brother has been alive this entire time, kept as a slave for a rival pack.

Fuck, what must she be feeling? What must *he* be feeling? He assumed his sister was dead, and now he's uncovered the truth that she's not.

Oh…fuck.

What's he going to do when he discovers the deal

between the packs? When he discovers that I have thirty days to win her over? When he discovers that she's my fated mate?

I rather like my balls connected to my body, thank you very much.

Grunt and I may be best friends, but he can be positively savage when he wants to be. There's nothing he cares more about than his family, despite believing they've been dead for years.

Over Blair's shoulder, Grunt begins to sign desperately, his fingers a blur of motion.

I keep my voice low and mechanical as I translate so she understands I'm simply speaking for him. "I thought you were dead. I was told you were dead. I had no idea you were alive." Grunt drops his arms to his sides as something despondent flickers in his eyes. "Percy? Mom and Dad?"

"They're dead," Blair whispers, a single tear cascading down her cheek.

Fuck it.

I can't stop myself from marching forward and pulling her into my arms. Grunt's eyes narrow at where I touch her, the wheels in his head spinning, but before he can question me, Blair fires off more questions.

"How did you end up here? How are you alive? I

just…" She shakes her head rapidly from side to side, and I use my thumb to brush away that pesky wayward tear.

Grunt glances at me, his expression solemn, before focusing his attention on Blair once more.

Once again, I translate for him as he signs. "I think we should sit down and talk."

FIFTEEN MINUTES LATER, WE'RE IN THE EMPTY apartment upstairs, seated around a rickety wooden table. The apartment used to belong to Grim, my father, but when he purchased the hotel, he decided to move there permanently. As such, the apartment has served as my home away from home for as long as I can remember. I've never officially declared the space as my own, but everyone in the pack knows it belongs to me. I have an official apartment located across town, one I plan to bring Blair to as soon as I'm able, but this one is closer to all of the big events and meetings.

Grunt leans forward until he's resting his elbows on his knees, his dark gaze faraway and distant. I sit beside Blair opposite him at the table, one of my hands inconspicuously rubbing at her knee. She doesn't push me away, which is the only evidence I need in order to know that she's as distraught by this discovery as he is. Her eyes are shadowed with pain, though I can't tell if it's because of her own memories or what she believes are his. Maybe a combination of the two?

Either way, I want to eradicate that look of hurt from her eyes once and for all.

Finally, Grunt sits back in his seat and begins to sign, his movements slow and sluggish as he gathers his thoughts. I imagine they're swirling rapidly right now, just as mine are.

"When we were attacked…" he begins, dropping his hands to his lap with an exasperated scoff. I can tell he doesn't know where to start his story, but I don't dare interrupt, allowing him to gather his thoughts in peace. Blair leans forward anxiously, her fingers tapping repeatedly against her knee in tandem to her rapidly racing pulse. "When we were attacked," I translate as he begins to sign again, "I thought you were killed. I saw those fucking wolves rip you and the others to pieces." Tears drip down his cheeks, but he doesn't lift a hand to push them away.

"I wasn't," Blair whispers. "Dead, I mean. I thought you were though. I thought everyone was dead. After I was attacked, I ran. And I just kept running. I mean, what did I have to go back to? A dead family? All I knew was that I needed to get as far away from those fuckers as possible before they decided to finish me off. I had no idea what was happening to me, only that I started to change. It was during one of those changes that Papa Gray found me."

"The leader of the bitten wolves," Grunt signs. He freezes once more, his hands stilling in the air, before continuing. "The same thing happened to me, only I wasn't taken in by Papa Gray."

"You were taken in by the Bloody Skulls," Blair finishes for him, and he nods sharply, his jaw clenched.

"I was," he admits with a helpless shrug. "I thought they'd be able to help me understand my wolf. In a span of seconds, my entire world had been tipped on its axis. My family was dead, my vocal cords were shot to shit, and I..." He squeezes his eyelids shut. "I could turn into a fucking wolf." His chest gives a rattling heave. "After you ran, that Davenport fucker—"

"Vincent's dad," Blair supplies, and my jaw clenches hearing my enemy's name leaving her perfect lips.

I hate Vincent Davenport more than words can describe.

Grunt nods solemnly. "He hurt me. At the time, I thought it was simply because he was a sadistic bastard, but now I wonder if he blamed me for allowing you to escape…despite the fact I had no idea you were still alive in the first place." Almost absently, he rubs at the back of his neck, and I wonder if he's remembering the feel of hands around his throat, of knives slicing at his skin. If he'd been bitten *before* those bastards destroyed his vocal cords, he would've at least had a slim chance of restoring his voice with his wolf's accelerated healing. Instead, the bastards stuck their teeth in his neck *after* the horrendous act already occurred, leaving him silenced for the rest of his life.

Another thing that exacerbates my rage whenever I think about those Davenport fucks.

"And then?" Blair barely seems to be breathing, her eyes saucers in her heart-shaped face.

"And then…" His hands freeze as he takes a shuddering breath. "He bit me—sunk his huge ass teeth into my fucking neck as I sobbed. Kicked me. Punched me. Laughed in my face as I writhed in agony on the floor. He would've killed me too if the shifter posing as a police officer hadn't told them that backup was on its way. I don't know if the Davenports were scared of the humans or if those mobsters just didn't want to deal with them. Either way, they fled, and I was put in the custody of a social worker. Well, in the custody of a woman who I *thought* was a social worker. As it turns out, she worked for the Bloody Skulls. She faked my records, allowing everyone to believe I was dead as well, and then brought me here."

"Brett..." Blair's eyes turn haunted, and I fucking hate that. And I hate even more that I had a part to play in her pain, though it was unintentional.

"It's okay, Bee-bear," Grunt signs as I once again translate in a robotic voice. "I met Mase because of all of this." He nods toward me, a smile tugging up the corner of his lips. "He's like a brother to me."

"But..." Blair appears generally flabbergasted. Out of the corner of my eye—because a part of me is always watching Blair, even when she's not aware of it—I see her brows furrow together and her lips purse delicately. Her eyes flicker in my direction, and a blush decorates her cheeks when she notices that I'm still staring at her. Silly girl. Where else would I look? I haven't been able to take my eyes off of her since she slid off my motorcycle at the club-house. Well, except when I'm forced to look at her brother to translate for him. But he's not nearly as sexy as my mate. "But the Bloody Skulls use bitten wolves as slaves."

There's no mistaking the horror in her voice, and shame immediately bombards me. Not because I've ever partaken in any particular cruelties against the bitten wolves, but because I've been complacent, which is just as bad.

Fuck, what must Blair think of me? Nothing good, that's for damn sure. And I can't even blame her. I've been horrible to bitten wolves my entire life. Sure, I never abused or bullied them, but I never stepped in either. The only bitten wolf I ever developed a genuine connection with is Grunt, and even that might be tarnished if he discovers my infatuation with Blair.

"Tell me about your life here," she whispers. "Tell me everything."

The two of them talk for hours, and I'm grateful to see a smile on Blair's face, transforming her from simply beautiful to absolutely breathtaking. My heart thunders with emotion the longer I stare at her, though I keep my face carefully blank and devoid of anything that will give my turbulent thoughts away. Grunt regales her with stories of his childhood growing up here and how he became friends with me.

"The dumbass tried to cheat at poker when he was just a pup," he signs, a smile pulling up his lips. "I stepped in before the other wolves could beat him to death."

"Hey," I laugh, using my normal voice so Blair knows I'm no longer translating. "You only caught me cheating because you were trying to cheat as well."

He shrugs in a 'what can you do' type of way.

"I needed the money," he signs.

I honest to god blush with embarrassment when Grunt jokes with Blair about how much of a player I am. Or was. My playboy ways have changed since I met Blair.

I notice that he *doesn't* mention the horrid way some of the other fenrir wolves treated him. He doesn't tell her about the time he was kicked in the ribs for stealing a chunk of bread or about the day he was locked in the basement with no food or water in one-hundred-degree heat after he stared at my asshole father a second too long.

Grunt shelters her from the horrors of his past, and my respect for him grows exponentially.

Blair tells us a little bit about her childhood with

Gray and the other bitten wolves. About the trailer park and recreation center. About her close friend, Martha or something, and Johnson, the head of security. I can see by just looking at her that she loves the makeshift family she created. Grunt can see it too, for a softness enters his eyes I've never seen before.

A yawn splits Blair's face in two, and I exchange an amused glance with Grunt.

"Bedtime?" he signs, a wry grin twisting up his lips.

Her entire face falls. "I don't know…" She glances at him as if he's going to disappear if she looks away, as if he's a mirage and she's afraid that one blink will have him disperse like grains of sand in the wind.

Grunt leans forward and takes her hand, giving it a squeeze. "I'll be here tomorrow," he promises her.

"Okay…" She glances at me hesitantly, and I nod toward the bedroom just behind us.

"You can take the bed in here for now until we can find you more comfortable accommodations."

She still seems hesitant, her teeth nibbling her plush lower lip, before she nods once, gives Grunt a hug and me a nod, and then moves toward the bedroom. I already had her luggage brought here from the Davenport residence, so I hope she'll feel more comfortable finding familiar clothes and belongings.

When I hear the door close, I turn back to Grunt…and find him staring at me with hate-filled eyes.

"Grunt…"

Before I can even finish speaking, he's around the table and gripping my blond hair tightly. Pure vitriol spews from his eyes as he glares down at me. I half want to laugh—mainly because I've never seen him so pissed before and he once found me fucking his girlfriend—but the rest of me knows that laughing is the wrong thing to do. I'll probably be cut into pieces if I dared to even smile.

And…

And I want him to like me, dammit. *Really* like me. I want him to see me as a perfect match for his sister.

He releases me to sign, his movements jerky with agitation.

"Don't hurt my sister." He flashes me a warning look, one that promises violence and pain if I choose to ignore his ominous warning. I wonder if he's aware of Blair's purpose here or if he came up with his own conclusions. Either way, he's not a happy camper. He's actually a very angry and stabby camper.

My lips curl away from my teeth. "I don't know what—"

"If you hurt her, I'll kill you," he warns. "I just got her back." A muscle in his jaw twitches as he stares down at me. "And I'll be damned if I lose her again."

3

BLAIR

DAY 2

That night, I dream I'm back in my house, laughing with my mom and dad while Brett holds Percy in his arms. And like the dream I have almost every night, the front door is kicked open, glass shatters, and the screams of my family permeate the night air.

Only this time, something's different. I can't place my finger on it until I sit up in bed, my breathing erratic and a fine layer of sweat coating my skin.

In this dream, I wasn't alone. My hand was clasped in Brett's, just the two of us against the world.

Brett, who is…

Who's alive.

I fall back onto the bed and work to modulate my breathing.

Brett's alive. Here. With Mason. Here. Oh god. Brett's alive. He's—

"Oh good! You're awake!" a far too chipper voice declares a second before the blinds of my room are pushed open. Bright, piercing sunlight spills through the window in ribbons of gold, and a groan tears itself from my mouth. I twist in bed and bring the blankets up over my head in order to escape the blinding light.

"Mason, what the fuck are you doing?" I grumble into my pillow.

I didn't see him at all last night after I retired to the room he indicated—consisting of nothing but a queen-sized bed, a dresser, a television, and a connecting bathroom. It reminds me of something you would see in a hotel, the immaculately made bed giving it an unused feel.

"I imagine you're hungry," Mason singsongs, tugging at the quilt covering me. I growl sharply, attempting to keep it pulled up to my chin, but he simply laughs and grabs at the blanket once more. It slips through my fingers before I can stop it and lands in a discarded heap at the foot of my bed.

"What the fuck, *stronzo*?" I hiss, sitting upright in bed and baring my teeth.

Mason smiles at me, already dressed and ready to start his day. His shoulder-length blond hair is wet from his shower, the ends beginning to curl slightly in the humid air. He wears his leather cut over a long-sleeve gray shirt. The ensemble is completed with a pair of ripped blue jeans. My eyes take him all in—sticking on the way his shirt clings to his muscular forearms—when I realize he's doing the same to me. I dressed last night in a simple cami and sleep shorts, and my nipples are beaded nubs, poking through the thin cotton material.

Instead of being embarrassed or even indignant, I push out my chest even further. A low groan escapes him before he can stop it.

"Fuck me," he growls out, and I smirk, kicking my leg over the side of the bed to stand.

"Nah. Not interested," I say as I stumble out of bed and into the bathroom. Mason follows me, apparently unperturbed by my ire. If anything, he seems amused, his smirk growing by the second.

"You will be. We're about to start stage one of

OFIL," he says casually, crossing his arms over his chest and leaning against the door frame.

"OFIL? What the fuck is that? If you think you're filling any of these holes, you're sorely mistaken." I sift through my duffle bag and grab a clean bra, panties, jeans, and top.

"Operation Falling In Love," he answers, his keen eyes fixed on me intently. I have no idea what he sees, but a chill cascades through me anyway, reminiscent of the breath of winter itself.

"Oh. You're talking about the moment you fall helplessly and irrevocably in love with me," I say with a nod of understanding, and he snorts.

"You wish. As I said before, I don't do love. But you, on the other hand, will—holy fuck." His eyes bug out of his head as I rip my sleep shirt clean over my head. He drops his eyes to my breasts, and his tongue snakes out to lick his lips. "Fucking hell, Blair."

"What?" I ask innocently as I slowly shimmy off my sleep shorts and panties. I spin, giving him my back, as I bend at the waist and pull the clothes down the rest of the way.

"Fuck. Fuck. Fuck."

"I honestly don't know what the problem is." I move toward the shower and flick it on, turning the temperature as hot as it will go. Steam wafts from the showerhead almost instantly as I push aside the flimsy white curtain and test the water with my finger. Finding it the perfect temperature, I step beneath the spray and tilt my head back. "Shifters get naked all the damn time."

Out of my periphery, I note Mason's hard cock straining against his jeans. His mouth is slightly agape, and there's a glaze to his eyes that hadn't been there prior.

"Blair…" His words are a low rumble—a threat, a curse, and a prayer all at once.

I roll my eyes exaggeratedly and grab a bottle of soap that Mason has supplied for me. Squeezing a generous amount into my hands, I begin to rub it over my body, starting at my toned stomach and then up between my breasts.

Mason's hands have dropped to his sides, and I see his chest rise and fall with his heavy breaths. His eyes are intent on me, laser-focused, and goose-bumps pebble on my arms despite the heat. Slowly, I bring my hand to my tit and begin to lather it in soap, pulling my nipple between my fingers.

"Fuck!" Mason curses again, his hand moving to his pants to cup his junk.

I bring my other hand to my neglected breast and

knead it gently, twisting and plucking at my own nipple under the guise of washing it.

Slowly, ever so slowly, I bring one hand down my stomach and between my thighs…

And then wrench the shower curtain shut with my free hand.

"I'll be out in a minute!" I call to Mason when he's completely obscured from view. Only his outline is visible through the flimsy fabric, his muscles coiled and ready to spring. Knowing he's able to see my profile as well, I run my finger through my pussy lips while my other hand continues to play with my breast.

Mason's as silent as a panther as he slowly frees his cock from the confines of his pants. All I can see is the outline of something long and hard in his hand as he strokes it. My mouth waters, my breaths turning shallow, and all I want to do is rip open the curtain and watch him unravel. I want to see his cock in his hand as he brings himself to the precipice of pleasure, all because of me. Because he wants me.

Mason begins to stroke himself faster, and the need to look is too strong to ignore. With a growl, I rip open the curtain to see Mason standing exactly where I left him…

With my dildo in his hand.

"What the fuck?" I ask, my eyes widening in alarm.

Mason grins like the cat who ate the canary as he slowly lowers my dildo back into my duffle bag.

"Oh, I'm sorry. Did you think that was my real cock?" Mason asks in mock surprise. When I glare at him, he winks and takes a step out of the bathroom. "You're only allowed to see my cock when you fall helplessly, head over heels in love with me."

"Not happening," I grit out angrily.

He pouts. "Awww. Too bad. So sad. Because if you don't, all of this"—he gestures crudely to his body and his thick, erect cock still straining against his jeans—"won't be yours."

"Why would I want that when I already had Vincent Davenport's?" I snark, wanting him to hurt.

Something dark and dangerous flashes in his eyes—something I would almost describe as jealousy and possession—before his flirty mask settles back into place.

"I'm more than just a hot piece of meat, Blair. I don't like always being sexualized by you." He makes another face at me, his lower lip trembling, and my eyes roll so far into the back of my head, I see brain matter.

"Fuck off."

"Or fuck in…as in, fuck *in* you." He quirks an eyebrow. "No? We're not doing that?"

"I'm not falling in love with you." I angrily shut off the water and step out. A breeze from the air conditioning blows over me, causing the tiny hairs on my arm to stand on end. Wordlessly, Mason hands me a towel from the closet, and I take it with a scowl.

"You are. That's the whole point of OFIL." He raps his knuckles against the wall and gives me another disarming grin. I'm sure it's capable of deteriorating the panties off most women, but to be perfectly honest…I'm not like most women. I refuse to fall prey to his charm. "Now, get dressed. I'm taking you out to eat. You haven't eaten since you left the Davenport mansion." His entire face seems to twist when he says the name Davenport, almost like a dark cloud moving in front of the sun.

"I'm not hungry," I snarl. As if on cue, my traitorous stomach gives a growl, that bitch.

Mason's smirk widens. "Not hungry, you say?" He shakes his head, his blond hair fanning out around him. "Get dressed. I'll be waiting."

And with that, he turns on his heel and slams the door shut behind him.

MASON CAN GO EAT A DICK. OR A PIECE OF SHIT. OR A dick covered in shit and sprinkled with poison.

Who the fuck does he think he is?

Who the fuck do you think you are? a snide voice inquires in my head. My mind conjures up images of Vincent the last time I saw him, the despondency in his gaze as he watched me drive away.

I know in my heart that I didn't do anything wrong. Vincent and I are not in a committed relationship, and I don't necessarily know if I believe that we're mates. Yes, I feel inexplicably drawn toward him, but I also feel the same way about Mason.

How can I be mates with one man and still be sexually attracted to another?

You know the answer to that, Blair. You just don't want to consider the implications.

As I finish getting dressed for the day, my eyes dip to the burner phone hidden inside of my duffle bag.

Should I call Vincent? A part of me worries what his reaction will be if I do and if I don't.

Does he even care that I left? Has he already

moved on with another girl? Was everything between us just a lie? I'll never admit this to anyone —not even to myself—but I already miss our late-night reading sessions in his study, the only sound the crackle of fire in the hearth. I miss his stoicism and the way his laugh bubbled out of him, almost as if he was just as surprised as me.

What the fuck is happening to me?

"Blair, are you ready?" Mason calls from the other side of the door, rapping his knuckles against the wood. "Our reservation is in a half hour."

A petty part of me wants to make us late to our "reservation," but a bigger part of me is curious about what he has planned. Mason is…confusing, to say the least. I can tell he's attracted to me on a visceral level, but he confuses the shit out of me. It's ironic, because most people would assume Vincent is the hardest to read out of all of the men I'm forced to date. That man takes aloof and ice-cold to an entirely new level.

However, he has nothing on Mason, whose hot and cold mood swings give me emotional whiplash. I never know if he's planning my death or wanting to eat me out. The smile on his face is nothing but a mask, though I don't know what will happen when that impeccably crafted mask shatters. I know innately I need to fear Mason, but at the same time…

Why does my body burst into flames whenever he stares at me?

"Let's get this over with," I grumble, throwing the door open and shoving past him.

I can hear his smile as he follows behind me. "That's the spirit."

We take his motorcycle—of course—and drive only five minutes before we pull into a cute Mexican restaurant nestled between a hair salon and a drug store.

I eye the restaurant with barely veiled disgust. "I don't want to get food poisoning and shit myself," I huff as I climb off the bike.

"Do you really think I'll do that to you?" Mason asks in feigned horror. He places a hand on the small of my back and leads me toward the front entrance.

This part of the city is just as derelict as the rest of it. I spot more than a dozen homeless people wandering around, and the streets are littered with trash and fast food wrappers. Still, Mason appears unperturbed as he leads me through the heavy wooden door.

The inside is surprisingly clean and cozy, especially considering the fading paint decorating the exterior. Bright colors give the room a cheerful feel, and the mahogany tables are polished to perfection. Almost every table is already full, and the waitstaff bustles to and fro, carrying trays of food and menus. A pretty, black-haired hostess leads us to a table near the back, where candles provide the main lighting.

Mason immediately moves to pull my chair out for me, and with a roll of my eyes, I oblige, allowing him to push me forward.

"What are we doing, Mason?" I question after the hostess hands us two menus and retreats.

"I told you." He doesn't look up from where he pores over his lamented menu, a tiny wrinkle materializing between his blond brows. "I'm wooing you."

"Wooing me?" I cock an eyebrow, my lips curling away from my teeth. "Why the fuck would you do that?"

He releases a long, haggard sigh, as if my constant questions are annoying for him. "I told you. By the end of these thirty days, you're going to fall desperately in love with me. OFIL."

"That's not going to happen," I scoff, dragging my attention to the menu. It's hard, though. I really, really want to continue glaring daggers at Mason.

"It will," he insists. "And it'll start with the best damn Mexican food in the entire city."

I roll my eyes again just as the waitress arrives to take our orders. I absently point to something on the menu—too lost in my thoughts to see what it is—and she smiles as she jots it down. Once Mason orders, she takes our menus and promises to return with our drinks. It's only when she's gone do I place my elbows on the table and lean forward, meeting Mason's penetrating gaze.

"I don't know what game you think you're playing—"

"No game." He holds his hands up in the air as if he means to fend me off, though that amicable smile on his face doesn't dissipate. "I'm dating you."

"Dating?" I narrow my eyes. "I heard that you don't even know what that word means."

He feigns surprise. "You've been asking about me? My, my, Blair. I'm shocked."

"Don't get a big head," I deadpan before pausing. Then I add, "Or an even bigger head."

"Oh, ha, ha." He lazily licks his upper lip with his tongue as the waitress returns with our drinks. He waits until she's gone before resuming whatever he was going to say. "I told you, Blair. I'm not the enemy here."

"You kept my brother as a slave for years," I hiss, making sure to lower my voice so the nearby humans won't hear. The truth of that statement stabs at me like a flaming sword, somehow doing very little to thaw the ice surrounding my heart.

Mason flinches almost imperceptibly and runs a hand through his shoulder-length blond hair. "I didn't know he was your brother."

"And you think that makes it better? You *stronzi* see bitten wolves as nothing but slaves and property. You see us as lesser—"

"Hey," he interrupts, the smile finally slipping from his face and his eyes turning cold. "Don't pretend to know what I'm thinking. Don't group an entire entity of wolves into one box."

"So you're saying that the Bloody Skulls aren't known bigots?" I fire back. "And that you're not the VP?"

Once more, he winces, a pained grimace distorting his handsome face. When he catches my gaze, he works to smooth out his features, adapting an inscrutable mask. "Just because I'm a part of something doesn't mean I agree with them," he settles on at last.

"And that's the sad part, Mason." I shake my head slowly. "If you just sit back and watch atrocious acts unfold, does that make you any better than the people actually performing said acts? Does that make you any less liable? Any less culpable? If a woman is choking and the crowded restaurant she's in refuses to help her, are they any less responsible for her death?"

Something unreadable flitters across his expression, there and gone faster than a shooting bullet. He steeples his hands together on top of his chest and reclines further back in the rickety wooden chair.

For a moment, he doesn't speak, his bright green eyes locked on mine. I cock an eyebrow, daring him to say something, anything, but he doesn't. At least, not right away.

After a moment, he whispers, "I'm happy you got your brother back." A muscle in his jaw twitches. "I'm happy at least one of our stories ended with a happily ever after."

There's so much I want to say—much I want to accuse him of—but I hold my tongue. Mason didn't know Brett was my brother, and from what I gathered, Mason looked out for him when I didn't. When I *couldn't*. I want to be thankful for him, but I can't ignore the incandescent anger that burns through me.

"Me too, Mason. Me too." My voice is nothing but a hushed murmur, but I know he hears me. His chin dips down toward his chest, an acknowledgment of everything I don't dare to say out loud.

We finish the rest of the meal in silence.

And Mason's right—it's the best Mexican food I've ever eaten in my life.

4

BLAIR

DAYS 3 AND 4

"You have got to be kidding me," I lament, glaring at the waterslide.

Mason's smile is decidedly boyish as he slings an arm over my shoulder.

"Come on. It'll be fun." He winks at me as he steers me toward the slide.

Pirate's Cove Waterpark is located just outside of town, in a neighboring city that has a rather small shifter population. After once again being awoken at the asscrack of dawn, Mason instructed me to wear a bathing suit and a coverup for today's OFIL adventure.

Fucking Mason.

I suppose a positive benefit is that the man himself is currently shirtless, standing beside me like some sort of Greek god, with his muscular chest on display and golden hair fanning out around him. More than a few girls have stopped to ogle at him, and each and every time, I have to rein in the impulse to growl. Or stab. Or murder.

Or all of the above.

It isn't like Mason is doing much better, though. My purple polka-dot bikini leaves very little to the imagination, pushing up my breasts and just barely covering my ass. With my brown hair hanging in loose waves around me, I'm vain enough to admit I look sexy as hell.

Something Mason did not take into consideration when he decided to bring us here.

As if he's reading my thoughts, the Bloody Skulls' VP releases another threatening growl, pulling me even closer to his side. His eyes narrow on the group of college-aged men checking me out, all of them fit and tan. One of them—the largest of the group with a chiseled jawline, high cheekbones, and copper hair —winks at me.

"I'm going to murder him," Mason mutters, too low for the human to hear. "I'm going to murder him and eat his remains."

A laugh bubbles out of me before I can contain it. "Oh, please. As if every girl in the park isn't checking you out." I nod toward a group of giggling women standing beside a water fountain sculpted to resemble a pirate. A busty blonde bites her lower lip as her gaze travels languidly over Mason.

His arms tighten around me almost imperceptibly.

"I didn't even notice." His voice is a low growl directly beside my ear. "I'm too busy staring at you."

My heart stutters and gets caught in my throat, though outwardly I keep my expression placid.

"Well, you're going to be staring at my ass in five seconds, because we're going down the damn waterslide." I nod toward the monstrosity in the center of the park, towering over all the other slides.

Mason jumps from foot to foot like a kid in a candy store as he releases me. Fuck, why is that so adorable?

"Really? You'll go on the waterslide with me?" He gives me these pathetic, guileless puppy dog eyes, and I feel my own roll back into my head.

"Race you to the entrance," I sing, already breaking into the run despite the blatant signs that state "NO RUNNING IN THE PARK." What can I say? I live life dangerously.

Mason whoops behind me, fist-pumping the air, and eats up the distance between us, his long legs easily able to catch up to me. His arms band around my waist as he gives me a twirl, depositing me on my feet behind him.

I growl in warning, though a smile slips across my face unbidden. "That's cheating!" I call to his retreating back.

"All's fair in love and war!" he hollers with another whoop. I watch his back muscles ripple and dilate as he races toward the stairs leading to the slide. Thinking quickly, I raise my voice just enough to have it be picked up by the ridiculous wolf shifter.

"Sure." I adopt a flirty giggle as I creep forward. "You can have my number. You're really cute." I probably look absolutely ridiculous speaking to nothing but air, but if it gets the job done…

Less than five seconds later, Mason is in front of me, his nostrils flaring and his eyes narrowed into slits.

"What the fuck, Blair?" he demands, his beautiful face twisting into a scowl. "Who did you just give your number to?" His eyes shine bright with his wolf, and his tone is acerbic, almost bitter.

Why do I have the distinct impression he'd hunt down this person and kill him?

"You want to know who I gave my number to?" I lower my voice to a conspiratorial whisper, and he instinctively leans in to hear me better. Fortunately, there's nobody around, and our position is obscured by the lockers on either side of us.

Which is perfect for what I'm about to do.

"Blair, I swear to God, if you—OWWW!" His entire face creases in pain as I kick him in the shins. Hard. "Blair!"

I snort, covering my mouth with my hand, before pushing past him and racing toward the waterslide.

"Fucking hell," I hear him gripe, but there's definitely amusement in his voice. When I glance over my shoulder, he's still bent over but smiling. He catches my eye, and something wicked flashes in his gaze. I have no idea what he's planning, but whatever it is, it doesn't bode well for me.

I cast a furtive glance in both directions, still ensuring we're semi-alone, before biting my lower lip. And then I grab the bottom of my bikini and raise it, flashing him.

His eyes go hooded with desire, his pupils dilating, as he stares at my naked tits. I can see the visible outline of his cock straining against his swim trunks.

"Fuck, that's not fair, baby," he growls, stalking closer.

I rub my nipple between my thumb and pointer finger, stopping him mid-stride.

"I can keep doing this," I warn him, taking a step backward…

Toward the busy part of the park.

Since it's a school day, there are very few kids in the park. There are, however, dozens of college men and women.

"Blair…" His voice rumbles through me, sending heat blazing through my system.

"What?" I cock my head to the side innocently, taking another step backward. One more step and I'd be in the direct line of view of almost everyone in the park with us.

Including the men who checked me out earlier.

"You don't want them to see my tits?" I mock, quirking an eyebrow.

Another growl escapes him as he folds his arms over his chest. Waiting.

Smirking in delight, I drop my top back down, covering the girls, and then turn on my heel with a giggle. Breaking into a run, I take the stone steps of the waterslide three at a time, dimly aware of Mason pursuing me now that the initial threat of absolute nipple-hilation is over.

I'm panting by the time I make it to the entrance

of the slide, placing my hand on the railing in front of Mason before he can cut me in line.

The worker—a twenty-year old man with acne and facial hair—gives us a bemused look. That look transforms into one of desire and lust when he catches sight of me.

Mason's light-hearted laugh immediately tapers off, and once again, he bands an arm around my chest, pulling me flush against his stomach.

"Mine," he growls, though I'm not sure if his words are meant for me or the worker. Either way, the worker snaps his attention toward the water near his feet and nods for me to step forward. He instructs me to lie on my back, fold my arms over my chest, and cross my ankles together.

Just before I go down the slide, I call back to a waiting Mason, "I win!"

My words are swallowed up by the water rushing up my nose and mouth.

The next day, Mason doesn't take me to a waterpark.

Instead, he drives us to an art museum located in the wealthier part of town.

The walls of the building are constructed out of white stone, providing a modernistic flare to the structure. Stone pillars stand erected in front of the entrance, each one painted a variety of colors—red, green, blue, orange, and yellow. According to Mason, each artist in the museum was allowed to paint one of the stones, and I can't help but admire the artistic styles, each one unique and beautiful. Some strokes are smooth and soft, while others are harsh and jagged. Some are light enough you can make out the gray color of the stone underneath, while others are dark and vibrant.

We step through the glass doors, and I'm immediately bombarded by the smell of acrylic paint.

"This place shows the art of local artists, correct?" I query as I glance around the room.

The smooth marble of the lobby transitions into bamboo floorboards when we reach where the art is displayed. It's surprisingly sparse, with only a few paintings nailed to the wall and even less sculptures visible. Two benches rest against either wall, allowing people to sit when they get tired of walking. More rooms branch off of the main exhibit, though I can't quite see what they contain.

"Humans and shifters," Mason supplies conversationally as he moves toward the front desk to purchase us tickets. It looks like something you'd see in a grand hotel, not a shitty art museum in a town stricken by poverty. The black granite is polished so meticulously, I can see my reflection in it. Light from the single window reflects off of it in shades of gold and white.

The middle-aged woman manning the counter smiles when she sees us.

"Two tickets please," Mason says, flashing her a charming smile. She types something into her computer as Mason fishes out his credit card. When I offer to pay for us, he looks so affronted that I can't help but laugh.

"Spoiler alert, Mason," I tease. "It's twenty-twenty-one. The ladies are in charge now."

He snorts and rolls his grassy green eyes. "You can start paying after you fall head over heels in love with me. OFIL, remember?"

A harsh bark of laughter escapes me. "Paying for dates isn't the way to my heart, Mase."

Instead of being upset by my words, his smile grows, revealing those delectable dimples I always ache to kiss. And punch. "First, you said dates." He sounds so proud of the fact that all I can do is gape at him, at a loss for what to say.

"Excuse me?"

He wags his fingers excitedly as the woman behind the counter grabs two tickets from her printer.

"Date! You said date! You finally agree with me that we've been dating the last three days."

"I…um…I meant…"

"And second," his smile broadens even further, his eyes sparkling enigmatically, "you called me Mase. I must be growing on you."

I scoff, attempting to backtrack. Something akin to fear curls through my veins like flames. "Yeah, like a fungus."

Real smooth, Blair. Real smooth.

"Fortunately for you, we're not going on a date today." He claps his hands together gleefully as my heart collapses in my chest.

"We're not?"

Fuck, did my voice sound as high-pitched out loud as it did in my head? Disappointment and relief flare to life in my stomach, a corrosive mixture. I can feel my heart migrate to my throat.

"Nope." Mason dramatically pops the P. "You're actually meeting someone else. Someone who should be here in…" A wide smile erupts on his face as he glances at something over my shoulder. Or someone. "Right now!"

I turn around slowly, every muscle in my body spasming, to face the newcomer. The whole world disappears, and my breathing transforms into nothing but a ragged sound, distant through the sloshing of blood in my ears.

"Valentina?" I can scarcely believe it.

Valentina Davenport is here. In the same room as Mason, her sworn enemy.

What the fuck is happening?

She looks exactly as I remember her, her dark hair coiffed into a bun and her pencil skirt and blouse emphasizing her soft curves. Her eyes are wide with alarm when she glances at Mason before she schools her expression with a monumental amount of effort.

Adopting her customary scowl, one befitting her nickname as the ice queen, she asks, "Did you miss me?"

APPARENTLY, MASON CALLED VALENTINA AFTER HE found her contact information in my phone. My real phone, not the burner Vincent gave me before I left. He knew I missed her fiercely and wanted to surprise me.

Of course, Valentina didn't tell Vincent where she was going, knowing what his reaction would be.

"I'm just as surprised as you are," Valentina confesses, smoothing out her skirt as she sits beside me on one of the benches I noted earlier. Mason is in a separate room, perusing the paintings on display. I lost sight of him over ten minutes ago when he decided to leave us alone to "girl talk and gossip about his sexy ass." His words. "Fuck, I missed you, girl." Valentina wraps me in her arms once again before immediately pulling away and attempting to compose herself. She takes a deep breath, her hands unclenching from where they've been balled into fists, and gently tucks a wayward strand of hair back into her immaculate bun.

Valentina—always the perfectionist.

"Please tell me the Bloody Skulls are treating you okay," she says earnestly, giving my hands a squeeze. "We've been worried."

"It's been going fine," I assure her, my heart becoming lodged in my throat. It warms my heart that Valentina has been worried about me. And that Vincent has too, though thoughts of him have my heart going into palpitations. It's not healthy for me to even think his name. "Mason has been...well...

Mason." I gesture vaguely in the direction he disappeared down, and her lips purse.

"I don't trust this, Blair." She pierces me with an unreadable look. "The Bloody Skulls...they never do anything out of the goodness of their hearts, you know? Especially not Mason."

"He's not doing this out of the goodness of his heart, Val." I inconspicuously glance over her shoulder, ensuring that Mason is still out of earshot, before continuing. "He wants me to fall in love with him."

She gasps, the only outward crack in her apathetic exterior, before releasing a strangled laugh. "That's ridiculous. I mean, he obviously doesn't know that you're Vincent's mate and aren't capable of feeling attraction toward him, but to think that..." She trails off at whatever expression she sees on my face. How do I tell Valentina that I do find myself attracted to Mason, just as much as Vincent? That I think about them both every damn day, even when I know I shouldn't? Her brows knit together with anxiety. "What?"

"What what?" I decide to play dumb.

"What's that look for?" Her lips compress in a grim line as her eyes narrow suspiciously.

"What look?" I part my lips in a perfect O, though I probably look more constipated than innocent.

"What aren't you telling me?" She taps her manicured fingers against her thigh, her ruby-red lips thinning even further. When I remain silent, she grips my hand once more and gives it another squeeze. "Blair, Vincent may be my brother, but I'm on your side. Always. What all of us are doing to you…" She swallows heavily, and something I would almost describe as guilt flashes across her face. "It's not right, and I'm sorry for the role I had to play in it."

"Val…"

"So tell me what's wrong," she insists.

I worry my bottom lip with my teeth, struggling to articulate an answer. A part of me wants to confide in Valentina, confide in anyone, but I'm not sure if it's wise, especially with the discourse between all of the packs.

I want to tell her that my brother is still alive, that he's a member of the Bloody Skulls. That I'm not sure if Vincent's my mate because I also have a very strong attraction toward Mason. That I'm confused and scared and want nothing more than to be comforted like I used to be when I was a child.

Instead of saying any of that though, I flash her a

sheepish smile. "I'm fine. I promise. Nothing's wrong." Her eyes narrow, and when she opens her mouth to chastise me, I cut her off, "How's...Vincent?"

His name feels like lead in my stomach, a heavy weight that settles until it's impossible to remove.

Why do I miss him so goddamn much? Why do my thoughts drift to him late at night, in the safety of my bedroom?

Our sex had been incredible, but our connection...

It feels more than *just* sexual. Our time together has inexorably connected us in ways I can't encapsulate with mere words. He's all rough edges and sharp knives—and I have the distinct feeling he's on the verge of slashing me to ribbons—but I can't seem to stay away. He draws me toward him like a moth to a flame, and I know if I get too close, he'll burn me to ash.

Does that mean he's truly my mate?

Is that what this feeling is, causing my heart to batter my ribs with a frightening speed?

Valentina's heavy sigh pulls me out of my thoughts. "He's a mess, Blair. An absolute fucking mess. I've never seen him like this before." She pierces me with a penetrating stare, one that holds a thousand words I don't quite know the meaning of. "He's willing to do whatever it takes to get you back and in his arms. Do you understand what I'm saying?"

For some reason, her confession causes my heart to shatter, every piece cutting up my insides like glass.

"Val…"

Abruptly, her mouth snaps shut as her eyes focus on something just above my shoulder.

If the vitriol spewing from her eyes is any indication, the person arriving is *not* a friend.

"Mason," she says curtly, moving to her feet and smoothing out the creases in her skirt.

He ignores her and focuses on me. "You enjoy your time with your friend?"

Before I can answer, Valentina places a hand on my arm. Mason's eyes narrow on where she touches me, a growl reverberating from his throat.

I elbow him in the stomach. Hard.

"I'll see you, Blair," Valentina says with a pointed look I can't quite read. She glances over her shoulder at Mason. "Swamp monster," she greets primly.

"Raging bitch," he responds chirpily, nodding his head.

With a huff, she grabs her clutch and marches out

of the museum, encompassing the regal demeanor of a queen but without any of the arrogance.

Valentina Davenport is going to rule the world one day, you mark my words.

"But seriously," Mason begins, pulling me into his arms. For some inexplicable reason...I let him, resting my chin on his chest and staring up into his painfully handsome face. "Did you have fun?"

"I did." A soft smile touches my lips. "Thank you, Mase. I mean it. I know it couldn't have been easy for you."

He snorts and begins to rock us back and forth. "I had to sell a piece of my soul and dignity to the devil to arrange this meeting, but it was worth it." He taps my nose with the pad of his pointer finger before shrugging. "I like seeing you happy."

His words stab at my brain like a flaming blade, and before I realize what I'm doing, I'm detangling myself from his arms with a nervous laugh.

"Me too. Happy. Yes. You. Thanks...Buddy." I punch his shoulder with another hysterical giggle.

What the fuck is happening to me?

I feel like I'm falling, but I have no idea where or why.

Will heaven await me on the other side of this hole...or hell?

5

BLAIR

DAY 7

I'm so fucking exhausted, I can barely think straight.

The last few days have been a whirlwind of activity—all of Mason's attempts to win me over.

As I move into my bathroom to shower, I replay all of the dates Mason took me on. My fifth day at the Clubhouse in BS territory, he took me bowling, though the bastard got way too competitive.

Well, we *both* got way too competitive. It became less about bowling strikes and more about disrupting the other person while they were attempting to bowl.

Day six, we went paintballing, my favorite date.

There's something immensely appealing about shooting Mason with a gun. Call me sadistic, but I took great pleasure in seeing pink splotches litter his safety vest and helmet.

And today, we went to a Major League Baseball game, where we sat directly behind home plate. Mason bought me popcorn and a giant pretzel, so I spent most of the game flicking popcorn at his head, trying to get one piece to fall into the pocket of his gray shirt. And he spent the entire game staring at me with an indecipherable expression.

The sun crests the horizon, ribbons of bright orange and red, as I strip out of my sweaty clothes and step underneath the tepid water. The humidity has been brutal today, and my body has paid the consequences, a fine layer of sweat gluing my clothes to my skin and causing my hair to spasm.

As I meticulously shampoo my hair, I think about everything that has happened since I arrived at the Bloody Skulls' Clubhouse. My dates with Mason, where I've come to the startling realization that I have feelings for him. My time with Valentina. My late-night visitations with Brett, where we catch up on everything going on in our lives. He isn't necessarily pleased about the bet occurring between the rival packs, but there isn't anything he can do about it. I hate that I'm causing strife between Brett and Mason—especially since I have the distinct feeling they don't have many friends outside of each other—but there isn't anything I can say to console either of them.

We're just…stuck. Stuck in quicksand, rapidly sinking with no chance of reprieve. I can feel the sand entering my mouth and nostrils, the texture gritty and unpleasant, but I can't spit it out. All I can do is fall, fall, fall and pray that relief will reach me on the other side.

And then there's Vincent.

My heart thunders in my chest when I think about the aloof mobster. I don't quite know if this is what it means to have a broken heart or if it's something else entirely.

Thoughts of him have my gaze flickering to my phone, still nestled in the duffel bag on the bathroom sink. Mason told me he'd move me to a different apartment, but that has never happened. I think he secretly likes having me nearby in his space. I feel slightly guilty that I'm taking his bed while he's stuck on the couch, but then I decide that it's his choice. After all, he kidnapped me, in a way. A lumpy couch is the least he deserves.

But that damn phone…

I haven't checked it once since I arrived at the Clubhouse, and that's not because I don't want to. The problem is I want to *too* much. Way too damn much. The intensity of my feelings terrifies me in a way not much is capable of.

Turning off the water, I stand in the tub, dripping wet and shivering. Goosebumps pebble across my naked body as I stare, just stare, at where the phone is burning a hole in my duffel bag.

A part of me is honestly terrified Vincent has forgotten about me, that our time together meant less to him than it did to me. I mean, it's only been seven days since we last saw each other. Does he truly miss me like Valentina claimed?

The frigid air dances across my skin as I step out of the shower, dripping wet and shivering. I blindly reach for a towel on the rack and wrap it around my body, tucking it in at my chest.

One step.

Two steps.

Three steps.

I reach into the pocket of the bag and grab out the tiny black burner phone. My heart races so fast, I fear it'll gain arms and legs and crawl out of my chest like the girl from *The Ring*.

What if he called me?

What if he didn't?

Why the fuck do I care so much?

With bated breath, I flip open the phone.

The words *twenty missed calls* dance across the screen, along with a single voicemail, left only an hour ago.

I can scarcely breathe as I click on the tiny phone icon, pulling up the message.

"Blair." Vincent's cold, collected voice cracks my heart in two, mainly because that single word is stated with a vulnerability and fear I've never heard from him before. "I need to see you. Please. Can you meet me at Oakland Park tonight at seven? You don't have to respond…but I just want you to know, I'll be there. I hope you will be too."

That's it. A simple message that wages an entire war inside of my body, wreaking havoc on my system. My skin feels too hot, but my hands are hewn from solid ice. My tongue has turned to cotton in my mouth, making speech utterly impossible.

Oakland Park.

Tonight.

Seven.

I glance at the clock on the phone, my breath catching when I realize it's already six thirty.

If I'm doing this, if I'm meeting Vincent…

Then I'll have to leave. Now.

Am I really doing this? I question, slipping on a pair of jean shorts and a pink tank-top. There's no doubt that Mason and the rest of the Bloody Skulls will be furious if they discover I'm sneaking out to meet with the enemy.

Yet I can't stay away.

It's like my soul is tied to Vincent's, and every time he tugs, I'm helpless to resist the pull, the compulsion. Whenever I'm in his presence, it seems as if my feet move of their own accord until I'm directly in front of him, desperately wanting to wrap my arms around his muscular frame and hold him to me.

Is that the mate bond speaking? Or are they my true feelings, the ones that developed after I learned about the real him and spent all those days by his side?

Confusion wars with the intense, all-consuming need inside of me. A need to go to him, see him, talk to him.

What the fuck is wrong with me?

I don't worry about that though as I shove the burner phone in my back pocket, slip on a pair of shoes, and stealthily open up the bedroom door just a crack.

Fortunately, I told Brett I was too tired to meet up, so he wouldn't be expecting me. Mason told me he had church today—the MC's version of a club meeting—so he'll be down in the main bar with the other fenrir wolves.

Still, I can't be too careful.

Ensuring the room is empty, I silently close the door and tiptoe out of the apartment, locking it behind me with the key Mason had given me. The hallway is clear too, and after a quick glance in both directions, I race toward the staircase that will hopefully take me out the back entrance. This is the only escape route I've been able to come up with that will make my interactions with the other wolves minimal at best.

If they discover you're leaving, Blair...

If they accuse you of betraying them...

I shove those thoughts aside and take the stairs two at a time, practically flying around the corners. My wet hair drips on the floor with every step I take, though I imagine the heat outside will dry the strands in minutes.

I've just reached the final step in the stairwell when voices reach me. I throw my body flush against the nearest wall and hold my breath.

It doesn't appear as if the men speaking are in the

stairwell with me, but just outside of it. Still, that doesn't mean it won't change. And if they see me…

Cold, insidious fear skates up my spine as I hold myself perfectly still, my heart battering my rib cage.

"…it'll be expensive," a familiar voice declares curtly. "But their resources will help significantly."

It takes me a moment to place where I recognize the voice, and when I do, my body tenses even further.

Grim.

The president of the Bloody Skulls and Mason's father.

The responding voice is unfamiliar, though if I had to guess, I would say it belongs to someone high up in the ranks. He speaks to Grim with a familiarity and casualness that hints at friendship or at least budding respect.

"Yeah, man. And you're positive they're on board?"

"Sarai wants the same things we do," Grim responds.

Sarai?

What does the leader of the Bloody Skulls have in common with the alpha of the Totemic Tribe?

"And your son?" the second man queries. "He won't be okay with this."

Grim's voice is harsh—a slash of a whip—when he snaps, "Leave the boy to me."

Mason?

What the fuck?

Their voices fade as they walk away, but I don't immediately move from my hiding space.

I feel as if I just heard something monumental, but what that thing is, I don't know.

Is what Vincent said true?

Are the Bloody Skulls and Totemic Tribe teaming up to annihilate the Davenports and bitten wolves?

Either way, I can't ignore the fact that a war is on the horizon.

And we all might fall prey to its bloodlust.

THE PARK IS EMPTY WHEN I ARRIVE, SILVERY BEAMS OF moonlight illuminating the sparse canopy of aspen and maple trees. The playset is shrouded in shadows, giving the entire place an ominous, eerie feel.

Unease pricks at my skin repeatedly like a rusty nail as I move through the metal gate separating the sidewalk from the park, searching desperately for Vincent.

When I don't see him, that unease transforms into panic and something akin to fear.

But fuck that shit.

If my life as a bitten wolf taught me one thing, it's that I can't become a victim to my terror. I have to conquer it in order to flourish, and this moment is no different.

Casting a pointed look in both directions, I unsheathe my dagger from its holster and spin it around my fingers. I truly believe every woman should know how to fight and defend herself, especially when they find themselves alone in unfamiliar situations. It's something I'd been working on with Valentina before I left the Davenport mansion about a week ago.

"Vincent?" My voice echoes as I take a tentative step forward, my heart thundering in my chest. "Where the fuck are you?"

When no one responds, any excitement I might've been feeling previously is eclipsed by terror.

Did something happen to him? Has he decided not to meet me? Is this a trap?

Something flickers up ahead, hidden behind the branches and boughs of trees. I quicken my pace as I head toward the light, unable to completely ignore my trepidation and wariness.

Rule number one of being a bitten wolf—always remain alert and vigilant.

I glide forward on my tiptoes, purposefully stepping over every wayward branch and leaf so I won't make a sound. I moderate my breathing until it's barely even audible to me.

And then, I step through the thicket.

Awe fills me, erupting through my bloodstream like thousands of meteors falling from the sky. All I can do is gape in disbelief as I take in the sight before me.

The forest has been transformed into a scene plucked straight out of a fairy tale. Bright, glittery lights have been strewn across the branches, flickering like fireflies. A large blanket rests in the center of a clearing, a collection of pillows resting on top. A picnic basket sits directly in front of the man currently waiting for me, his hands clasped behind his back and his profile to me.

Vincent Davenport.

As always, my breath catches when I see him, utterly enthralled by his ethereal beauty. It's a beauty that has been indelibly tattooed onto my soul. Our separation has only emphasized my attraction to him. There's something so predatory about him, so innately lethal, that danger radiates off of him in tangible waves.

He's wearing another suit today, this one dark brown with a plum-colored tie. It accentuates his naturally tan skin and dark brown hair, currently brushed away from his chiseled, arresting facial features. Normally, Vincent's clean-shaven, but I can't help but notice the tiny bit of dark scruff coating his jawline. It somehow adds to his sexy allure, exacerbating the danger he exudes.

Vincent Davenport is combative, ornery, cantankerous…and mine. If I allow him to be.

I clear my throat as soon as I step into the clearing, and his head whips in my direction.

"Blair," he chokes out, emotions distorting his features.

I don't know how it happens—if he runs forward, or if I do. If he takes me in his arms, or if I take him in mine—but the next thing I know, his lips are devouring my own. His pine scent washes over me, as familiar to me as breathing. He pries my lips apart with his, his tongue darting in, and I eagerly open for him, accepting everything he wants to give me.

I…

I missed him.

A lot.

And that revelation slashes at my heart until the organ is barely recognizable.

Am I allowed to miss him while still developing feelings for Mason? What does all of this mean?

Either way, I lose myself in his kiss, in him, until he reluctantly pulls away, peppering gentle kisses to the corner of my lips.

"Fuck, I missed you. I missed you so damn much," he whispers reverently, peering down at me with eyes as black as obsidian stones.

"I missed you too," I confess, my voice nothing but a whisper.

His answering smile to my confession is glorious, his teeth blindingly white in his handsome face. He plants a tender kiss to my nose before releasing me, intertwining our fingers together and leading me toward the picnic.

"I can't believe you're stuck with the goddamn Bloody Skulls," he growls out, something dark coloring his features.

I want to assure him that, besides the first day there, the members of the Bloody Skulls have left me alone. That I've actually been enjoying my "dates" with Mason. That I was able to see Valentina.

But I keep my mouth shut.

For reasons I choose not to look at too closely, my words feel like a betrayal, though I don't know which guy I would be betraying. Vincent, who made passionate love to me and claimed I was his mate before I was forced to leave him? Or Mason, who sets my skin on fire with a single, demanding look? The two of them are fire and ice, a perfect dichotomy if I ever saw one.

"I don't want to talk about that," I tell Vincent instead, giving his hand a soft squeeze. My insides twist into thousands of intricate knots, and I swallow heavily. "I don't want to talk about any of that. You already know how I feel about all of this."

"Blair…" Vincent's voice is a plea, but I shake my head before he can get more than my name out.

"No, Vincent. I don't want to hear it. You may have," a golf ball-sized lump gets caught in my throat, "developed feelings for me, but that doesn't change the fact that I'm a pawn in a war I don't want to be in. The last thing I want to do is draw the bitten wolves, my family, into a war we can't win."

Vincent growls. "I told you." His tone is almost harsh, though I know his ire isn't directed at me but the situation. "We can protect you."

"And I told you," I say, licking my upper lip, "I

wouldn't need your protection if I wasn't pulled into this mess in the first place."

Resentment bubbles up inside of me, nearly over-shadowing everything else. It's true, in a twisted way, that I wouldn't be in this situation if Valentina hadn't tried to win me for her brother. If the three wolf packs hadn't decided to fight over me like a damn chew toy.

I could've been safe at the compound with my found family, planning to escape before shit hit the fan.

And now, I'm smack dab in the middle of it, unwittingly dragging my family into it as well.

Though, would I have wanted anything to change?

I mean, I met Vincent because of all of this. Mason too. And I discovered Brett was alive, which is greater than any gift the universe could've given me.

"So," I clear my throat, desperate to change the subject, "I see that you decided to recreate our first date."

Another tentative smile pulls up his lips as he glances around at the lights hanging from the trees. "I don't know if I'd technically consider that our first date…"

"Vincent," I give him a droll look, "you can't seriously consider the time you shot that guy in the head a date."

He looks moderately affronted. "Don't tell me you're secretly squeamish, Blair," he teases. "You're the big, bad, scary assassin."

I giggle and shove at his shoulder. "And you're just big, bad, and scary."

"Big?" His eyebrows touch his hairline as he glances at his cock. "Yup, definitely big. Bad?" He taps a finger against his chin in contemplation as I roll my eyes at his ridiculousness. "Hmm. I suppose you could say I'm bad. And scary?" Before I can retort, Vincent tackles me to the ground and begins to tickle my sides. I laugh helplessly, twisting my body in a desperate attempt to escape his wandering fingers.

"I'm going to stab you!" I threaten around peals of laughter, and Vincent flashes another disarming smile.

I've never seen him so…carefree. Happy. There's a joy emanating from his gaze that feels foreign, and it causes my heart to increase speed.

He's handsome all the damn time, but when he smiles, he's otherworldly.

"Say mercy," he taunts. His fingers are licks of fire on my bare skin where my shirt has risen up.

"Make me!"

He laughs, the noise soothing my frayed nerves, as I bite my lower lip. I could easily get away from him if I desired, but I don't want to. At all.

Slowly, his fingers still on my skin as his eyes drop to my lips. The lust in his gaze is impossible to ignore, and I know it reflects the need in my own.

"I missed you so damn much, Blair," he whispers as he lowers his head. "I need you to come back."

"Vincent." My hands snake up of their own accord, running through his immaculately-styled, dark-brown hair and messing it up. He slowly brings his lips to mine, teasing my tongue with his, as his hands push my shirt up over my breasts, baring my lacy bra to him. He cups my breast as a single finger enters the waistband of my shorts, fiddling with the hem of my panties.

"Blair…" My name is a whisper on his lips—a prayer, a promise, and a threat all in one. I can hear his need for me, his love, and something inside of me shatters irreparably.

I've never been in love before, but I imagine this is how it feels. A sense of completeness permeates the air as I surrender to Vincent's bruising, possessive kiss. It's a merging of souls, of hearts, and I feel something begin to solidify inside of me—something flimsy but growing stronger and stronger with every flick of his tongue against mine.

Is that...? Is that the mate bond? I haven't felt it this strong since we had sex back at his mansion.

The connection feels tenuous and almost inconsequential, but I know it has the power to change my life drastically. All I need to do is grab on to it and reinforce it with love and passion.

It's real. It's not a mirage or an illusion or anything else I thought it was.

Vincent is truly my mate.

I just need to—

"Blair."

The masculine voice has us pulling apart, a growl rumbling from Vincent's throat as he attempts to shield me from the intruder.

I sit up in alarm, my shirt still bunched around my bra and one of my tits spilling out. My shorts are unbuttoned, revealing a sliver of pink panties, though I don't immediately cover myself.

Instead, I meet the bright green eyes staring at me with a mixture of horror and betrayal.

"Mason." My voice is throaty, though I'm not sure if it's because of the desire still coursing through me or because I'm trying to hold back tears. My emotions are a strange and confusing cocktail.

The Bloody Skulls' VP gulps, his eyes traveling to me before resting on Vincent. The hatred radiating from his gaze is impossible to miss.

"You went missing, so I followed your scent," Mason says in a deadened voice. He looks so… different. The man I've spent the last seven days with had been full of life and joy, his lips in a perpetual state of some sort of smirk and his eyes glimmering mischievously.

This new Mason is devoid of anything that I have come to admire about the old one. His eyes are bland and vacant, barely sparing me more than a fleeting glance.

I think I broke his heart, and God, if that doesn't fuck me up inside.

"Mason," I begin helplessly, but he cuts me off by raising a single hand. He doesn't scream or yell or even get angry. He just appears…defeated, and that cuts me up more than anything else.

"It's okay, Blair," he whispers, dropping his gaze to the ground. "You don't have to explain yourself."

"You better not tell anyone what you just saw, pup," Vincent growls, still covering me with his muscular frame.

Mason's head snaps up, and the darkness I've seen in his eyes before, the darkness that beckons me to him like a lighthouse, materializes in his green gaze. "My father would kill her if he discovered she was," his face twists with unabashed disgust, "*fraternizing* with the enemy. I don't want to see her dead."

"Then what do you want?" Vincent barks, and I see him once again adopting his cold, glacial mask. It's the same mask he wore when I first met him, over a month ago—shutting the world and everyone in it out completely. Locking his true emotions behind impenetrable walls of steel.

Mason doesn't answer Vincent's question, though his eyes flicker toward me for a fraction of a second. It isn't long enough for Vincent to see it.

But I do.

"Mason," I try again, but for the second time tonight, he cuts me off.

"Not now, Blair."

Blair. Not baby girl.

And also…

I fucking hate when he cuts me off.

"*Vaffanculo*," I mutter under my breath. *Fuck off.*

Vincent growls low in his throat, his eyes spewing animosity and vitriol. "How do I know you won't hurt her?" he demands, placing a hand on the small of my back.

Mason's eyes widen in disbelief before he smooths over his expression. "Hurt her? What makes you think I'd hurt her?"

"Because you're a fenrir wolf. The VP of the Bloody Skulls," Vincent spits out. "Pain is in your blood."

This time, Mason's mask doesn't crack—doesn't even chip. He stares blankly ahead with his arms folded over his chest. A muscle in his jaw twitches, though he doesn't rise to the bait.

"And isn't it *your* father who killed her family, Vincent Davenport?" Mason retorts.

Vincent's back muscles tense and ripple as he hurls daggers with his eyes at the other man.

"I'm not responsible for the crimes my father committed," he bites out scathingly.

"Neither am I," Mason snaps.

Silence descends as I struggle to fix my clothes. All I can hear is Vincent's ragged breathing as he struggles to regain control of his wolf. Mason's eyes flash brightly—strong indication that his own wolf is rising to the surface—before he wrestles it back under control.

"I'm also the one who'll reunite Blair with her family," Vincent grits out.

It feels as if a heavy stone has been dropped in my stomach, causing the acid there to ripple and churn. The temperature rises a dozen degrees as sweat breaks out on my skin. I can barely breathe, barely think, only aware of the drumming in my head.

"What?"

Is he talking about Brett? Does Vincent know that Brett's alive?

Vincent doesn't take his eyes off of Mason, though his words are intended for me. "I found your family," he says softly, the tenderness in his voice belying the rigidness in his entire frame as he glares at Mason. "You told me before that you never knew your mother's side of the family, but I found them. Your aunts and uncles, cousins and grandparents. I found them all. They live only an hour or so away from here."

His words flood my veins, followed immediately by a spark of electricity that has my muscles spasming.

My…my family?

I'd given up hope that I'd ever meet my blood. After my parents died, I lived on the streets, shuffling from box to box until I ran into Papa Gray. It wasn't because I didn't know I had family left, but because I had no way of getting a hold of them. I was a child too frightened to contact the police.

Even now as an adult, my thoughts still sometimes stray to the family I never met, the family who I never got the chance to love and be loved by.

I don't know if I hate Vincent right now or love him.

"You found my family?" I whisper, shock percolating in my stomach and intermingling with the nerves already present there.

Mason looks as if he's seconds from screaming, a vein in his forehead bulging. His hands clench into fists by his sides as he glares at Vincent, radiating an incandescent fury that siphons all of the oxygen out of the room.

"Of course you fucking did," he growls. "The perfect psychopath."

"Fuck off!" Vincent hisses before shifting slightly to face me as well. "But Blair, yes, I found them. I did some digging and found a cemetery near your grandmother's house. Blair, they think you're *dead*. Your gravestone is there, along with the rest of your family's." Pain shadows his eyes as my heart beats erratically in my chest

My family.

Alive.

And they *care*. Well, at least they care enough about me—a child they never knew—to place me in their family cemetery.

What does this mean? For me and for Brett?

"I can take you to them, Blair. You'll be able to meet your family." Vincent's voice is a soothing plea, and all I want is to put my hand in his and allow him to take me away.

But then Mason's voice cracks across the field like thunder. "She has a fucking family, mongrel."

Vincent scoffs. "You?"

"Her brother." Mason's face distorts in twisted delight, especially when Vincent frowns. "Oh, she didn't tell you?" He turns to me, feigning surprise. But the little shit knows exactly what he's doing. "Blair, I can't believe you didn't tell your lover that your brother is a member of the Bloody Skulls."

Vincent has gone absolutely rigid, his fingers elongating into claws. His words are nothing but a growl when he speaks next. "Blair, is that true?"

Mason laughs, cold and caustic, and I whip my head around to glare at him. "I find it difficult to believe that she'll choose to leave her beloved brother once the ninety days are over, don't you?" he taunts, cocking his head to the side. A strand of silky blond hair bounces in front of his face, though he doesn't lift a finger to push it away. His body thrums with barely contained energy, an entire electrical storm racing just beneath his skin.

"Mason," I warn as Vincent lunges forward, looking like a tall, dark avenging angel in his suit coat. "Vincent!"

"Do you really think she's going to choose to stay with you?" Vincent sneers at the other man as I struggle to get in between them, one hand going on either chest.

"Don't underestimate me, fucker," Mason seethes, baring his teeth.

"Guys." The second my hands make contact with their chests, I feel it. There are no words capable of describing the sensation, but it's almost like thousands of butterflies have been set free in my stomach. Heat migrates from where we touch, creating an inferno in my lower belly. It runs through my veins like magma. I want to ask them if they feel that, the connection between us, but they're too preoccupied with glaring at each other to even notice me.

"I'm going to kill you," Vincent growls.

"And risk something happening to Blair?" Mason scoffs. "Not likely. We both know that if you kill me, my father will go after her. And I know we both don't want that to happen."

"You don't know what I want!"

"I have a feeling I do." Once again, Mason's eyes dip to mine before focusing over my head once more. "And it's never going to happen." The smile carved into Mason's luscious mouth is grim and weary, the crack in his enigmatic personality as visible as it has ever been. "Because guess what, lycan trash?" He takes a step closer until his chest brushes my arm, forcing me even further against Vincent. I'm sandwiched between them, but I don't feel help-less or even frightened. Is it wrong that I'm... aroused? "I still have twenty-three more days with her. And at the end of those twenty-three days?" He pauses to place a hand on my hip, where my shirt has risen up. "She'll be desperately in love with me."

6

BLAIR

DAY 15

I haven't seen Mason since the incident with Vincent, and for reasons I don't want to examine too closely, that cuts a hole in my chest. It's almost as if I can physically feel my blood drip from my open chest cavity and spread across the floor in a canvas of thick, potent red.

It's been days, *days*, and the Bloody Skulls' VP has made himself scarce. Sometimes, I'll see his shock of golden hair in the bar downstairs, but when he catches sight of me, he'll walk out the door. I get the impression that he wants to be near me and as far away from me as possible at the same time.

The sensation his absence leaves behind is like

tar on my skin, like skittering insects I'm desperate to brush off. I feel it keenly, though I don't know why. I should hate him, and maybe a part of me does, but the rest of me…

The rest of me is devastated that I broke his heart.

How can I have such strong feelings for Vincent and still be lusting after Mason? How can my heart be pulled in two separate directions?

The only good news about this whole fiasco is now that my days aren't taken up by Mason and his dates, I get to spend more time with my brother. I'm not yet proficient in sign language, but I'm learning a little more every day. Brett has taken to communicating on a whiteboard Mason supplied for him whenever we have conversations. I haven't told him what exactly went down between Mason, Vincent, and myself, but he's smart enough to know something happened.

"He's brooding," Brett writes now, flashing his board for me to see.

I push my lips out in a scowl. "If he's that upset, he can come see me," I retort.

Before I have even finished speaking, Brett's already shaking his head and moving to write something else on the white board. "No can do, little sis.

Men like him have too much pride. You broke his heart."

Broke his heart.

Those words do something to my own heart, something that claws and stabs at me. Rather than focusing on the myriad of emotions coursing through me, I ask instead, "Is this weird for you?"

When Brett simply raises an eyebrow, I hurry to elaborate. "You know, me being here. 'Dating' Mason, if you can even call it that. Being…" I trail off, but when a shadow crosses over Brett's face, I know he can fill in the missing word.

Being alive.

It takes him a while to write out his reply, the marker tapping repeatedly against his chin. He reclines back in the uncomfortable wooden chair resting on the other side of the apartment's dining room table before flashing me the board.

"It's still surreal," it reads. "I sometimes think I'm going to wake up and discover this has been nothing but a wonderful dream. I thought you were dead for so damn long, that it's strange to know differently. But it's the best damn feeling in the world."

A soft smile curves up my lips as I place my hand over the top of his. "It really is."

We talk for another hour before Brett excuses

himself for the night. When he pulls me into his strong arms, the familiar sensation of being home, of being where I belong, crashes over me like a tsunami. Everything feels right at that moment. The world is exactly the way it's supposed to be.

Brett pulls back, his eyes misty, and grabs his white board once more.

"When I saw you at the bar, I thought I was imagining things. I still can't believe this is real."

"Wait." I glance from the board to his expressive eyes. "You saw me before?"

He nods sharply, twisting the board back toward him to write on it once more. "I thought I did. I would spot your eyes from miles away, Blair. I've never seen eyes as blue as yours, except for Mom's. You look exactly like her."

His words fill me with emotion, and I drown in the waves of it. I don't remember much of my parents, but I do recall my mother smiling down at me with eyes the exact same shade as my own. Her hair had been slightly lighter though, more gold than brown, and hung in short curls around her cherubic face. I got my dad's dark brown hair highlighted with gold and red.

"I miss them," I confess in a breathy exhale. "A lot."

"There's not a day that goes by when I don't think about them, you, and Percy," Brett responds.

We chat for another few minutes, both of us reluctant to part after spending years away from each other, before Brett sighs heavily, kisses my forehead, and leaves the apartment.

His departure siphons all the oxygen out of the room, and I can't help but place my back to the door and take a deep, ragged breath.

What the fuck is happening to me?

For years, I've locked all of my emotions in a steel box, refusing to even acknowledge them, but they're coming back to the surface like a pesky tide that carries dead fish to shore. First Vincent, then Mason, and now Brett. I'd thought my heart to be hewn from stone, impenetrable and closed to any affection, but I was wrong. So, so wrong.

A knock on the door startles me out of my thoughts, and I spin, half expecting it to be Brett or Mason. Still, I grab my dagger out of its holster and hold it at the ready. You can never be too careful.

The knock sounds again, louder and more demanding this time, and my unease amps up. I move on the balls of my feet and peer out the peephole.

What the fuck?

Grim, the president of the Bloody Skulls and Mason's father, stands on the other side of the door, his handsome features twisted in irritation.

Slowly, I drop down to my feet and slide the deadbolt away, opening the door. I don't trust Grim further than I can throw him, but the last thing I want to do is offend him by ignoring his knocks. For the next fifteen days, I'm his bitch. As much as I hate that—and him—there's nothing I can do about it.

"Grim, what a pleasant surprise," I say cordially as I move to stand in front of the open doorway, barring him entrance. My smile is more of a grimace —a baring of teeth—but if he notices or cares, he doesn't show it.

"I see my bastard son finally got sick of your pussy," he responds vulgarly, and my upper lip pulls away from my teeth in a snarl. I remind myself that I'm in the midst of my enemy's territory and the last thing I'm allowed to do is stab him in the neck and watch him bleed out.

"Can I help you with something?" This time, I don't bother to hide the animosity saturating my voice. He's a fucking prick who deserves to suffer at my hand.

I hate that when he smiles, he looks like Mason. Normally, it's easy to differentiate between the two of them, but when Grim smiles, he looks so similar to his son, it's uncanny. Same white-blond hair, same green eyes, same dimples. But Grim's eyes? They're cold. Empty. Dead.

"Look, if you have nothing to say—" I begin to shut the door when his hand snakes out, catching it before it can close completely. With a considerable show of strength, he pushes it open the rest of the way and stalks into the room. I growl at him in warning, but his smile only broadens, and he continues grinning like a crazy motherfucker.

"I wanted to see for myself what everyone finds so attractive about the little bitten wolf." He offers me a leer that has goosebumps pebbling on my arms. Disgust swarms in my stomach like acid, but I don't let that show on my face.

"You looked. You saw. Now leave." I point toward the door, holding my ground despite how rapidly my heart is beating inside of my chest. I know men like him—can see the malicious intent in his eyes— and I'd die before I allowed him to touch me.

"How about we make a deal?" He takes a step closer to me, and I counter it by moving backward. "All I want is to try out your sweet pussy. Just once. Then—" As he takes another step closer, I lunge forward at the same time, twisting my body until I'm behind him with my knife at his throat. He stills instantly, though I can't see the expression on his face.

"I think you need to leave now," I hiss, digging the knife into his skin slightly for emphasis.

This is bad. This is very, very bad.

Grim surprises me by throwing back his head in laughter. "All right." I spin both of our bodies until we're facing the door once more and then give him a shove, keeping my dagger at the ready.

"Leave, *pezzo di merda*." A growl rumbles up my throat as I narrow my eyes at his retreating back. *Piece of shit.*

Grim casually sticks his hands into his pockets and begins to shuffle out the door before whirling back toward me with eyes that gleam like fire.

In the next instant, he has my wrist in his hand and twists it hard enough that I drop the knife. Anyone else might've screamed in agony at the pressure he applied to my poor, abused bones, but only a hiss of pain escapes me.

Allowing him to think he has the upper hand, I make my body go limp and pliable—clay for him to mold the way he wants.

Another cruel laugh escapes him as he leans

forward, his rancid breath tickling the hair by my ear. "Good girl."

Still holding my wrist in one hand, his other hand slides down my tank until my bra-covered tit springs free.

Let him think he won.

Let him think he owns you.

His thumb moves to stroke over my nipple, but before he can make contact, I lift my knee and slam it into his dick. Hard.

He bellows in pain, instantly releasing me, and I waste no time spinning around to punch him in the face, imbuing it with the strength of my wolf. The force of it causes him to topple, and I fall with him, landing on his stomach and straddling him.

I continue my assault on his smug, smiling face, uncaring of what this means for me. He'll kill me—of that I have no doubt—but it'll be better than anything else he might've done.

"I love the fire in you," he purrs as I punch him in the face again. Abruptly, he grabs my fist and gives it a twist, and a scream escapes me as my wrist officially breaks. It'll heal in hours with my wolf's accelerated healing, but fuck! That hurt like a bitch.

He takes my momentary lapse of concentration to roll me onto my back and hover over me. A clawed finger lowers to my shirt and tears it down the middle, breaking through my bra as well. His eyes gleam with malevolent hunger as he stares at my bare breasts, his tongue wetting his upper lip as if he's thinking about tasting them.

Using all of my ab muscles, I lift my upper body to headbutt him as hard as I can. He grunts, releasing me, and I waste no time shrugging out of my destroyed shirt. At the moment, my naked chest is the least of my worries.

His eyes are gold—a solid, liquid gold that indicates he's not in control.

His wolf is.

Unlike bitten wolves, fenrir wolves don't change form. Instead, their eyes change and they maintain their human body while still exhibiting behaviors of wolves. It's what makes them immensely dangerous and terrifying—animal characteristics in a human shell.

Grim lunges at me, his claws extended, and embeds his nails in my thigh. I growl, attempting to kick him off, but he simply howls in mocking laughter.

Fuck. Fuck. *Fuck!*

I curse at him as he attempts to straddle me once

more, his hands grabbing both of mine and thrusting them above my head. My screams echo off the walls as I thrash and kick, swear and bite, ignoring the agony radiating from my wrist as I fight for my fucking life.

The sound of the door banging open reverberates through the apartment. My heart soars in my chest as I expect to see Brett.

But it's not him.

Mason takes one look at the scene before him—me, penned beneath his father, my breasts on display and my wrist mangled—and something I've never seen before crosses over his expression. Something dark and dangerous and so unnerving, I find I can't look away.

And then, he attacks.

He charges at his father with a roar of fury and tackles him off of me. Grim bucks and hisses, swiping claws at his son's face, but Mason will not be deterred. At that moment, both are more beast than human.

I shuffle backward until my back is flush against the wall, cradling my wrist to my chest. I'm desperate to cover up my nude body, but I don't dare move. I'm a fucking wounded animal, cornered and bleeding profusely. Any second now, one of the apex predators fighting will get a sniff of my blood and come for me.

I can't allow that to happen.

Something glints in the corner of my vision, and I lunge for my discarded knife. Pain explodes inside of me as I practically fall on my stomach, landing on my wrist, but I ignore it as I clamp my fingers around the knife and drag it toward me. I bare my teeth as I twist my head to see if their fighting will come to me, but it never does.

Because Grim? He's unconscious, his head lolling to the side and his eyes shut. And standing atop him is a snow-white wolf nearly the size of my own. When he glances in my direction, his eyes remain the same emerald green I remember.

But...

But that's impossible.

Fenrir wolves don't transform fully into wolves. Unless...

Unless Mason isn't a fenrir wolf. Or at least, he isn't a *full* fenrir wolf.

He stalks toward me, his muzzle covered in blood and sticking to his fur, and waits for my reaction. I don't know if he expects me to run, scream, or stab him, but all I do is place a shaky hand on his snout and give it a quick pet.

I'm strong, but fenrir wolves are significantly stronger. Deadlier.

Mason saved my life. He went against his father, the man capable of destroying him, for me. He did it for *me*. He easily could've looked the other way—most men would've—but instead of cowering, he fought back with everything he had. I'm in one piece because of him. Maybe Grim wouldn't have killed me, but I have no doubt what he had planned would've been immensely more damning than any knife in the chest would've been.

A light, airy emotion swells inside of me, threatening to pop like a bubble at any moment.

"Thank you," I whisper breathlessly. "Thank you for saving me."

He makes a noise that might be a yip before lowering his head into my lap. And for just a brief, brief second, the rest of the world falls away. Grim didn't just try to rape me, I didn't attack the leader of a savage motorcycle club, I'm not falling in love with two men simultaneously, and there isn't a war on the horizon.

It's nothing but a fever dream, but it's nice to imagine, right?

7

———

TAI

DAY 15

There's something that happens to a man when he becomes separated from his mate.

There's an aching hole in my chest, reminding me distinctly of a puzzle missing one single piece. I can't quite be complete without it. Everything hurts —my head, my body, my very fucking soul.

I fucking hate it.

And a part of me hates Blair for making me so needy and dependent on her, on a stranger.

But when I close my eyes, I can envision her cascading brown hair highlighted with strands of gold. I can see her bright blue eyes, seemingly capable of staring into the chunk of coal that serves as my heart. She's a fire that burns so hot, she draws all of the oxygen out of the room, leaving you feeling oddly bereft.

And now, she's in the home of my enemy.

I curl my lip away from my teeth as I lean against the graffiti-covered store directly across the street from the Bloody Skulls' Clubhouse. With my sunglasses on and a ballcap on my head, I pray no one will be able to recognize me. The last thing I need is someone declaring war on us because the prince of the Totemic Tribe was spotted in enemy territory.

But fuck, I can't just leave her unattended.

My need to take care of Blair, to watch over and care for her, has grown into an obsession. I can't quite function when I don't have my eyes on her, ensuring for myself that she's alive and okay. That Mason hasn't killed her.

Over the last fifteen days, I watched her go on a series of dates with him, completely oblivious to my presence. A part of me I fucking hate—a part of me I want to tear apart until it's unrecognizable—feels a sting of hurt over that. How can my soul recognize hers from miles away while she seems utterly unaware of mine? How can she be my fated mate, sent to me from the moon goddess herself, yet still regard me as a stranger?

Fate is a twisted bitch, one that deserves a million spankings, for pairing me up with a girl who, for all intents and purposes, is my "enemy."

Yet I find that I wouldn't have it any other way.

Blair is that one damn flower erupting in a field of weeds. She's sunlight and water and everything else that is necessary for survival.

And though I hate the fact my mate is someone who despises me, I know in my heart that I wouldn't want anyone else. I already hate the fact I have to hide what she means to me around my father and even my mother. I want to scream from the rooftop that she's mine—or soon will be—but I don't dare.

My dad destroys the things and people I love, and I'll be damned before he does the same thing to her.

I eye the sleazy-looking bar intently, as I have done the last fifteen days. Ever since Blair snuck out in the middle of the night to see Vincent fucking Davenport, she hasn't left the apartment. I would've thought Mason had done something to her if I hadn't seen him walking the streets like a kicked puppy with his tail between his legs, his expression one of absolute devastation and pain.

My mind races back to when Vincent kissed

Blair on the picnic blanket in the woods. Jealousy burned a hole in my chest at seeing another man—especially a motherfucking *Davenport*—kiss my mate, but accompanied by that insidious emotion was something akin to lust. My cock hardened in my pants as I watched him pull up her shirt, revealing her perfect breasts and dusky nipples. Those little mewls that escaped her parted lips were music to my ears...

I scowl darkly at the memory.

Never in a million years have I heard of men being okay with other men touching their mate. It just wasn't heard of. When we found the one fated for us, the wolf who called to our own and whose soul lit a fire in our bodies, we became insanely possessive and protective of them. I should've wanted to tear Vincent apart limb by limb.

Instead, I wanted to join.

I wanted to press my cock to her ruby-red lips and push inside of her inch by inch until that delectable mouth was full of me. And then, I wanted to fist her hair and squeeze her throat as Vincent licked and sucked at her pussy. I wanted her to scream for me, for us—

I shut that shit down fast, unsure why that

strange image popped into my head in the first place.

Mate, my wolf whispers in my mind, pacing. His tail swishes back and forth as the enormity of his emotions for the petite female mingles with my own. He's already head over heels in love with her, while I'm unsure how I feel.

I know I'm ridiculously attracted to her—as in, my cock refuses to work for any female who isn't Blair Windsor—but I honestly don't know much about her.

Like, what's her favorite television show? Favorite movie? Color? Food?

My wolf growls in my head, reminding me that it doesn't matter, that she's our mate, but I shush him.

It does fucking matter. By the time I'm done with Blair, I'll know everything there is to know about her, including how hard she likes to be choked in bed.

My cock swells with excitement at the thought, and I want nothing more than to break through the Bloody Skulls' front door, grab my sweet mate, and remind her who she belongs to. But since it seems as if she doesn't feel the mating bond the same way I do, she's more liable to stab me than kiss me back.

Though the thought of her stabbing me while I'm balls deep inside of her only amplifies my desire.

Fuuuck.

Movement in my periphery drags my attention away from the bar and toward an alleyway nestled between two nondescript stores. My ears sharpen, listening intently, as I hear the pounding of footsteps as the figure lurks closer, staring in the same direction I am.

Normally, I wouldn't be suspicious, but I can never be too careful with Blair's life on the line.

A growl breaks through my chest as I begin to stalk toward the figure, but he—or she—has already begun to walk down the street in front of me. He has a gray hoodie pulled over his head, making it impossible to make out any distinguishing features, but I would have to guess he's a male based on his considerable bulk.

I quicken my pace as he slides into a beat-up car parked in front of the hotel. And when he grabs binoculars and aims it at Blair's apartment window, I. See. Red.

"What the fuck do you think you're doing?" I bellow, pulling the door open and sliding into the passenger seat. My ass has just touched the cold leather when the barrel of a pistol touches my temple. Slowly, I twist my head to meet the obsidian gaze of Vincent Davenport.

He's almost unrecognizable. In his attempt to blend in, he's no longer wearing his customary suit and tie. Instead, he has on a pair of gray sweatpants and a matching sweatshirt. His normally slicked back hair is loose of its gel, the ends curling slightly.

"What are you doing in my car?" he demands.

Ah. There's the voice of the asshole I know and hate—cold as ice.

"Why are you spying on Blair?" I counter, not at all perturbed by the gun pointed at my head. The last thing Vincent will do is shoot me and risk pissing off my family, provoking a war he cannot win.

He doesn't have to know that my father will celebrate in the streets if I die.

Honestly, the only reason the sick bastard doesn't kill me himself is because he's afraid his "subjects" will revolt if I'm murdered. And the last thing he needs is a rebellion, especially when his leadership is contested regularly.

"What are *you* doing?" Vincent hisses, baring his teeth. He flicks his gaze toward Blair's apartment over the top of the bar and then back to me. After a long moment, he lowers the gun from my head and clicks the safety on.

"Doesn't fucking matter," I hiss.

"Are you stalking her?" Vincent demands, and he sounds so fucking outraged by the fact, that I have to laugh.

"Says the person staking out her apartment," I retort with an eye roll. He opens his mouth to no doubt argue when the front door to the bar opens and the object of both of our attentions steps out.

"Shit," I hiss. "Get down." Before he can protest, I slam my hand onto his chest and push with all my might. He's a strong bastard...but I'm stronger. Over two hundred pounds of solid muscle, baby.

"What?" Vincent whips his head toward the street, where Blair steps into the sunshine with that prick Mason. Is it just me or does she look abnormally pale? Why does she hold her wrist to her chest like that? And why does she keep casting Mason speculative glances? What the fuck happened?

"Get down," I instruct Vincent again as I slide further down the seat. Vincent curses but complies, squeezing himself underneath the steering wheel while simultaneously threatening me bodily harm. "Oh, shut up," I deadpan.

"Fuck you," he seethes, tossing me a frosty glare.

"Fuck—oh shit." My head, which has been poking

up to catch sight of Blair, snaps down when I make motherfucking eye contact with her.

Fuck.

My.

Life.

"Shit. Shit. Shit. Shit."

"What?" Vincent demands, awkwardly crouched beneath the steering wheel.

A second later, someone taps on the driver's side window. Vincent and I both lift our heads to meet Blair's amused stare. Mason stands over her shoulder with his arms crossed and a wry smirk pulling up his lips.

Still crouched down, Vincent lifts an arm to roll down the window of his car.

Neither of us move. I don't know if we're pretending to play dead or what, but moving feels like the wrong fucking option.

"Um…hello?" Blair tilts her head to the side curiously, and a thousand questions spring to the tip of my tongue. "What are you two *stronzi* doing?"

But instead of asking any of them, though, I bark out, "Why the fuck do you look so pale?" Horror squeezes my heart. "And why is there a motherfucking bruise on your neck? And why are you holding your wrist like that?"

So fast that I might've missed it if I'd blinked, Blair's eyes flicker to Mason, who has gone rigid. Incandescent anger burns white-hot in my veins, liquifying them. If he hurt her, if he's the cause of those damn bruises, I'll make him wish he had never been born. I'll have him screaming in agony as I dance over his bruised and beaten body. I'll lick his tears from his cheeks and piss on his corpse and—

Blair rolls her eyes and waves a hand in the air dismissively. "That doesn't matter. Mason has nothing to do with any of this. He's actually taking me out for lunch to take my mind off of things."

"Taking you out?" Vincent growls, and I detect a hint of jealousy in his voice.

Blair's eyes sharpen. "You know you guys shouldn't be here. This is enemy territory."

She's right. It *is* enemy territory. I'm literally staring into the faces of two of my greatest enemies right at this fucking moment.

So why don't I feel even a trickle of unease? Why do I know innately that Mason won't turn me in to his sadistic gang and Vincent won't slit my throat?

Maybe I'm broken.

That sounds like a pretty reasonable explanation.

"We wanted to make sure you were okay," Vincent grits out, and I can't help but fixate on his use of "we," almost as if we called each other up and arranged a stake out of the girl we're both obsessed with. The only difference between the two of us—Blair's my fated mate and not his. He can be in love with her for all the shits I give, but he'll never have her. Especially not after she discovers the truth about our connection.

Blair's eyes soften at his words as Mason scoffs. She shoots a glare at him over her shoulder, and he smiles sheepishly.

"Have you ever noticed…?" She trails off as her gaze flickers from Mason to me and then back to Mason. When we both stare at her intently, waiting for her to continue, she frowns. "Never mind." She bites down on her lower lip before focusing on Vincent and me. "But seriously. You guys can't be here."

Vincent growls sharply. "Why the fuck not?"

"Because it's not safe, man," Mason interjects, and both of us whip our heads in his direction. Mason meets Vincent's eyes first, and something undefinable passes between them. An understanding of sorts? Something else entirely?

What the fucking hell is happening?

Pack, my wolf pipes up, opening a single eye sleepily.

I snort at the idiotic creature.

Not pack, I tell it, scowling.

Pack, my wolf insists.

"You need to go. Now." Blair glances over her shoulder warily, a delicate crease appearing between her brows. "Grim will be pissed." Something dark flashes in her eyes at the name of the rival pack leader, but I don't dare push the issue. I don't know Blair well enough yet.

But Vincent? He doesn't fucking hesitate.

"What the fuck happened?"

"Nothing," she answers. He opens his mouth, but she simply leans forward to place her small hand over it. A bark of laughter escapes me as Mason smirks. Vincent's eyes widen almost imperceptibly. I imagine it's not often that someone basically tells him to 'shut the fuck up.'

"Damn, baby girl," Mason coos, and Vincent and I both growl at the ridiculous nickname he has for her.

I wanted to call her baby, for fuck's sake, and now I need to change my goddamn nickname for her because of that asshole.

"Leave. Now. I'll talk to you both later." She shifts her eyes to include me as well before removing her hand from Vincent's mouth, grabbing Mason's sleeve, and stomping away. Both of us watch her go, our eyes glued to her swaying ass. I should feel annoyed that Vincent is enjoying the show also, but…I don't.

"Do you think something happened?" Vincent asks after she disappears around the corner with Mason.

"Obviously, but with whom? Mason?" I query, but he shakes his head.

"No, with Grim. Did you notice how she tensed up when she said his name?"

"I'll kill him if he'd touched her," I growl, and Vincent rumbles out his agreement.

"Get in fucking line."

Silence stretches between us, but surprisingly, it isn't uncomfortable. It feels almost…companionable?

What. The. Hell?

This is Vincent Davenport, for fuck's sake. I should be trying to kill him, not sitting in a fucking car with him in amicable silence. If witches existed, I would've believed someone placed a spell on me. This can't be normal.

Echoing my thoughts, Vincent muses in a cold, detached voice, "This is weird."

"Very," I agree, still not making a move to get out of the car.

A second later, I hear the click of a safety being turned off and a gun is once again pressed to my head.

"Get the fuck out of my car before I blow your brains out," Vincent growls, and surprised laughter erupts out of me.

"Damn." Ignoring the gun to my head, I turn to smirk at him. "Still pissed that I beat your ass back in the ring?"

He snorts, shoving the gun even further against my skull. "You didn't fucking win."

"Did too." I smile triumphantly.

"Doesn't matter. I got to go home and pound into Blair's sweet pussy," he taunts.

And yup, my smile fades.

"Fucker." My heart thrums madly in my chest. I should be fucking furious by his proclamation, but instead, I feel…turned on? The fuck?

Vincent stares at me for a long moment, his eyes unreadable, before moving the gun to the center of my forehead. "You have five seconds."

I roll my eyes at his dramatics before unfolding my huge body out of his car and standing on the sidewalk. I've only just shut his car door when the car speeds off in the direction of his mansion—leaving me with the biggest sense of 'what the fuck' in my life.

WHEN I CLIMB OFF MY BIKE A FEW HOURS LATER, IT'S to see my pack in disarray.

A large semi-truck rests in front of a corrugated iron warehouse that usually houses our supplies. I stride toward it, something akin to anxiety twisting up the muscles in my stomach.

Crate after wooden crate is being unloaded by the males in my tribe, including my best friend Paco. My father, the sadistic fucker, stands slightly apart from everyone else, a wide smile brimming on his face.

As I watch, horrified, one of the men opens the nearest crate, revealing numerous automatic assault rifles.

What the fuck?

It looks as if we're preparing for fucking war.

But what war? And why?

As I stare even harder at the unloaded crates, I can dimly make out a symbol carved into the upper right corner.

A skull weeping tears of blood.

Why the fuck are the Bloody Skulls supplying my father weapons?

Alliance, my wolf whispers, and I can't help but nod in agreement.

So if we're teaming up with them…

What does that mean for the bitten wolves and the Davenports?

8

BLAIR

DAY 16

"Rise and shine, sleepy head."

Once again, the blinds to my window are pulled open, and a snarl is ripped from my lips.

"*Stronzo*," I hiss in Italian as a rather cheerful Mason smirks down at me.

His sinfully plush lips purse out into a pout when I don't immediately rush out of bed to do his bidding. To be completely honest, my heart is racing so fast, I'm not sure I'd even be able to.

Besides when he saved me yesterday, Mason hasn't said more than two words to me after the whole incident with Vincent. Even when he took me out to lunch—bringing me to the same Mexican restaurant as before—he didn't speak.

I desperately want to ask him how he was able to transform into a full wolf when he's a fenrir, but I don't dare. I suppose it's just a secret he'll have to learn to trust me with over time.

"OFIL is back on," Mason says cheerfully, somehow easily able to read the disbelieving expression on my face.

I blink at him as I sit up in bed, my covers pooling around my waist. Lifting one hand, I rub sleep out of my tired eyes, half wondering if I'm still dreaming. "What?" I ask wearily.

"OFIL." His smile broadens.

"Mason," I begin cautiously, "is that really the best idea? Especially after Grim…" I allow my words to taper off, trying to ignore the sudden tightness in my chest. I had trouble sleeping last night, even with the doors locked and Mason right outside on the couch.

Whenever I close my eyes, I see Grim's malicious sneer and narrowed-eyed glare. I have the distinct impression that he'll want revenge for the slight against him. He doesn't like the fact that I kicked his ass…and that his own son turned against him. Well, maybe he *did* like the fact that I fought back, though the thought of him getting turned on by me fighting for my life makes vomit churn in my stomach.

Something insidious flashes in Mason's eyes, but unlike with his father, it does the exact opposite of scare me away. There's something about the darkness in Mason that calls to the hungry beast roaming beneath my skin. A part of me, the same part that revels in Vincent's ice-cold attention, wants Mason to carry me into the shadows that surround him until we rule over the darkness together. His blue eyes carve a pathway of fire all the way to my very soul.

"Grim won't come for you again," Mason all but growls, his lips peeling away from his teeth.

"How can you be sure?"

Because unlike Mason, I don't believe for a second that Grim won't come after me again. But this time, I'll be ready. Grim took me by surprise the first time, but I refuse to let it happen again. I didn't become the best assassin and spy for the bitten wolves by being scared and weak. He's larger than me, yes, and maybe even stronger, but he's not smarter. If he comes for me, I won't hesitate to do what needs to be done, consequences be damned.

"Grim is too prideful," Mason confesses. "He can't stand the fact that he lost to me and you, and he'll keep his distance until he feels as if he actually has a chance of beating us." A wicked smile curls up his lips, and I feel my eyes lower to them instinctively. "But since I don't plan on leaving you alone anytime soon, that won't happen." He leans down to give my ankle, hidden beneath the covers, a tap. "Now, get up. And dress in something warm."

Dress in something warm?

It's ninety freaking degrees outside, but I learned long ago not to ask Mason questions.

Still…

"I thought after you saw me with Vincent—" I cut off abruptly when a low growl rumbles from his chest. His eyes flash, his wolf making an appearance, before he takes a deep, shuddering breath and squeezes his eyelids shut.

"It doesn't matter," he says through heavily clenched teeth.

I snort. "You guys both acted like it mattered at the park the other day," I point out. "But I'm a wild wolf, Mason. And I'll never allow myself to be tamed or leashed by only one man."

"I know that," he bites out, his cheeks hollowing as he inhales sharply. "And…I've accepted that."

My eyebrows shoot upward. "You have?"

"I'm going to fight for you, Blair. And if that

means I need to fight against my enemy, then so be it." He stalks toward me until his large, imposing frame is towering over my much slighter one. Still, I don't cower, don't look away, maintaining eye contact as he attempts to intimidate me. His hands lower to either side of my head as he looms above me. "I told you. You're going to fall in love with me, and there's nothing anyone can do about it."

"And I told you," I hiss, placing a hand in the center of his stomach and pushing him back a step. "*You're* going to fall in love with *me*."

He doesn't scoff or laugh or do any of the things I expect him to. Instead, he simply bares his teeth in a semblance of a smile, forks his fingers through his shaggy blond hair, and straightens.

"Get dressed."

And with that, he's gone.

"YOU NEED TO STICK IT INSIDE," I TELL MASON breathily as his scowl deepens.

"I'm too big," he protests.

"Just push it in. Here. You push forward and I'll push backward at the same time, okay?"

We both do as I suggest, panting and gasping.

"Fuck, it won't fit!" Mason growls. "I told you I'm too big."

"The hole isn't that small," I protest. "Maybe just put the tip in and try to squeeze it in as far as you can go?"

"Okay, on the count of three," he agrees with a head nod. "One, two—" Before he can get to three, I grab the skate and shove it onto his foot.

He yelps, his features creasing with pain, and I roll my eyes.

"Don't be a big baby," I lament as I finally—*finally* —get the skate on his big ass foot. "You're the one who didn't think to call ahead and make sure they had skates that actually fit us." I smirk up at him, and he scoffs, crossing his arms over his chest and pouting petulantly.

"I didn't expect the ice skating rink to be this busy," he confesses, still pouting.

I'm happy I listened to Mason and brought a sweater and leggings to change into, because the interior of the rink is shockingly cold. Goosebumps had pebbled on my arms the second I stepped into the large building.

Music blares from the speakers up ahead, playing some eighties pop song as people skate around, holding hands. There are a few kids stumbling across the ice as well, all of them wearing matching party hats.

"I don't know how the fuck I'm going to get my other foot in," Mason grumbles, glaring at his second skate distastefully. "It feels as if my poor toes are doing gymnastics and backbending."

"Oh my gosh." I straighten from my kneeling position in front of him, almost immediately toppling to the side as I struggle to regain my balance. "You're being a massive baby."

"Oh shut up." He grabs a rolled-up straw wrapper and tosses it at my head. I squeak and attempt to move to the side but overestimate my sense of balance. Mason roars with laughter as I fall unceremoniously onto the floor, my legs extended in front of me and my arms sprawled on either side of my head.

"Owww," I moan dramatically as he laughs even harder, clutching his stomach.

"And you say I'm the massive baby?" He guffaws, pointing at my sprawled form. Snarling, I lean forward and grab his foot in the skate, pressing down on his cramped toes. He releases an embarrassingly high-pitched squeal. "Owww! My toesies!"

I stare at him—just stare—before laughing so

hard that tears cascade down my cheeks. "Holy fuck! Did you just say toesies?"

He growls. "No."

"You totally just said toesies."

"I don't know what you're talking about. I coughed," he protests stubbornly.

"Yeah, coughed up your masculinity, because you, my friend, just said toesies."

He places a hand to his chest in awe. "Did you just call me your friend, baby girl?"

"Don't go getting a big head about it," I scoff as Mason's phone pings on the bench beside him.

That's the sixteenth time it has vibrated in the last hour. A tiny trickle of jealousy snakes down my spine as I glare at his phone. Who the fuck is texting him nonstop? I know it's not his father or Brett, so I can't help but think it's another woman.

Though…

Why the fuck do I even care?

"Aren't you going to get that, *stronzo*?" I taunt as his eyes flicker to the phone before flashing back to my face.

"No," he bites out. "It's not important. I don't even know how this person got my number in the first place."

"Oh." I glance down at my own skates sticking

out in front of me, pretending I'm not interested in his mysterious texter. Nope. Not me. I have better things to do than fret over some person who may or may not be texting a guy who is definitely *not* my boyfriend.

"He just keeps fucking texting me," Mason growls. "I have no idea how he got my number or—why the fuck is he stalking me? How did he know I was here?"

"He?" My brows touch my hairline as I whip my head in Mason's direction, but his attention isn't on me. It's on the figure entering the skating rink like a dark, brooding angel.

My throat dries as I watch Tai stalk toward us, his black hair cut close to his scalp and drawing attention to his harsh, masculine features—his chiseled jawline, straight brows, and slightly crooked nose. His tribal tattoos flex and ripple like they're alive as he marches to stand directly in front of us, his eyes lowering to me on the ground before fixing on Mason.

His nostrils flare. "You haven't returned my calls."

Mason leans backward on the bench with feigned casualness, but I can see the tightness in his jaw and shoulders. "I didn't know we were texting buddies."

Standing so close together, I can't help but note how similar the two of them are in appearance. Of course, the similarities are minuscule, considering the fact that Mason is pale and blond and Tai is tan and has black hair, but their strong features are eerily similar. And I swear they have the exact same smiles…

"How did you find me?" Mason's voice is almost a snarl as he eyes Tai with barely veiled distaste. His hand balls into a fist, and I honestly fear that the two will go to blows at any damn second.

Cursing in Italian under my breath, I stumble to my feet, placing one hand in the center of Tai's chest and the other on Mason's shoulder to steady myself. Instinctively, Mason places his hand atop mine and Tai captures my hand in his own, but the two of them don't turn away from each other.

"I tracked your phone," Tai says without remorse. Mason's eyes flare.

"Why the fuck would you do that?"

"Because," Tai's chest heaves as he inhales and then exhales, his facial muscles twitching, "I think our fathers formed an alliance."

I whirl to face Tai so suddenly, my hair whips into Mason's face.

"What did you discover?" I bark, my stomach

muscles clenching. Vincent told me about his theory of an alliance between the two packs, but so far, I haven't heard anything concrete, even with my ear to the ground.

Tai briefly lowers his eyes to meet my own, and they're shadowed with pain, pain I doubt he'll allow himself to feel normally. "I spotted my father unloading crates of guns with the Bloody Skulls' MC logo on the front."

"And you think...?" Mason trails off, horror infusing his words.

"I think that they made an alliance." Tai nods his head once, his features grim.

Something dark and sinister explodes inside my chest as the ramifications of his words crash over me like a tsunami. If that's true...

Then it means that the Totemic Tribe and the Bloody Skulls are officially declaring war on the Davenports and bitten wolves.

It's not just "talk" anymore. It's real and dangerous and deadly.

It means that none of us are safe.

"Why are you telling us this?" I demand at the same time Mason barks out, "How can we trust you?"

Tai turns to answer Mason first. "You can't." He

lowers his eyes to me, and I lose myself in the brown orbs flecked with gold. "Because, Blair," he lifts a hand as if to cup my cheek before immediately dropping it, his jaw flexing, "I don't want to see you hurt."

There are a thousand things he leaves unsaid, but I can read between the lines easily enough.

What the Bloody Skulls and Totemic Tribe are doing is an act of war in the eyes of the other wolves. They know it; we know it.

Everyone fucking knows it.

It won't be long until it's brother against brother, sister fighting sister, bitten wolves attacking born wolves and vice versa. The streets will run red with blood, and the entire city will be a battleground for a war the humans know nothing about.

And there's not a damn thing I can do about it.

9

BLAIR

DAY 20

"We'll be okay, kid," Papa Grayson assures me on the other end of the line.

"I know." I throw myself onto my bed and rub a hand down my face, my heart thumping like crazy in my chest. "I just…"

"Worry?" I hear distinct amusement in the old man's voice, and if I were near him, I would've hit him.

"I don't like not being there," I confess on a sigh, and he laughs gruffly.

"Worried you're going to miss out on all the fun?" he taunts in a singsong voice.

I snort. "Oh, please. You need me to protect your old ass, admit it."

Genuine laughter escapes him, and I feel my own lips twitch upward instinctively. "Girly, this ass may be old, but it can still fight with the best of them."

Silence reigns as we both think about what to say. I've never been the strongest at articulating my emotions, but then again, neither has Papa Gray.

"Just...be safe, okay?" I all but plead into the phone. "If the Totemics and Bloody Skulls are already compiling weapons..."

"We will be," Papa Gray promises. "Especially with the extra security the Davenports gave us. Blair, I promise you that we'll be fine. It's *you* we're all worried about."

I release a slightly hysterical laugh as I squeeze my eyelids shut, fighting off a headache. "I can look after myself. You know that."

"But should you?" he retorts immediately. Muffled voices on the other end of the line capture Papa Gray's attention, and he places his hand over the speaker to respond to them. I recognize Johnson's deep, gravelly voice and Martha's high-pitched one. "I have to go. But you'll look after yourself, won't you, girly?"

I snort before I can stop myself, the noise leaving

me without conscious thought. "I have too much to live for to die. You know that."

"Enjoy your time with your brother, kid." I can hear the awe in Papa Gray's tone. When I told him I reunited with Brett, he was overjoyed for me. He, more than any other wolf, knows the horrors that plagued my childhood. All he has ever wanted for me was a chance to find a family of my own and be happy. And now that my happiness is within my grasp, he wants me to hold on to it with all my might and never let it go.

"Love you, old man." My throat closes with emotions for the man who plucked me from the street, gave me a home and love, and called me daughter when his own family had perished many years before. I don't know if I'll ever truly be able to repay him for all he has done for me and all he continues to do.

"Love you too, girly. Be safe."

"You too."

We hang up after that, and for the longest time, I can't peel my eyes from the now dark phone screen. A snarl bubbles up my throat like steam in a kettle, and all I want to do is throw my phone across the room and watch it shatter.

I should be with Papa Gray and the others, not in

some fucking apartment above a shitty ass bar. Because of this damn bet, I'm away from my family, and I hate that more than I can put into words.

"Uh oh." Mason's amused voice has me whipping my head in his direction, surprised to see him leaning against the door frame with a wry smirk pulling up his lips. "Whenever you snarl like that, it means you're planning someone's death."

I growl at him in warning, not in the mood for his shit today. Since Tai's confession four days ago, we haven't seen each other that often. I've been busy organizing things with Gray and Vincent, while Mason has been spying on his father, searching for any information that might help us.

One thing is clear—Grim and Sarai are working together, but we can't quite figure out what their endgame is.

Complete annihilation of all the lycans and bitten wolves in the city?

Something else entirely?

The mere thought has centipedes crawling across my skin.

"You look tense," Mason points out, and I bare my teeth at him.

"You don't fucking say," I bite out. The bun I have haphazardly thrown my hair into has come loose, a few long strands tumbling around my face. With a growl, I rip my hair the rest of the way out of the bun and work on braiding it away from my face. I'm sure I'm a sight for Mason to see—disheveled, messy, and covered in stains. With everything that has been going on, I haven't been taking the best care of myself, a fact that's impossible to hide.

"Want to talk about it?" He folds his arms over his chest and quirks a blond brow at me.

"Talk about what?" Harsh laughter escapes me as I sit further up in bed. "I'm worried sick about Gray and the rest of my family. Grim no doubt wants to murder me because of what happened the other day, though I haven't seen that sick bastard since he tried to rape me." I ignore the way Mason's eyes darken at the reminder. "The Totemic Tribe and Bloody Skulls are going to declare war on us any day now, and I have no idea what that means for me or the people I care about. Everything is going to shit, Mase, and I'm right smack dab in the middle of it all."

With every word I speak, Mason stalks a step forward until he's directly in front of me.

"Take your clothes off," he instructs as I blink up at him, at a loss for words.

"Excuse me, *pezzo di merda*?" My words are practically a purr, but no one can miss the unveiled threat in them.

Mason rolls his eyes as if I'm being overly dramatic. "I'm not going to jump you, doofus." He has the nerve to squeeze my nose like it's some sort of squeaky toy or shit. "You're too tense."

"And how is getting naked going to help anything?" I bark out, seriously considering the merits of knocking him unconscious. It's so fucking tempting…

"I'm going to massage you." He rolls his eyes again. "And you'll be covered by the blanket. Now stop complaining, take your clothes off, and get on your damn stomach. Before I change my mind."

I balk, unsure of what to do, and he simply sighs and gives me his back.

Quickly, before I can lose my nerve and change my mind, I whip my shirt over my head and remove my bra as well. I scramble onto my knees before sliding down my pants and underwear. Once I'm completely naked, I twist so I'm lying on my stomach, the blanket covering the curve of my ass.

"Are you decent?" Mason asks, and out of my periphery, I watch as he turns around, one of his hands covering his eyes. "Not that I care either way. I mean, I've seen you naked so many times, I can probably draw you."

"You going to draw me like one of your French girls, Mase?" I tease, quoting a line from *Titanic*.

"I'm going to make a stick-figure drawing with a big ass and a nice pair of tits," Mason counters immediately, moving his hand from his eyes and grinning when he sees that I'm covered. "That's the extent of my artistic talent."

"Hopefully your massage skills are better than your art ones," I quip as he places his hands on my shoulders and begins to knead the skin. A low moan rips itself from my mouth as my eyelashes flutter shut.

"I believe that moan answered your question," he points out, digging his thumbs into the tense muscles of my neck.

"I moan for many things…" I breathily exclaim. "Pizza is one of them. Are you comparing yourself to pizza, Mason?"

I can hear the smirk in his voice when he says, "If the shoe fits. I mean, I never heard of someone getting a lady boner for pizza before, but I suppose there's a first time for everything."

"I'm not getting a lady boner for you," I retort automatically. But truth be told…I definitely am. His hands are positively magical on my bare skin, and liquid fire rushes through my veins, setting me aflame.

"Sure you're not," Mason purrs, elongating the 'sure.'

"Lady boner. Regular boner. Is there really a difference?" I mumble, my words slurring together in my lust-fueled haze.

"You're just rambling now." Mason chuckles. "I doubt you have any idea what you're saying anymore."

"Tomato. Tomahto."

"Yup. You're officially lust-drunk," he says, snorting.

"Your face is lust-drunk."

Blair—one.

Mason—zero.

"Do you have any lotion?" Mason inquires, his hands stilling on my back. I practically let out a pathetic whimper before mumbling something that I'm pretty sure translated to "bathroom."

Mason leaves, returning less than a second later with a bottle of my fruity lotion. I watch as he squeezes a generous amount into his palms before rubbing them together. Then, he moves onto the bed, his knees on either side of my hips, and begins to massage me once more.

I fucking *purr.*

"Did you turn into a cat when I wasn't looking?" Mason teases as he lowers his hands to my sides, lightly rubbing them across the side of my boobs. Heat licks down my spine from the menial touch, and an entire fireworks show erupts inside my stomach.

Before I can stop myself, a moan is pulled from my throat, the noise carnal, hungry, and dripping in sin.

Mason growls sharply, his hands flexing on my naked skin, before he takes a deep, calming breath and forces himself to relax.

"If you keep making those noises, baby girl, we'll have a problem." His words rumble through me, dark and decadent like a fruit from the forbidden tree. I know I shouldn't have a bite…

But I desperately want to.

"Distract me," I murmur sleepily.

"With what?" His voice is a hushed whisper as he continues to knead the sensitive muscles of my shoulders and upper back.

"Why?" That one word hangs suspended between

us, though I can tell he doesn't initially comprehend its meaning.

"Why what?" His hands still, and I all but cry out, shifting in the bed to encourage him to continue. He chuckles darkly before pushing his thumbs into the skin of my neck, rubbing soothing circles. "Why am I so good looking?"

"Why are you a part of the Bloody Skulls?" My words are almost slurred with fatigue, but I can tell they penetrate his defenses when he stills once more. "I mean, you're not like Grim and the others."

"How is that?" His voice is deceptively light, though I can sense the undercurrent of warning. Or maybe it's wariness? It's hard to say for certain.

"You're not cruel," I reply. "You don't hurt people just to hurt people. I think you're actually…" I hesitate over what to say next before deciding on honesty. "Gentle."

"Trust me, baby girl." A bark of harsh, self-deprecating laughter tumbles out of him. "I'm the exact opposite of gentle."

"You're gentle with me," I point out, and I hear him blow out a breath above me.

"That's different." His words are almost a growl, and when he resumes his massage, his fingers dig into my skin punishingly hard. A swarm of buzzing bees fly around in my stomach, and I can't help but smile against the pillow. A part of me loves the fact that Mason is only gentle with me. I don't know how to encapsulate it with words, but I don't want him to act like this with anyone else. The mere thought has me seeing red.

"You never answered my question." With my head twisted sideways, I can only see one of his legs and the width of his forearm, but I imagine his lips are curled into a frown.

"About why I'm a member of the Bloody Skulls?" he asks for clarification. He doesn't give me a chance to respond before forging on. "Besides the fact that I grew up here and these men are quite literally my family…" A strangled noise escapes me as he presses down on a particularly sore portion of my spine, but he doesn't let up. "I like to ride. Love it, really. Sometimes, I'll just climb on my bike and ride until my skin is sunburnt and my body aches. It's exhilarating. I've never been flying before, but I imagine it's somewhat similar. I feel…empty, like the ghosts of my past don't haunt me when I'm on my bike. I can just leave everything behind. You know?"

"I know," I whisper breathily. "It's probably how I feel when I'm in my wolf form."

Silence stretches between us, and I know he's

thinking about the secret that was unintentionally revealed when he attacked Grim in his wolf form.

"I can see your mind steaming, baby girl." Mason's voice is almost wary. "You know you can ask me anything."

I try to resist, to bite my tongue, but he dangles answers in front of my face so enticingly, I can't help but bite down. "How is that possible? How are you a full wolf? Fenrir wolves aren't supposed to be able to shift completely."

"I'm not only a fenrir wolf, Blair." He moves down the curve of my spine, applying just enough pressure to balance that line between pleasure and pain.

"What is that supposed to mean?"

"It means that my mother was either a totemic wolf, a bitten wolf, or a lycan," he answers, his tone devoid of any inflection. "I wouldn't know, though, because I never met her."

"Mason…"

"Enough. I don't want to talk about my fucked up family…or lack thereof. Not with you naked in front of me, looking so fucking delectable that I want to bite your ass."

"Bite my ass?" I huff out a laugh at his choice of

words, while behind my rib cage, my heart begins to beat like crazy.

"You have to know what you do to me," Mason deadpans. "You're every dirty thought I ever had personified. But if you're a demoness sent to drag me straight to hell, I'll go willingly. I crave to live in sin with you, Blair Windsor."

When Mason's hands lower to the curve of my ass, massaging my cheeks through the flimsy sheet that covers it, I lose all sense of reasoning. I'm pretty sure my brain turns into a literal puddle of goo as coherent thoughts flee.

Before I can think better of it, I flip onto my back, the blanket falling to my knees.

Mason's breath hitches where he still hovers above me, his eyes devouring every inch of skin exposed. The heat emanating from his bright gaze lights a fire in my soul, and I know without a shadow of doubt that he wants me. He'll never admit it out loud—he's too fucking stubborn—but he wants me with every dark and twisted facet of his soul, the same as I do.

He tries for a cocky smirk, but the confidence he attempts to emulate is eclipsed by the wanton need in his gaze.

"Baby girl, we talked about this…" His hands

travel to my breasts, tentatively at first but gaining strength by the second. At first, he simply kneads the tender flesh, staring intently at my beaded nipples, before his thumb lashes out to flick one. He watches in rapt fascination as it immediately settles back into place. "Fuck…"

He pushes both of my breasts together, a slight sheen on my skin from the lotion, before lowering his head. His tongue curls around my right nipple, eliciting delicious tremors through my body, before he sucks it entirely into his mouth. When he releases it, he immediately kisses his way over to my left breast and gives it the same treatment.

"Mason…" I gasp as a thousand words jump to the tip of my tongue.

We shouldn't do this.

We need to stop.

We can't go any further.

But what comes out is, "Kiss me." It's a low, throaty plea, and when he growls, I lose all sense of self. I'm desperate for him, desperate to be reminded that war doesn't necessarily mean the end. That death isn't lurking over our heads like the blade on a guillotine.

When he begins to kiss up my neck, eagerly

seeking out my lips, I tangle my fingers in his blond hair.

It's a kiss that ends all kisses.

Nothing exists in that moment except his lips on mine, his tongue plundering my mouth like he'll fucking die if he doesn't taste me. I meet him stroke to stroke, a growl leaving my throat as I tighten my hands in his hair.

He kisses me like he owns me, but we both know that isn't true.

I own *him.*

His large body fits perfectly between my spread legs, and I widen them even further as one of his fingers begins to circle my clit.

"You drive me fucking crazy," he all but roars against my lips as he breaks the kiss, panting down at me. His eyes scream words he doesn't dare say, and I get the impression that he's pissed at me, but for what, I don't know. Despite the fierceness in his gaze—the corrosive mixture of lust and hatred radiating from his eyes—his fingers don't leave my pussy lips as he strokes them.

"Why don't you do something about it?" I taunt, widening my legs even further to grant him better access.

Without warning, he moves off the bed, drops to

his knees before me, and grabs my legs, hitching them over his shoulder. This new position puts my core at level with his face, and his eyes gleam mischievously as he eyes my glistening pussy lips.

"Are you wet for me already, baby girl?" he practically purrs as his tongue snakes out to lick a slow, sensuous pathway. My toes curl, and I dig my hands into the blankets on either side of me, fisting them the same way I want to his blond hair.

"Don't tease me," I growl.

"Unfortunately for you...Tease is my middle name." He winks at me before dropping his mouth to my core once more, pulling my clit between his luscious lips and sucking.

He starts to fuck me with his fingers, his mouth suctioned to my clit, as I try to remind myself how to breathe. Pleasure turns my blood into molten lava as I thrash on the bed, arching my back.

"Scream for me, baby girl, and maybe I'll let you come." Mason's voice is low with wicked intent and dark promises—promises that are only ever made between the sheets late at night.

My back arches off the bed as I ride wave after wave of pleasure, my fingers and toes both curling simultaneously. I scream Mason's name as he licks and sucks me through my orgasm, his free hand sneaking up my stomach to cup my breast.

"Fucking hell," I curse as I fall from the heavens and back onto earth.

Mason lifts his head, his lips sparkling with the evidence of my arousal, and lazily licks it away. Slowly, keeping his eyes trained on me, he stands and removes his cut, revealing a lean and muscular chest sprinkled with fine blond hairs. He reaches for the waistband of his pants, but before he can remove them, a tiny noise of dissent leaves my lips.

"Wait."

He pauses, his hands on the waistband of his jeans, and I watch his blond brows raise. Something akin to hurt flashes in his gaze.

"Do you not want me?" He tries to smile, tries to adopt his cocky mask, but I can see the cracks in it, the ones he tries to quickly refill with plaster.

"Mason, there's something I need to tell you," I confess breathily, my chest heaving.

"If you don't want to do this—"

"I want to—fuck, do I want to—but you need to know something." My heart hammers a staccato in my chest, and no amount of moderated breathing can get it under control. "It's something that happened with Vincent when I stayed at his house."

"Vincent." Pure rage flashes in his eyes as a growl breaks free. He stalks toward me like some type of angelic entity, though his wicked scowl conjures up images of the devil. "Why the fuck are you talking about Vincent?"

"He claims I'm his mate. And...and I believe him. I feel the bond," I blurt out, knowing my confession will alter something irrevocably between us. A part of me believes Vincent, but...

But another part of me doesn't understand how I can still have such strong feelings for Mason if I truly *am* Vincent's mate. Unless there's something fundamentally wrong with me, that shit just doesn't happen.

How can you explain the bond, Blair? The feeling of completeness when Vincent's with you? The bond that seems to shimmer like starlight whenever he's near?

A myriad of emotions cross Mason's face— surprise, shock, confusion, and then something far more sinister.

A nice girl would run kicking and screaming from the dangerous expression that distorts his beautiful face. But I've never been a nice girl. Instead of running, heat pulsates between my thighs and my skin erupts into goosebumps.

"Vincent's lying, baby girl," he purrs as he crawls

over my body, his naked chest pressing against my own.

"Mason, I don't think—"

"You can't be his mate," he insists as he sucks on my neck hard enough to leave a hickey.

"How can you be so confident?" I gasp, twisting my neck to grant him better access.

"Because you're *mine*."

10

VINCENT

DAY 20

I press my back against the wall, nothing but a shadow in the gray sky. My mask is in place, impeccably crafted as always, and my gun is in my hand.

Tonight, I will see my mate.

I can't ignore the need inside of me, pressing on my chest and making breathing immensely difficult. Every day that we've been parted has been goddamn torture.

And I'm determined more than ever to end the agony that has been riding me since I watched Blair walk away from me with that fuck, Mason, a few nights ago.

When she hears what I have to tell her, she'll jump into my arms with a beatific grin on her beautiful face. She'll thank me, and I'll soak up her attention eagerly, for once bringing hope into someone's life instead of darkness.

A memory assaults me, so staggering with its intensity that I have to press my palm to the wall and take a deep breath.

"FATHER." MY TONE IS CURT AND SHARP AS I NOD toward the domineering man sitting at the head of the table. "Mother." My gaze travels to Annabelle Davenport, her fluffy blonde tresses coiffed into a bun at the top of her head. Finally, I rest my eyes on one of the only people in this world I can claim to truly love.

Valentina lifts her chin and gives me the slightest nod —our secret code. With that one nod, I know a few things.

One, that she's okay. That when our father returned home from his trip to London, he hadn't taken his rage out on her. Not that he hurts Valentina often. She's not his preferred punching bag, something I'm grateful for every day, but there are times when his rage gets the best of him and she's the only one in the immediate vicinity.

And two, that Father is in a surprisingly good mood.

"Sit! Sit!" He gestures for me to claim my seat to the right of him, opposite my mother, just as the servants hurry into the grand dining room, carrying trays of meat, vegetables, and freshly baked rolls. Their enticing smells do very little to settle my roiling stomach.

Once the staff sets down the last plate and then departs back into the kitchen, my father indicates for us to dig in.

As I scoop some broccoli onto my plate, I take a moment to survey my father, gauging his mood.

I hate how similar we look to one another. Same dark hair, same pitch-black eyes, same chiseled features and cheekbones. I like to believe that I'm kinder than the man who sired me...but that would be a lie.

I love to kill, and more than that, I'm damn good at it.

"How was your trip, honey?" my mother inquires softly. Does my father notice that she flinches when he turns his obsidian gaze in her direction?

Does she flinch when I stare at her?

The thought of being more like my father than I thought sours my stomach.

Ignoring my mother, Father turns to me with a bright smile, one that sends prickles of unease shooting up and then back down my spine.

"I have a surprise for you, son. Meet me in the basement after dinner."

Oh...fuck.

I have no idea what this surprise is, but it sounds ominous. My father isn't the type of parental figure to bestow gifts upon his children. Whatever he wants to show me, it can't be good.

Throughout the rest of the meal, we don't talk. Valentina tries to meet my gaze, but I purposefully avoid her. Even my mother tries to distract Father, talking about a new purse she bought, but he dismisses her with a simple wave of his hand.

By the time dinner ends and our plates are removed, there are a thousand different knots twisting together in my stomach. Pain explodes behind my eyes, but I ignore it as I get to my feet, keeping my face impassive.

My mask.

My perfect, cruel mask.

Father doesn't say a word to any of us as he stalks down the hall toward the door that leads to the basement. He doesn't need to say anything. Where he goes, I follow. That's the way we work.

His loafers clack against the smooth white tiles as he plugs in the familiar combination on the keypad adjacent to the door. The light overhead turns green, and the door swings open on silent hinges.

I've always hated the basement and what it repre-

sented. *I swear I can scent death in the air before I've even ventured down a single step.*

Don't let your mask break, Vincent. If your father wants a monster in his image, then that's what he's going to get.

I repeat that mantra in my head as I descend the staircase, my back perfectly straight and my chin lifted, emulating all of the confidence a sixteen-year-old boy is capable of possessing.

The cloying scent of blood barrages my senses when I finally climb down the last step, squinting in the blindingly bright room below our mansion. It's ironic, really, that the wicked deeds most people would do in the dark, my father does in the light. After all, with the power he wields, he doesn't have any reason to hide his sins from the world.

My father stops suddenly, forcing me to a halt as well, and when he moves to the side, I'm given a view of the woman strapped to a metal table in the center of the room.

She's naked, her pasty skin covered in bruises and bloody wounds. Blood drips down her chin as she turns toward me.

"Please, help me," she begs, sobbing. "Please. You have to help me. I have a family. Please."

My father slowly, almost indolently, rolls up the sleeves of his dress shirt and moves to grab a knife off a table opposite her. I fight with all of my strength not to flinch, not to cry out, as she wails in agony.

"I thought it was time you learned how to be a man, Vincent," my father tells me, circling her nipple with the tip of the blade. "And what better way than with a piece of shit totemic wolf?"

My father isn't torturing this wolf shifter because she's a woman. No, I've seen him torture both male and female. Gender doesn't matter to him. Neither does age or race.

He'll hurt and destroy any wolf who isn't a lycan like us.

"Please!" The woman begins sobbing in earnest as my father grins at me.

"If you don't support us, you're an enemy," he tells me, still moving the blade in a leisurely circle around her nipple. "And if you're the enemy, you end up here."

He positions the blade between her breasts, directly over her heart...

And then plunges it inside of her.

I just barely stop myself from crying out in alarm as blood bubbles out of the woman's mouth, her eyes turning glazed in death.

"So tell me, Vincent..." He casually removes the knife from her chest and wipes it on her stomach. I can't seem to pull my gaze away from her sightless eyes, still laced with

agony even in death. "What will you do to protect this family?"

I WONDER IF THE SURLY, SADISTIC BASTARD STILL would've killed that woman if he knew that, one year from then, her husband would cut off his head in retaliation, killing him instantly.

I never killed anyone on behalf of my father, but he *did* transform me into the monster the world sees today. A monster who won't hesitate to kill for the people he loves and the family he vowed to protect.

And now, that protection extends to Blair and her family of bitten wolves.

Shaking off the memory, I continue across the street and through the back door of the bar. With my gun in hand, I feel like a harbinger of death, coming to seek retribution on all the men and women who tried to take Blair away from me.

There's only vengeance on my mind—only pain —and I covet both emotions fiercely. They're the only ones I'm capable of feeling without Blair beside me.

Blair…

My mate who still refuses to accept that the bond

between us is real and vibrant and the only bright thing in my life.

Voices sound from the right of me, and I stealthily move into the shadows of the stairwell, holding my breath as they pass. I don't want to have to shoot anyone today—but I will. I won't even fucking hesitate. Nothing will stop me from seeing my mate.

Logically, I know this is a dumb idea. My appearance here will mean war against the Bloody Skulls, and with the mounting tensions between all of our packs, I'm not prepared for it.

Though I do relish the prospect of shooting heads off of some of these fuckers.

My research—ahem, stalking—has shown me that Blair lives in the apartment above the bar. According to my sources, Mason was supposed to move her to his own apartment complex across town but decided against it, wanting her to remain close to her brother Brett. Mason apparently sleeps on the couch in the living room, and I honestly don't know how I feel about that.

On one hand, I want her to be protected, despite knowing she can protect herself, and on the other...

The thought of them alone together at night makes me want to kill somebody. Well, not just anybody. *Him.* I want to put the barrel of my gun between his eyes and press down on the trigger, watching in grim satisfaction as his body falls backward in a pool of blood.

There aren't even words capable of describing the need waging a war inside of me. It's not just a want, but something intrinsic to my survival.

Mason will pay for trying to take Blair away from me. That's a promise.

I move like death itself up the stairs, ducking my head out the door to ensure that the hall is clear. Silence greets me, cloying and pronounced, and I finally place my gun back in its holster and stalk toward the apartment. I don't bother knocking as I push it open and glance around the modestly furnished living room.

I'll need to remind Blair not to leave her door unlocked. Any insane murderer can just sneak in, and she'd be none the wiser. Case in point.

Fortunately, she only has ten more days she has to stay in this hell hole. Ten more days...until she travels to Tai's home for an additional month.

The thought has me biting down on the growl that wants to escape.

But then I remind myself that Blair is my fated mate, that the moon chose her for me, and the anger percolating in my gut evaporates like sizzling water over a stovetop.

Without preamble, I turn in the direction of her bedroom and throw open the door. I've been staking out the bar all day, and I know for a fact she hasn't left. I expect her to be reading one of those damn reverse harem books she seems to love so much or even talking to Papa Gray on the phone.

What I don't expect to see, however, is my mate naked with that fucker Mason leaning over her.

For a brief minute, I see red. The color seeps over every available surface, painting my surroundings in a garnet sheen. All I'm aware of is the pounding in my head, almost like a drumline, distant but growing louder as the seconds drag on.

Is he hurting her? What the fuck is he doing to my mate? Is he—

Blair definitely doesn't look like she's in distress, staring up at Mason with wide, lust-filled eyes.

The two of them don't seem to notice I'm in the room, too preoccupied with each other.

Betrayal stabs at me, flays me open, and I place a hand against the wall to steady myself.

How can Blair do this to me?

But then I remember one of our last days in my mansion, where she adamantly insisted that she wasn't my mate. When she denied the mate bond I knew we both felt.

We've never declared ourselves to be exclusive, but I'd assumed…

I wrongly assumed that she wanted and desired me as much as I did her.

That she loved me as much as I loved her.

Apparently, I was wrong.

Every muscle in me tightens, coiling together like a nest of slithering snakes, as I stare at the love of my existence naked beneath my sworn enemy.

And…

I can't even be mad at her. I know in my heart that I didn't fight for her hard enough, that I didn't fight for her family hard enough, and because of that, she chose to reject the mate bond. I hate myself more than I hate her.

But him? Him, I can kill.

"Get your fucking hands off my mate," I growl out, something dark and insidious taking root in my stomach. Mason scrambles off of her as if his ass is on fire, his eyes widening in alarm before narrowing. Blair simply sits upright in bed, not bothering to cover her bare breasts.

"Vincent? What are you doing here? How did you get into the Bloody Skulls' clubhouse?" Confusion laces her tone, though I barely pay her a glance. It hurts too much to stare at her.

"I'm going to fucking kill you!" I roar, running at Mason with all the strength my wolf possesses and throwing a punch at his face. I could use my gun and end this here and now, but where's the fun in that? I want him to bleed for touching what's mine. I want him to pay with his life, my fists pounding repeatedly into his smug, pretty boy face.

He's shirtless, a fact that only exacerbates my rage, but at least his motherfucking pants are still on.

"You're fucking dead!" I seethe, raining down blow after blow as he smiles up at me. Blood stains his teeth, but if he's in any pain, he doesn't let it show.

"Jealous, lycan?" he taunts, spitting out the mouthful of blood.

I simply roar in rage and punch him again as hard as I can, watching as his head twists to the side with the force of my hit.

"You guys are being absolutely ridiculous," Blair deadpans from somewhere behind me, sounding absolutely fucking nonchalant about this all.

Before I can stop myself, I whirl around to face her, allowing her to see the agony etched across my face. The betrayal. The hurt.

"How could you?" I snap, wanting nothing more than to go to her and…

And what?

Take her in my arms and never let her go? Run away with her? Spank her perfect ass for hurting me as much as she did?

A delicate wrinkle appears between her brow as she moves gracefully forward, her naked body doing things to my cock that is completely inappropriate, considering I'm straddling another man and beating his face in.

"Vincent, there's something we need to talk about —" she begins, but she's cut off when Mason begins to laugh.

"Is that boner for her, or are you just happy to see me shirtless?" he queries with a mocking grin.

I bellow in rage, prepared to punch him again, when Blair appears behind me, capturing my wrist and holding it hostage. I twist my head to stare at her in betrayal.

"You're defending him?" I don't even bother to hide the hurt permeating my words.

"I'm defending my mate from my other mate," she snaps, and my heart lurches at hearing her refer to me as her mate for the first time in her life.

But then her words pierce the haze in my mind.

"What?" Mason and I both ask in unison.

She releases my wrist and moves to sit on the edge of the bed, crossing one leg over the other.

"It makes sense, don't you think?" she asks, running a hand through her loose hair. "Why I'm attracted to both of you at the same time. Why I have all of these goddamn fucking feelings for you guys that I can't understand." She makes a face at the latter statement, but my damn, traitorous heart once again leaps for joy.

Feelings?

"When Mason told me that I was his mate, it finally clicked inside of me," she confesses, placing a fist against her bare chest, directly over her heart. "It's not an either-or situation. I'm not just one of your mates. I'm *both* of yours."

"What?" Mason balks, shoving at my chest until I reluctantly get off of him. "How is that possible? You're *my* mate!"

"No, she's mine," I hiss out, baring my teeth. I feel like a feral wolf, cornered and caged and just waiting for a chance to bite into his throat.

"I think..." Blair takes a deep breath. "I think I'm both of your mates. And maybe even Tai's."

"Tai's?" Mason snaps, running his fingers through

his shoulder-length hair. "The prince of the Totemic Tribe? That fucking Tai?"

"You're the only three wolves I'm attracted to." She shrugs her shoulders. "I can't even explain it in words, but—"

"You want me to share my mate?" I interrupt incredulously, jabbing a finger in Mason's direction. "With *him*? Not fucking happening!"

"I'm not asking anyone to share me," Blair bites out, and for the first time since I stormed into her bedroom, I see a flicker of irritation in her gaze. Not shame or even embarrassment, but...annoyance. At me? At both of us? "I'm just telling you what I suspect. I'm being honest with you."

"Honest?" I bark out a laugh, smoothing out a wrinkle in my pristine, five-piece black suit. "Maybe you should've been honest when I was balls deep inside of your cunt." The crude words are meant to remind her of our time together...and also piss off Mason. If I happen to hurt her in the process, then so be it. That pain has nothing on the agony she caused me.

Am I hearing this right?

She thinks we're *both* her mates? That Tai might be too?

What the fuck is she even suggesting?

"I didn't know Mason was my mate when we had sex," she argues, growling. "And I never promised myself to just you, Vincent."

Her words stab at something already bleeding in my chest, and I can't help but stagger back a step as if I've been physically assaulted.

"So I really mean that little to you, huh?"

Why does it feel as if my heart's breaking? As if I'm being run over repeatedly by a truck while she watches and laughs?

"You know that's not true." She licks her upper lip as she seems to consider her next words. "But I also know I can't choose just one of you. And if you guys are both truly my mates, then you shouldn't ask me to. It'd be like asking me to give up one of my fucking limbs."

"What you're asking is too much," Mason spits out, and for the first time in my life, I have to agree with the not-wolf.

"Ho bisogno dell'aria per respirare. Per favore, non andartene. Per favore, non chiedermi di scegliere." I don't understand a word she's saying, but there's a plea in her voice I never heard before. She's begging, and I have the distinct impression I know what for. Bright blue eyes, reminiscent of the sea itself, peer into my soul as her Italian words rush over me in a

blaze of pure sunlight. I shiver before I can stop myself.

How is this girl capable of carving down my defenses with a single look?

How can she destroy me one second and then piece me back together the next?

"Blair…" I take a step closer, but my movement is impeded by Mason placing a hand on my shoulder. He spins me around to face him, and I growl low in my throat in warning.

"Don't you dare fucking hurt her," he bellows.

"I would never fucking hurt her!" I take a step closer until I'm in his face, my hand twitching to draw the gun from my holster and shoot him between the eyes. If he's dead, maybe Blair will stop spouting all of that ridiculous nonsense about being mates with both of us. "I'm telling the truth when I say that she's my mate. I care about this woman more than I care about most people in this entire fucked up world." Before Blair, I was known as being the man hewn from ice. The man who felt nothing for the people in this world. But now, I'm fire, burning white-hot and blistering.

Burning for her.

"And you're saying I don't?" Mason glares at me.

"I never said that, now did I?"

"I'm not a fucking idiot," he hisses. "I can see it in your eyes—"

"Ohhhh." Blair's breathy moan has us turning to face her, still sitting on the edge of the bed.

"What the fuck?" Mason breathes in wonder, but I'm incapable of speech.

Her legs are spread open to reveal her wet pussy, and two of her fingers are currently sheathed inside of her tight hole. She cups her breast with her other hand, twisting her dusky red nipple between her thumb and forefinger.

My cock feels like granite in my pants as I practically pant with the need to claim her, taste her, own her.

One time with Blair Windsor just isn't enough to satiate me. I need more—I need everything.

"Fucking hell, baby girl," Mason remarks, and for a brief, brief second, I don't even care that he's in the room with me, watching the same show I am. I don't give a fucking damn that he's supposed to be my sworn enemy.

All I can focus on is Blair.

Her thumb circles her clit as she stares at us through heavily hooded eyes, her lips pursed. Her tongue darts out to lick her plump bottom one as she continues to hold both of our stares.

"Does this bother you? Me putting on a show for both of you at the same time?" Her voice turns into a whimper as her fingers begin to move faster inside of her tight pussy. "Because you sure as fuck don't look bothered."

"I…" Words rush onto the tip of my tongue, but I don't say them. I can't say them.

Because they would be lies.

To be completely honest, Mason's presence in the room doesn't bother me in the least. If anything, the fact that he's watching the same show I am, the fact that he's getting turned on by it, only amplifies my own desire. It's like Blair's a damn temptress, a siren, and we're incapable of resisting the spell she casts over us. She lures us in with every sinful word, every heated glance, every thrust of her fingers in that perfect pussy.

We're hers. Both of us.

I exchange a long, loaded glance with Mason, and I can see the same acquiescence in his own gaze—for a few minutes, we'll forget about the feud and hatred still consuming both of us. We'll forget about the war between our packs. We'll forget about anything and everything that doesn't have to do with this goddess spread out before us.

That isn't to say that we're suddenly best friends

or anything. I still hate this fucker with everything that I am…but I don't want him to leave. I want him to watch me pleasure my girl. Hell, I want to watch *him* pleasure her as well, because I know for a fact that there's nothing in this world more arousing than watching Blair's orgasm face.

What the fuck is happening to me?

I don't dare look at it too closely as I carefully, methodically, unbutton my suit coat and drape it over the chair in the corner of the bedroom. The last time I took Blair, it'd been a frenzy of bodies and a gnashing of teeth. It was wild and primitive and everything I never knew I wanted. I still remember how it felt when I marked her with my teeth, the bond between us strengthening with every passing second. I remember the way my cock knotted inside of her.

Fuck…

"One night only," Mason rumbles, recapturing my attention. "For one night only, we forget about all of the shit between our packs and share her."

A myriad of emotions floods me.

A part of me knows I should rebel at the prospect of sharing my mate with my mortal enemy, but the rest of me might quite actually wither to dust and die if I can't have her. Would it really be that horrible to share her with him? I'm aroused by the prospect of him watching, but can I handle him touching her? Kissing her? Claiming her?

"One night only." The words spill from my mouth before I can take them back, but the second they're out in the world, I find that I don't regret them. At all.

Besides, by the time I'm done with her, it's going to be *me* she remembers, not the fucker standing next to me.

As one, Mason and I turn back to face Blair.

For her, I'll do just about anything.

And apparently, that includes sharing her with my enemy.

11

BLAIR

DAY 20

The two of them standing before me—one dark and the other light—is like every wet dream I never allowed myself to have, mainly because it seemed too improbable.

These two alpha men would never in a million years agree to share me, yet I know in my heart that what I told them is true.

They're both my fated mates, and they may not be my only ones.

But at that moment, as they advance on me like malevolent, angelic deities, no one else matters except for them. I want to lose myself in their touches of ice and fire, surrender to the darkness they exude. Our pack alignments don't matter. Nothing matters except tasting them.

My eyes glue to Mason first, still shirtless and emanating an aura that's ten parts innocence and five hundred parts danger. I then glance toward Vincent as he undoes the last button of his dress shirt, unveiling skin that is darkened by the sun and chiseled to perfection. They're as different from each other as night and day—ice and fire—but their differences call to a primitive part of my soul. I want to freeze in Vincent's coldness and burn in Mason's heat.

Mason reaches me first and grabs a fistful of my hair, pulling me to my feet and claiming my lips with a bruising intensity that I've come to associate with him. Everything about his kiss is possessive, and I find myself weak in the knees as I surrender to each punishing thrust of his tongue in my mouth.

His hands grope my bare ass, massaging the skin the way he did earlier, and I groan against his mouth, wanting more from him. Wanting everything. I can feel how hard his cock is through the fabric of his jeans, and my hand moves without conscious thought to stroke him through the rough material.

Abruptly, Vincent grabs my shoulders and spins

me to face him. His mouth meets mine, the sensation electrifying, as he presses my ass against Mason's rock-hard cock.

"Fucking hell, baby girl," he groans, gyrating his hips against me. I shamelessly rock back and forth between the two men, reveling in the taste of Vincent and each possessive stroke of his tongue against mine.

With my lips still meshed to Vincent, I don't see Mason until he's on his knees to the side of me, one of his hands making a leisurely pathway up my inner thigh. I break my mouth from Vincent's to gasp, staring down at the strong and arresting man kneeling before me.

I part my legs eagerly as Mason dips one finger inside my core, his gaze never leaving mine.

Vincent growls with lust and something almost possessive as he grips my chin and reclaims my lips. His free hand creates a pathway of fire down my stomach until he, too, is able to enter my slick channel. When his finger accidentally brushes Mason, both men release warning growls.

"Fuck off, asshole," Mason hisses, but Vincent doesn't dignify him with a response, still kissing me passionately as his finger thrusts in and out of my pussy.

In the next second, I feel a wet tongue caress my slit, and I jerk in Vincent's arms, breaking free of his kiss. My eyes slide downward to see Mason grinning devilishly, his tongue circling my clit directly beside Vincent's hand.

"Do you like that, Blair?" Vincent grabs my chin and forces my attention back on him. "Do you like seeing him on his knees before you? You're so fucking greedy, aren't you? You like knowing you have both of us wrapped around your little finger."

"Fuck, I need you, Vincent." I lower my gaze back down to Mason, where his tongue continues to lick my entrance. "I need you both."

I watch the two of them exchange an unreadable glance, and I swear Vincent even bares his teeth. For a single second, no one moves. Mason remains between my thighs, that cocky smirk plastered firmly in place, and Vincent keeps his hands clasped on my shoulders.

As if they've come to some silent agreement, they jump to action, pushing me backward until I fall on the bed, my hair cascading around me. Vincent moves to stand between my legs, but before he can take a single step, Mason is there, shoving at his shoulder.

"Mine," Mason growls as he drops his pants and boxers, his hard cock springing free.

Vincent's eyes turn pitch-black, almost like two cauldrons of ink, so dark I can't even make out his pupils.

"Watch it, pup," he warns as he removes his own pants, crawling onto the bed beside me. He catches my face between his hands and tips my mouth up to meet his lips once more. Mason growls, seemingly annoyed that my attention isn't on him, and with a gasp, I pull my mouth away from Vincent's and twist to face my second mate.

"I need you *both*," I remind them, my voice a breathy plea. And I do. I need them with the intensity of the moon in the sky and the stars winking into existence across the velvety black canvas. It's something innate within me, something I can't articulate with mere words. I know in my heart that I'm meant to be with both of them, and while that prospect terrifies me, it also exhilarates me like nothing else is capable of. I thought there was something wrong with me for wanting them both, but now I know that this is fated. My feelings for them are normal.

I just want them to drop their barriers and be with me freely, the way our hearts and souls yearn for. They don't have to start sucking each other's dicks or anything—though I wouldn't protest if that was what they wanted—but they do need to learn how to share.

For tonight, I'm going to indulge myself in the fantasies I haven't dared allowed myself to dream. I won't deny myself the pleasure of feeling both of them inside of me, our hearts beating as one and our souls tangled together.

Mason crawls up my body, his hard cock pressing against my stomach, as he twists my head toward his and kisses me passionately. Vincent releases a low, dangerous growl, one that has my toes curling, and attempts to steal my lips for himself.

"Share," I snarl in warning, sitting upright and nearly knocking my head into Mason's as I dart my glare between the two of them. He rolls onto his side, and I can't help the desire that snakes through me at seeing the two of them like this—naked and lying side by side in my bed.

Vincent opens his mouth as if to make a retort, but I stop him by placing my hand around his dick. His eyes widen, lust seeping into his hard gaze, before he moans low in his throat. Mason watches the two of us with barely concealed jealousy, but when I grab his dick as well, that jealousy dissipates.

"This will only fucking work if you understand that I want you both. Not just one of you. Do you hear me?" I plant a tender kiss to Vincent's inner thigh, and he hisses out a breath through clenched teeth. I twist my head to give Mason the same treatment, my hands working in tandem up and down their dicks. "Do you understand?"

"Baby girl…" Mason moans.

"Blair…" Vincent growls.

Smirking darkly, and feeling like a goddess in control of two Herculean-like gods, I bend over completely and take Vincent into my mouth. His hard cock reaches the back of my throat as I swallow him like a champ, my breasts brushing against his thigh. Before he can place his hands in my hair, I release him with an audible pop and move to Mason, running my tongue over his slit before swallowing him whole. My hand wraps around Vincent's cock as I work them both.

Something snaps inside of them at almost the exact same second as their lust for me overrides their hatred toward each other. Mason's hips begin to buck up and down, his cock hitting the back of my throat, as Vincent's hands roam over my body, caressing my nipples and stomach and thighs—anywhere he can reach me.

I pull my lips from Mason and lick away the evidence of his arousal.

Their hands are everywhere on my skin, sending licks of fire and ice straight to my core. I'm burning for the two of them, and it's the best damn feeling in the entire world.

"Suck Vincent off, baby girl," Mason purrs as he guides my head to the other man's long cock. "I want to eat your pussy again."

I part my lips, taking Vincent's length eagerly, as Mason positions himself at my entrance once more, his tongue flicking out experimentally. I shift onto my hands and knees to grant him better access as I bob my head up and down, allowing my tongue to trace the vein on the underside of Vincent's cock with each ministration.

"She tastes so fucking good," Mason pants from between my pussy lips, and Vincent groans low in his throat, thrusting his hips upward. When Mason begins sucking on my clit, suctioning it between his lips, I stop automatically, Vincent's cock sliding free from my lips. "I didn't say you could stop sucking him, baby," Mason chastises, removing his lips from my pussy as well. I want to cry out, to scream at him, but he simply guides my head back over Vincent's hard length.

"You're so fucking perfect," Vincent grunts, his tone pained.

Mason's hands grip my thighs, hoisting me higher into the air so his tongue can destroy me.

And fuck, does it destroy me.

I swear I feel my soul leaving my body, orbiting around the sun a few rotations, before snapping back into place. I combust into thousands of pieces before being remade as a new and improved Blair Windsor.

My body starts shaking as Mason expertly and passionately licks my pussy, and before I know it, I'm releasing Vincent a second time and bathing in the ecstasy of my release.

"I love watching you fuck his face, Blair," Vincent says, pulling my face down to his so he can whisper in my ear. He lazily rolls my nipples between two of his fingers. "Do you know that you make the sweetest fucking cry when you come?"

"I need someone to fuck me," I all but sob, thrusting my ass against Mason's face. He chuckles darkly, flipping me in his arms so my head is now in Vincent's lap and Mason's standing over me.

"Greedy, greedy girl," Mason tsks with a disapproving head shake. "Did you really think we were done with you yet? I've been waiting for this moment too damn long to finish this early." His cock bobs against his stomach as he stalks forward, crawling across the bed so he's beside me.

"I know exactly how perfect that pussy feels around my cock," Vincent retorts smugly, sounding like a bragging teenage boy instead of the stone-cold killer I know him to be. And honestly, I don't give enough fucks to call him out on it. He can brag all he damn well wants…if he just fucks me.

"I haven't even begun to pay attention to these perfect breasts yet," Mason murmurs, dropping his head to kiss a fiery pathway down my neck and to the swell of my right tit.

Vincent carefully moves from above my head and positions himself on the other side of me. His eyes are intense on Mason—almost a glare—as he watches the other man kiss a lazy pathway around my nipple.

After a moment of careful watching, Vincent follows the same pathway on my left breast, though he makes sure to leave behind a trail of saliva from his tongue. And when he bites down, I know he's marking me.

Mason growls, his eyes shifting to Vincent's face,

as he suckles on the skin just above my breast, no doubt leaving behind another hickey.

This is a fucking pissing war…but with orgasms. And I think I'm okay with it.

Vincent's tongue circles my nipple as I bring my hands up, tangling them in both of their hair. Mason's is soft to the touch, the long strands easily able to fit around my fists, while Vincent's is cut short, making it impossible to fully grab on to it.

"Fuck, Vincent. Mason," I cry out, and Vincent smirks in satisfaction as he sucks my entire breast into his mouth before releasing it.

"She said my name first," he taunts.

Mason hisses and begins to suck on my nipple with vigor, his teeth grazing the sensitive nub.

"Fuck, Mason," I whimper.

"Ha!" Mason releases me to grin over my body at Vincent. "Now it's *my* name she's moaning."

"You guys seem more into each other than me right about now," I bite out, resisting the urge to pout. The two of them exchange another one of those eloquent glances, mischief burning in their eyes, before turning toward me as one.

"Is my little mate feeling neglected?" Vincent questions in a singsong voice.

"*My* mate," Mason corrects.

"Someone fuck me," I interrupt, knowing that their cantankerous and combative personalities can stop this party before it can even truly begin.

Mason and Vincent turn toward each other once more, and as one exclaim, "Rock, paper, scissors, shoot!"

Vincent scowls when Mason unveils a paper to conquer his rock.

"Ha!" Mason says smugly, and I resist the urge to roll my eyes. Still, a giddy smile erupts on my face as Mason positions himself on top of me, every inch the dangerous and sexy biker.

He grabs my left wrist and directs my hand toward Vincent's aching cock. I immediately wrap it in my fist as the tip of Mason's hard cock touches my entrance.

"Blair?" he whispers silkily, pushing a strand of sweaty hair away from my face. "I think you won the bet."

He claims my body with a powerful thrust of his hips, and I gasp out loud, arching my back as ecstasy floods my veins. I try to get used to the fullness of his length inside of me, the feeling of him pressing against my walls, but he doesn't give me a chance to adjust as he pistons in and out of me.

With one hand still stroking Vincent, I wrap my

legs around Mason's waist to allow him better access. He fucks me hard, every thrust a promise of more to come. A tiny part of my brain switches off, but the rest of me focuses on his confession just before he entered me.

Did he mean...?

Coherent thoughts flee as his pace turns punishing, every thrust of his hips reminding me who I belong to. My screams echo off the walls, and I just pray Brett isn't anywhere nearby to hear this.

My body tightens around Mason's thick length, and I open my mouth to plead with him for...something...when he unsheathes himself from my folds and flips me onto my stomach.

"Suck him, baby. Suck him while I ram my cock into your tight pussy," Mason growls, tangling his fist in my hair as he lines up with my entrance once more. I position myself on my hands and knees as Vincent knee-walks across the bed, stopping when he's directly in front of me.

It could be my imagination, but I swear even their touches emit different temperatures as Vincent reverently clasps my cheeks, guiding my face toward his hard dick. Vincent is all ice, the frigidness of his touch seeping past my defenses, while Mason is nothing but fire and heat.

This time, when Mason thrusts into me from behind, Vincent does it from in front. The two of them work in unison to bring me to the precipice of pleasure. They're not gentle with me, but I don't expect them to be. I'm not made of glass, and they know that more than anyone else.

Vincent's dick slides down the back of my throat, and I moan in encouragement, wanting more from him. More from Mason. More from both of them.

Right then and there, the three of us are connected in a way we've never been before. It's like our souls are merging, becoming one, and I can't differentiate where I end and they begin. I can't remember a time I felt so complete, but there's no denying that with the both of them inside of me, my entire body is coming alive in flames.

Mason's grip in my hair is unyielding but not painful as he guides my mouth up and down Vincent's shaft. His balls slap against me with every forward thrust of his hips, our combined lust potent and all-consuming in the tiny room. I want to drown in it, in them, as pleasure overwhelms me, blocking out all other sensations.

A sharp jolt of arousal shoots through my body, almost as if every nerve-ending has been set on fire, and I fall apart, squeezing Mason's shaft for all it's worth. I cry out around Vincent's cock as Mason ruts into me wildly, like a man possessed. My body shatters into pieces and then reforms all in a span of a second. I scream, and scream, and scream, my orgasm ripping through me.

The two of them come as one, Vincent shooting ropes of cum down my throat as I swallow it all. Mason jerks his hips erratically, his hands leaving my hair to cup my breasts and pull my body flush against his. His teeth bite into my neck, hard enough to sting, but the pain is immediately eclipsed by the sensation of love and laughter. I can feel his cock swelling inside of my pussy, and I know immediately what's happening.

He's knotting.

"Holy fuck," Vincent breathes in awe as Mason's cock tightens inside of me, touching every wall and setting me on fire. "It's true."

He's knotting, something that only occurs between fated mates. The male's cock enlarges inside of the female, prohibiting him from removing it for an unspecified amount of time.

As Mason slides slightly to the side, practically crushing me against the mattress, I know that he's stuck inside of me.

And that he's truly my mate, just as Vincent is.

I can feel the bond caused by his bite thickening and strengthening like strands of silver rope, just as Vincent's does whenever we make love. The two bonds connect my heart to theirs, my soul to their souls, and I know that there's no power in the universe capable of dissolving them.

"Fuck, this feels incredible," Mason moans as he peppers kisses up and down the back of my neck.

"It's true," Vincent repeats, still appearing stunned. Behind me, Mason begins to move, shallow thrusts of his hips, and I grit my teeth against the cry that wants to escape.

I twist my head to the side, and Vincent complies to my unspoken demand easily, claiming my lips in a sweet kiss.

"We're both truly your mates, aren't we?" he whispers as he finally pulls away.

The bond between the three of us shines brightly, illuminating the dark room in ribbons of silvery light.

"It is," I reply. "And that's good, because I don't know if I can let either of you go."

"You're ours, baby girl," Mason whispers as he continues to rut into me softly.

Ours.

Fuck, I love the sound of that.

Relief crashes through me like a tsunami that he's not rejecting the bond, that he's not pushing me away because of my connection with the Davenport heir. He may not be happy with it, but he's also not running to the hills, crying and screaming. He's here, with me, and bubbles erupt in my stomach at the thought of a future with both men.

Vincent moves until he's curled around my side, looking uncharacteristically vulnerable.

"What about Tai…?"

"Hey," I lean forward to plant another kiss on his swollen lips, "don't worry about that. Don't worry about anything, okay? Tomorrow, we'll face the rest of the world, but today, it's just the three of us."

"And tomorrow morning," Mason murmurs. "And maybe tomorrow afternoon."

Vincent barks out a laugh, the sound seeming to be pulled from him without conscious thought. He actually seems surprised by it, his eyes widening. "To be completely honest, I never would've expected this to happen when I came here to tell you the news."

"What—" I cut off as Mason hits a sweet spot inside of me with his cock. I let out a cry of pleasure and arch against him. "What news?" I repeat breathily.

One of Vincent's arms wraps around me, not

even seeming to care that in the process, it coils around Mason as well. "I got into contact with your birth grandma," he confesses. "I told her that you and Brett were still alive, that you're safe. She wants to meet you."

My heart stutters in my chest, skipping an entire beat before starting back up with a vengeance. "What?" I gasp.

"I was thinking you could meet her," Vincent replies softly. "If you want to, that is."

"I…I do." Tears burn my eyes, and a foreign emotion invades my heart and soul. Is this what love feels like? I wouldn't know because I've never been in love before, but I can't imagine feeling anything stronger. "But only after all of this shit between the packs is over…"

"Of course," he rushes to assure me. "Whenever you and Brett feel comfortable. I know how to get in contact with her."

"Thank you, Vincent," I whisper softly, pecking him on the lips.

"Anything for you," he replies.

Three words are on the tip of my tongue, but I don't dare say them. Not yet. They'll open up a wound I'm not sure I'll ever be able to stitch back together. There's a part of me that wonders if I'm even capable of being vulnerable with these men after the life of pain I've been through. I'm too broken, too jaded, and my pieces will never fit together properly.

But maybe, just maybe, they're healing me.

"That's wonderful and all," Mason grunts out, "but can we not talk about relatives while I'm balls deep inside of her? I swear I'm going to un-knot myself just thinking about Blair's brother right now."

Vincent and I both snort out a laugh.

I meant what I said to them earlier.

Now that I've had both of them, now that I know in my heart and soul that this is where we belong, I'm never letting them go.

War can come for us, and I have no doubt that it will, but with them by my side, I can face anything.

12

BLAIR

DAY 21

I wrap the robe tighter around my body as I venture into the kitchen, squinting my eyes against the blinding morning sun.

Vincent sits at the head of the table, his lips compressed in a thin line as he pores over the local newspaper. A mug of coffee rests before him, and he absently takes a sip as he reads.

Mason stands in the kitchen, the sound of sizzling bacon filling the air as he moves from pan to pan, cooking everything from eggs to pancakes.

I notice he has only two plates, however, and I imagine it's a slight against Vincent, who's purposefully not looking in his direction.

Baby steps, Blair. Baby steps.

"Good morning, baby girl," Mason greets when he catches sight of me. He must've changed his clothes some time before I woke up, for he's wearing a clean gray shirt underneath his cut and a fresh pair of jeans. His messy blond hair is combed into a low ponytail, a few strands coming loose and framing his arresting face.

"Um…good morning?" My greeting turns into a question as my eyes shift back and forth between the mobster drinking coffee and the motorcycle VP cooking breakfast.

I'm surprised they're even in the same room together, let alone doing something as domesticated as this.

A muscle in Mason's jaw twitches as he scoops a pancake, eggs, and bacon onto one plate and slides it across the bar toward me. Still, despite the minuscule facial tick, his smile remains firmly in place. I've come to recognize it as his mask, though I don't dare call him out on it.

Both Vincent and Mason wear masks, but Vincent's is designed to keep people out of his head and scare them away. Mason's is the exact opposite —its sole purpose is to entice and lure you into a false sense of security and safety. Just when you think you know what's happening, he rips the metaphorical rug out from underneath you.

All of us are uniquely adapted to the darkness and shadows. But now, it's hard to return to the abyss we once hunted in.

I move to claim the seat beside Vincent as Mason walks over as well, his own plate of food in his hands. Vincent's eyes narrow on the steam wafting up from the eggs, but he doesn't comment as Mason immediately digs into his plate with gusto.

"I see that you guys are getting along well," I quip as I cut off a sliver of pancake.

"Fucking peachy, baby." Mason throws me a wink before turning to face Vincent. When Vincent continues to glare, Mason opens his mouth wide, revealing a mouthful of half-chewed food. "Isn't this yummy?"

"You guys are children," I sigh.

"Kinda gross, considering you fucked us both last night," Mason retorts without skipping a beat, and I seriously consider the merits of stabbing my fork into his neck.

"And this morning," Vincent points out, his expression carefully blank.

"And—"

"All right!" I throw my hands up into the air with

an indignant grunt. "I get your point." Shoving another piece of pancake into my mouth, I swivel on the wooden chair to face Vincent. "What are you still doing here?"

"Trying to kick me out, Blair?" He folds his hands on his stomach and reclines backward in his seat. If anyone else did that, he would look casual and nonchalant, but I know Vincent well enough to see the tension in his shoulders and neck.

"No," I snarl. "Of course not. I'm just worried—"

"We need to talk about this," Mason interrupts. He drops his fork on the table with a clank and leans forward, bracing himself on his elbows. "*All*," he moves his pointer finger around in a circular rotation to encompass the entire table, "of this."

A knot forms in my throat as I drop my silverware as well. Something akin to panic builds inside of me as a frown pinches Mason's brow. Fear and anxiety light my heart on fire as I brace myself for whatever he's going to say.

But...he doesn't speak. Neither does Vincent as he takes a silent sip of his coffee.

The slightest downward tilt to Vincent's lips commandeers my attention, and I find that I can't look away.

When I feel like I'm going to fucking suffocate, I grit out, "You guys can't handle this, can you?"

Both of them turn to face me in unison. Silence spreads over the tiny room, washing over me in a torrent, almost painful in its intensity.

"Blair—" Mason begins softly.

"You guys can't handle *this*." I gesture vaguely between the three of us. "Sharing me. Caring about me. Your hatred toward one another has been ingrained inside of you for too damn long to change now." I swear my stomach is physically spasming, threatening to expel its meager contents across the table. "So…what does this mean? You guys want me to choose one of you, don't you?"

And just like that, my heart shatters into thousands of irreparable pieces.

Last night had been…well, it'd been fucking amazing. My body still feels as if it's on fire, my veins electrified by their touches. They worked together so perfectly to rip me apart and then sew me back together. But maybe, just maybe, their hatred toward one another is too strong to be broken by one night together. Maybe their feelings for me aren't strong enough to overcome years of hatred and rivalry.

But how can I choose only one when I know in

my very soul that we all belong together? How can fate ask that of me?

I need Vincent's ice-cold protectiveness and the feeling of safety that accompanies it. I need late nights in his library, silently reading as we enjoy one another's company.

And I need Mason's boisterous personality and the way he never fails to make me laugh and smile. There's something broken about the angelic-looking man, but that only adds to his allure. I don't want to fix him or anything like that because I honestly don't believe he *needs* to be fixed. He sees the darkness inside of him as a curse, but I recognize it for what it truly is—a part of him.

"I already told you." My spine straightens with resilience as I force myself to meet each of their eyes. "I'm not choosing."

"I don't know how you expect this to work, Blair," Vincent grits out, the hand around his coffee mug tightening almost imperceptibly until I'm afraid he'll break it. Which would be a shame, considering the fact the mug reads *Hot for Cock*. "A timeshare schedule? I get you one weekend, and Mason gets you the next? And don't even get me started on Tai."

"Our packs are at war, baby girl," Mason points out, his tone gentle but chastising. "We agreed to put rules to hell for one night, but now that the sun has risen…"

"What?" I scoff. "Now that the sun has risen, you're going to what? Pretend that what we had together never happened? Pretend that we're not mates? Because I *know* you both feel the same connection I do."

"No one wants to pretend that," Vincent snaps waspishly, a crack appearing on his mask.

"But you only want me to acknowledge one of you as my mate, is that it? Despite the fact that we *all* know that's not the case."

"Goddammit, Blair." Mason throws his fist down on the table, causing our plates to shake. "You need to choose. Him or me."

The breath leaves my lungs in a swooshing exhale. My heart pounds between my ears as I stare first into a pair of eyes so green, they look like emeralds, and then into a gaze as dark as pitch. Both men beseech me with their stares to claim them, go to them, love them.

But trying to choose between the two of them is like asking me to choose between lungs.

"No." I shake my head. "No, I'm not fucking doing this."

"Blair!" Vincent growls, but I'm already pushing

away from the table. I'll spend the next nine days hiding in my bedroom if I need to, but I'm not having this fucking conversation. "Don't you walk away from us."

"Me?" I whirl around to face him, my anger bubbling to the surface like boiling water in a kettle. If they come any closer, I'm liable to burn them both. "I'm not the one who turned his back on his fated mate."

"That's not fucking fair," he grits out, his teeth clenched together.

"No?" I pretend to think about it for a long moment, tapping a finger incessantly against my chin. "So can you both acknowledge the fact that you're my mates?" I query, watching their reactions carefully.

Vincent's jaw clenches, drawing attention to the frown marring his face, while Mason stares stonily at his plate of food. Both refuse to acknowledge my question, but I prattle on anyway.

"And you both acknowledge that Sarai and Grim are allying their packs to eliminate the bitten wolves and lycans?" I continue. "And you both agree that's fucking wrong?"

Again, not a single response, but their silence is all the confirmation I need.

"Maybe instead of fighting amongst each other, we can actually work together to figure out how to get out of this *goddamn mess*," I finish, my chest heaving as I struggle to regain control of my emotions.

"As if I'd trust the Bloody Skulls' goddamn VP." Vincent jabs a finger over his shoulder at Mason, his eyes spewing fire.

"Do you think I like the way my father handles his business?" Mason jumps to his feet, knocking back his chair in the process. "Do you think I like the way he treats my best friend? My *mate*? The other bitten wolves?" A growl tumbles from his lips as he advances on the other shifter. "You should know better than anyone that some apples fall far, far from the tree."

"You don't think I'm aware of that?" Vincent's hand twitches, almost as if he's dying to pull out his favorite gun and shoot Mason between the eyes. He won't—not when he knows it'll hurt me—but I can see the need brimming behind his black stare. "You don't think I stay up at night, thinking through my father's crimes and wondering how I can fix everything?"

"Does one of those things you need to fix include

Blair?" Mason taunts. "Are you embarrassed of your little bitten mate?"

I know his words are meant to be a jab at Vincent, but I can't stop the stab of pain that cuts through me.

Abruptly, Vincent is across the room, his hands wrapped around Mason's throat as he shoves him against the wall. He takes a step closer, breaching his personal space, and bares his teeth.

"I have committed many, many sins, none more than in the last five years," he hisses. "I've never atoned for any of them before. Why should I, when all I was trying to do was protect my family and the people I love? I don't kill just to kill, unlike you and your fucked up family." He spits near Mason's feet, though the other man doesn't even flinch. "I'm a murderer, a serial killer, an avenging angel who takes the law into his own hands. But you want to know what my gravest sin has been? The one that's surely going to send me straight to hell?" His hand still around Mason's throat, he whirls him around to face me. "Loving her. Coveting her. Desiring her, even when I know I shouldn't.

"I'm not trying to gain any penitence for that. How can I, when I effectively destroyed her life just for being who I am?"

"Vincent..." I begin, but he continues like I haven't even spoken.

"I'll never apologize for caring about her. And I'll never, *ever* be ashamed to call her my mate." He releases Mason with a disgusted huff, twisting slightly as if he means to turn his back on the Bloody Skulls' VP.

"How the fuck would it even work? Sharing one mate?" Despite his words being directed at me, Mason doesn't peel his gaze off of Vincent's back.

My mobster moves toward the window sill, the blinds drawn shut, and places a single hand against the wall, lowering his head. His breathing is soft and even, but it's almost *too* soft and even, as if he has to consciously remember to modulate it.

"We figure it out as we go," I whisper. "Do you think I'm not absolutely fucking terrified? I've been alone for so, so long, and now I discover I have two mates, potentially three. And you guys want to leave me—"

"No!" Mason hisses out.

"Absolutely not," Vincent agrees vehemently, spinning around to face me.

The two of them still at the passion in their shared reply, exchanging wary, distrustful glances.

"I suppose we're at an impasse, then," Mason

muses, running a hand down his cheek. "We both don't want to let her go."

"So that means we have to share her?" Vincent shakes his head in denial, his features rife with frustration. "No. Not fucking happening."

"We don't have a goddamn choice!" Red splotches erupt on Mason's cheeks as his hands clench into fists. "We either share her…or lose her. And I, for one, have no intention of losing her. Do you?"

Vincent locks his teeth together before slowly shaking his head no.

"So what the fuck do we do?"

"We do what she suggested." Mason turns to me, and I hold my breath, not allowing myself to hope. "We take it one day at a time and try not to kill each other. If that means we have to add Tai to the group as well, then so be it. But for now, that's the least of our worries."

Vincent looks like he wants to argue, his jaw unclenching and his mouth opening, before he glances in my direction and immediately snaps it shut. He runs his hand through his dark hair, causing the strands to become wildly disheveled.

"We need to figure out how to handle Grim and Sarai. They're both power hungry, malicious bastards," he informs us before turning toward

Mason completely. "They won't hesitate to kill every single fucking wolf who opposes them, including Blair. They won't stop just because she's your mate."

"I'm aware," Mason fumes.

"So can you do what needs to be done against your own father?" Vincent raises an eyebrow, waiting for Mason's answer.

"Is this really fucking necessary?" I demand. Grim is Mason's father, for fuck's sake, and though he's a murderous, rapist piece of shit, Vincent can't surely be suggesting—

"I'll do what I need to do," Mason sneers.

"How can I believe—"

"I'll do what I need to do," he repeats, louder this time, his voice dripping with scorn. "But my father knows I don't trust or agree with him. He's been holding church without me present."

"And that's out of the ordinary?" I ask.

"Very." Mason nods his head before turning to face Vincent once more. "But I can try to figure out what the fuck is going on. I can't promise that it'll work, but it's the only option we have."

"I can pool my sources together as well," Vincent offers, running another hand through his inky strands.

When both men turn toward me, I nod in acquiescence. I may not have any spies on the inside of the Bloody Skulls, but I can keep my ear to the ground and dig up what I can. And when I get to the Totemic Tribe in nine days, I can press Tai for answers. I don't know if I can trust the handsome prince, but if my theory is correct, if he truly *is* my mate as well, then he'll tell me what he knows.

Besides, he willingly told Mason about Grim supplying his pack with weapons. If he's willing to go against his own father, he surely can't be a bad man, right?

"Just…just be fucking careful, all right?" Vincent demands, marching forward and gripping my chin. He plants a chaste, lingering kiss to my lips, one I feel all the way to the tips of my toes, before releasing me and turning to glower at Mason. "Take care of her, okay?"

"Always." For once, Mason's voice is devoid of anything teasing or mocking. There's a solemn edge to it that I don't hear very often.

When Vincent continues to stare at him, seemingly gauging his sincerity, Mason's lips twitch into the beginnings of his customary, devilish smile.

"She is my mate, after all," he says lightly. "So I suppose you're my mate-in-law. My brother mate? My brother husband?"

Vincent growls low in his throat, kisses me once more, and then rips open the door to the apartment.

He leaves as silently and as stealthily as he arrived, and I feel his absence as keenly as a missing limb.

"It's going to be okay, Blair," Mason says softly from behind me. His hand comes down on my shoulder. "It's going to be okay."

I don't know if he's talking about the impending war, my mate bond with the two of them, or all of the above. Either way, something that feels awfully like a premonition grabs hold of my heart and refuses to release it.

This will only end once we're all dead.

13

BLAIR

DAY 30

It's not easy to say goodbye.

The last few days have been an oasis in a desert, an escape from reality. Between my phone calls with Valentina and Papa Gray, I've been able to forget the rest of the world and the horrors plaguing it. I haven't seen Mason and Vincent that often since our explosive sex session...and then our explosive argument immediately following it. Vincent is preparing himself and his family for the inevitable war, while Mason spends his time roaming the halls of the bar, picking up any information he can from the drunken wolves who frequent there.

A few things become clear.

One, Sarai and Grim have definitely started an alliance, though according to our sources, there's a lot of tension reverberating between the two men.

Two, Sarai and Grim are both bigoted assholes who wish to eliminate lycan and bitten wolves from the city for good.

And finally…

I'm not safe.

None of us acknowledge that blade glinting over all of our heads, just waiting to drop, but even with Brett or Mason with me twenty-four hours a day, we're all on edge. Grim has, fortunately, stayed away since the incident fifteen days ago, but I don't believe that means he's given up. I haven't seen the surly bastard, but for some reason, I feel like he's aware of every move I make, every word I say. It's like I can feel his eyes on me all the way across town, a penetrating, stomach-churning caress.

And by the end of my thirty days with Mason, I can't say I'll miss the constant fear that Grim will return for me. I don't like being on edge, and even sleeping with a knife doesn't provide me the comfort I so desperately need.

I stand in front of the bar with Brett on one side

of me and Mason on the other. I feel physically sick to my stomach as I wait for Tai to arrive and take me to the Totemic Tribe.

"Stop fucking growling," I hiss at Mason, jabbing my elbow into his side. "You're giving me a stress headache."

"I fucking hate this," he bites out, his tone scathing. He twists his head to pierce me with a bright green gaze, one that I lose myself in momentarily before blinking myself back to the present. "I don't trust Tai or the Totemics or Sarai...I don't trust anyone, really, besides me." As an afterthought, he adds, "And my cock. I trust my cock."

Brett releases an indignant huff and reaches over my head to smack Mason's cheek.

We haven't told Brett the truth yet about our tenuous relationship and mating bond. It's not because we don't trust him—the exact opposite—but I know my big brother and how he'll react. Since we found each other thirty days ago, Brett already proved to be immensely protective of me, to the point that he wants to rip Mason's head off daily for even daring to flirt with me. I can't imagine what he'll do when he discovers that his long thought dead baby sister is mated to two guys, one of them being his best friend and the other a known serial killer.

Yeah. Not looking forward to that conversation.

Thoughts of Brett inevitably lead to ones about my estranged family. A family I barely remember, who apparently grieved my death.

A memory tugs at my consciousness, and I allow myself to fall into it eagerly, remembering a conversation with Brett only two days earlier.

"She's beautiful," I whisper reverently, pushing the pad of my thumb against the picture Vincent sent me to trace her elegant visage.

My grandma is an older woman, in her late seventies, with surprisingly voluminous brown hair streaked with gray. Her button nose, bright blue eyes, and dimples give her an elfin appearance, but the haggard lines marring her face makes her look years older. This is a woman who has definitely been through some rough shit yet still manages to get out of bed every day, fake a smile, and go about her life.

The last time I saw her...she had been in Italy on her deathbed. It was one of the last family vacations we took before Vincent's father murdered my entire family. She had cancer, and everyone assumed that she wouldn't make it. But she pulled through with steely determination, looking death in the face and laughing smugly.

At least, that was what the news article said when they described her recovery.

She moved back to the States shortly after to be closer to her family, only to discover the horrifying truth—that her daughter and son-in-law had been slaughtered, alongside her three grandchildren.

I was so young at the time, I barely remember her. I can vaguely recall her baking bomboloni while singing in Italian, but even that might be nothing but a fabricated dream I conjured up.

"Nonna," Brett writes on his whiteboard, a tiny smile pulling up his lips. He then repeats the word by opening up his hand and separating his fingers. He places his thumb to his chin and then moves it forward in one arc followed immediately by a second one.

"Nonna," I say, repeating the movement. He nods in encouragement, his smile broadening, before it fades from his face.

Turning his attention back to his whiteboard, he writes out, "Are you scared to meet her?"

"Scared?" I sit on the edge of the bed and lean forward,

resting my elbows on my knees. "No, I'm not scared. Why would I be...?" My words taper off at his disapproving frown, and I sigh. "Of course I'm scared. I'm fucking terrified. I thought I didn't have a family left, you know? And now, I discover I have a brother and a grandma and aunts and uncles and cousins." I run a hand down my face, feeling oddly distraught. "What if they...I don't know...blame me for what happened to Mom? What if they hate me or think I'm weird? Obviously, I can't tell them about the whole shifter thing, but—"

Brett cuts me off by placing a hand over my mouth. My brows rise with surprise, but he doesn't give me a chance to chew him out as he writes rapidly with his free hand. Finally, he lifts the board for me to see, still keeping his hand over my mouth.

"I know you're scared, and I completely understand the reasoning behind it. But, Blair, they're going to love you. I promise you that. How can they not, when they realize how fucking amazing you are? And I'll be there every step of the way. If for some reason we discover they're assholes, then we'll take off running in the opposite direction and never look back. Okay?"

I glance back down at the picture again when he drops his hand, my heart thumping wildly, before sticking my pinky out and linking it with Brett's.

"Deal. But...if we have to run, just know that I'm faster than you and will probably leave you in my dust."

I SMILE AT THE MEMORY, BUT IT IMMEDIATELY FALTERS when I think about what I'm going to be doing in less than a few minutes.

Traveling to the Totemic Tribe.

Spying on Sarai and feeding information back to Papa Gray, Vincent, and Mason.

Deciding if Tai is a friend or a foe.

And hopefully, not get killed in the process.

"I don't think I can do this," Mason snarls under his breath, too low for Brett to hear even with his advanced shifter hearing. "I don't think I can watch you walk away with my enemy."

"Then don't." I spin to face Mason, my heart leaping to my throat. Anxiety has wrinkled his blond brows, and I yearn to smooth them out. I can practically sense the protective fury and worry pouring off him in palpable waves. "I'll tell you what I told Vincent when I left him thirty days ago."

"I finally understand his pain," Mason murmurs.

I ignore him and push myself onto my tiptoes. "I need to do this. We both know it's true. But I promise you, Mason, that this isn't a goodbye. I trust Tai to keep me safe—"

"You barely know the man," Mason bites out, but he stills when I run my fingers through his shaggy blond hair. I don't even care that Brett is at my back, watching us with too keen eyes. I just want to comfort the man that the universe has decided is my fated mate.

"And if he doesn't keep me safe, then I'll keep myself safe. I'm not a damsel in distress, Mase." I offer him a cocky smile. "Just because I like pink doesn't mean I can't kick major ass."

"Grim nearly…" Mason trails off, swallowing heavily. I can hear Brett make another strange noise in the back of his throat, and I mentally curse Mason for almost giving away my secret.

"But you were there." I lower my voice to a whisper and press my lips directly to his ear. "There always seems to be this idiotic mentality that a woman is either a complete badass and never needs a man in her life to protect her, or she's weak and constantly needs to be saved. Why can't someone be both? A lot of times, I *can* save and protect myself, but I'd be the first to admit that time with Grim wasn't one of them. I'm not going to lie to you, Mason. Your father fucking terrifies me. He was so much stronger than me, and he took me unaware. If you hadn't gotten there when you did…"

"But I did get there," Mason stresses, bouncing on the balls of his feet. His silky blond hair tickles my cheek as he leans in close, his stubble grazing my skin. "If this is a pep talk, then it's not really working. You're only making me more fucking anxious about letting you go."

I snort before stepping back, allowing my hands to remain on his shoulders. "I told you that so you'll understand that I'm honest about my limitations. That time with Grim, I couldn't protect myself, but I'm more prepared now. I know for sure who my enemies are, and I won't hesitate to do what needs to be done. I was scared of hurting Grim and starting a motherfucking war, but war is inevitable now, don't you think?"

"Just be careful, baby girl." He opens his arms to encircle me in his embrace. "I can't lose you."

"When did you get so mushy, baby boy?" I taunt, tilting my chin back to stare up into his arresting, elegant face.

"When I fell in love with a bitten wolf," he answers without pause, holding my stare and drawing me into his green gaze. I swear, his words stab at my brain like a flaming blade. My chest constricts, crushed under the weight of my feelings for him. Love for him sinks its teeth into me, and I have the distinct impression I'm on the verge of being slashed to ribbons. Ripped to shreds.

"I…" My confession cuts off by the sound of a car pulling to a screeching halt directly in front of the Bloody Skulls' bar.

Tai unfolds his massive body from the driver's seat of the muscle car and stalks forward, all predatorial energy and rage. He glances from me to Mason and then back to me, a scowl pulling down his lips.

I take a step back from Mason immediately, my heart migrating to my throat. I ignore the flash of hurt I see in his eyes, telling myself that I'm not saying the words back only because Tai is here and I don't want him to know the truth of my feelings.

But the truth is? I'm a fucking coward.

I spin on my heels and throw my arms around Brett, pressing my body as close to his as physically possible.

"I'm going to miss you so damn much," I whisper as he returns my hug just as tightly. I'm sure there are a thousand things he wants to say, a thousand things he's unable to say, but his embrace articulates them all. "And don't kill Mason while I'm gone," I add as an afterthought, and he makes a low noise that I translate to mean, "No promises."

Oh yeah.

Brett knows. There's no fucking doubt about that. I mean, it's not like we were being subtle with our affection toward one another.

I reluctantly pull myself away from my brother before turning to meet Mason's eyes one last time.

He swallows, shoving his hands into the pockets of his loose jeans, before turning to Tai, almost as if it pains him to stare at me for too long.

"Take care of her."

"I will," Tai bites out, already opening the passenger door for me. "Let's go."

My heart in my throat and my stomach in knots, I take a tentative step toward the car, stopping only once to stare over my shoulder at Mason.

One last time.

He looks as if he's in the midst of heart palpitations, his arms extended as if he wants to yank me to him and throw me over his shoulder. His eyes are darkened with fury and possessive, protective intensity.

Brett, no doubt seeing the same thing I am, rushes forward to place a restraining hand on Mason's shoulder.

"I'll be okay," I tell them both, infusing as much sincerity into my voice as I can.

As I slide into the car, my hands shaking ever so slightly, I can't help but feel as if I just told the biggest lie I've ever spoken in my entire life.

THE TOTEMIC TRIBE

TAI

DAY 1

Her sunshine and floral scent fills the car, waking up my wolf and causing my hands to clench around the steering wheel.

I want to drown in that addicting scent, but I force myself to play it cool.

Blair seems subdued, almost despondent, her gaze glued to the window as the busy city transforms into fields of corn and silos the farther north we get.

Home.

I'm bringing her to my home.

Bile rushes up my throat before I can contain it at

the thought of bringing Blair anywhere near my father and brothers. She's a strong, fierce wolf, but they'll still eat her alive and then spit her back out. She's nothing but prey to them, a game that they can play, cheat at, and then destroy as soon as they win.

But I can't imagine they'll win against Blair fucking Windsor. She's a hurricane, a force to be reckoned with, and I find myself desperate to know what put that hardened glint in her eyes.

"Music?" I grunt out, nodding toward the radio.

One word sentences, Tai? Really? What are you, a caveman?

"No, I'm fine," Blair dismisses, not peeling her gaze away from the window. For reasons I don't care to look at too closely, that bothers me. A fucking lot. I want her gaze to be on me, watching me as intensely as I do her.

For the millionth time since she got into my car, I glance at her out of the corner of my eye, noting the goosebumps that have pebbled on her smooth skin.

Fuck, is she cold?

I hurriedly glance toward the air conditioning unit and turn it down to stop the blast of cold air bombarding her.

Idiot, Tai. Idiot.

"Jacket?" I bite out, my eyes continuously dropping to the goosebumps on her arms. She's wearing a tank top that molds to her tits and flat stomach and a pair of jean shorts. If I'd been thinking with anything other than my dick, like my brain, I would've known not to turn the AC up for the half hour drive to my packlands.

"Jacket?" Blair finally turns to stare at me, and I lose myself in her Caribbean eyes...before remembering I need to focus on the goddamn road.

"I have one," I mumble, nodding toward the jacket tossed over the center console.

"Oh, um, thank you." My heart judders in my chest as I watch her slide the jacket on, the leather material practically devouring her dainty frame. I can feel my cock begin to harden once again in my jeans, and I mentally curse the fucker for being so damn excited all the time. But fuck, she looks phenomenal in my clothes, and the wolf inside of me sighs in satisfaction at the prospect of surrounding her in our scent.

Mine, he growls, desperately wanting to be set free. My canines expand, and all I can think about is marking her neck with my bite. Claiming her.

But I can't do that. Not yet. She doesn't know me from Adam, and the last thing I want to do is terrify her.

My heart races the closer we get to my mother's house, and I wonder if she can hear the rapid *thump-thump-thump* of the organ working overtime in my chest. Sarai insisted he greet her personally before we head to my apartment, and though the thought causes fire ants to skitter across my skin and acid to percolate in my stomach, I can't refuse him.

When I say no, he gets angry. And when he gets angry, he hurts the people I care about.

And now, that includes Blair.

"Whoa." She leans forward in her seat, her bright eyes widening as she gets a glimpse of the Totemic Tribe packland for the first time. It has been in my family for hundreds of years, but it never fails to inspire a sense of awe and wonder.

The trials we faced, the horrors we endured, brought us to this moment—where we're a thriving civilization, self-contained and self-disciplined. Respect for my ancestors rushes through me, and I just barely hide my smile as Blair devours the scenery with fresh eyes.

The fields of corn gradually give way to perfectly manicured green grass. White houses, some the size of trailers and others as large as farmhouses, decorate the large expanse. Gray roofs, resembling a clump of mushroom caps, peek through the dense maple that grows in thickets around the property. Pebbled pathways connect building to building, flowers growing on either side of the aperture. In the distance, cows graze the field, and a well stands adjacent to a flowing stream. The community I live in never fails to amaze me.

Correction—the community I *lived* in.

Kind of hard to be home when your father's a sadistic piece of shit.

"This is beautiful," she breathes, and the deference in her tone has my heart pounding even faster.

"Most of these buildings haven't changed much from when my ancestors first arrived," I confess, throwing a surreptitious glance in her direction before focusing back on the dirt road. "Though I am grateful that we actually have indoor plumbing now. Leaves and holes in the ground aren't exactly good for the ass."

She lets out a twinkling laugh, one that does absolutely *nothing* to help with my boner situation, before the smile slips from her face.

"Is Sarai…?" She trails off, absently fiddling with the ends of her long brown hair. The silky strands catch in the light, and I swear I almost see shades of sunlit gold woven throughout.

But then I remember what she asked me, and the lust I felt over her appearance fizzles and dissolves.

"Yes," I manage to say through clenched teeth, "he's here."

"And I have to meet him?" Her voice is deceptively light, almost nonchalant, but I swear a muscle in her jaw twitches, capturing my complete and undivided attention.

"Unfortunately."

Silence stretches between us, and I hate how uncomfortable I'm making my mate.

Fuck, say something, Tai! Anything!

I wonder if Blair's thoughts are on the same wavelength as mine, because it's her that breaks the silence first.

"I like your car," she praises, rubbing her hands over the seats of the upholstery.

I clear my throat, trying not to puff my chest out in pride. "It's a 1964 Ford Fairlane Thunderbolt. Got her a few years back. Worked at the grocery store since I was fourteen and saved up every penny for this beauty."

What would it feel to take Blair inside of this car? To push down the seats and bury my cock in her slick folds?

The fantasy has me clenching my teeth against

the searing pain in my dick. If I weren't driving, I would squeeze my eyelids shut and imagine old ladies naked to kill the boner from hell.

"Well, I like it," she says simply, offering me a timid smile. "It suits you."

"I usually ride my bike," I confess, releasing the steering wheel with one hand to run it through my short-cropped black hair. It's a little longer than I'm used to but still much shorter than most guys prefer to wear theirs. "But I didn't want to take you on it."

"Why not?" A wry grin twists up her lips, and I have the distinct impression she's teasing me.

"Not safe," I grunt out, dropping my hand back to the wheel. "A lot of accidents."

And the thought of Blair being in one of those accidents makes me want to stab someone.

"You do realize I've ridden on the back of Mason's bike loads of times?" she points out, and I swear to fuck my jaw clenches so tightly, I hear my molars break.

An irrational part of me wants to call Mason up and ask him if he at least had her wear a helmet, but then I remember that I despise the punk, we're not texting buddies, and that I just stole the girl he's obviously infatuated with. He'll probably drive that damn bike down to my apartment and run over my face with it.

Pack, my wolf boasts in my head cryptically. I shush the furry bastard and focus on Blair once more.

She's silent, her lower lip caught between her teeth, before she whispers, "You guys are a lot alike, you know?"

"Who?" I turn the car into a parking space on the grass in front of my mother's tiny cottage that's painted white like the rest of the buildings in the vicinity.

"You and Mason."

I can't quite read the expression on her face, but I would almost describe it as...curious? Cautious? Wary?

What the hell?

"I'm nothing like that murderous asshole," I bite out scathingly, ripping open the driver's side door and racing around the front of the car. I open Blair's door before she can and immediately wrap my hand around her tiny forearm. For a moment, I'm enraptured by the difference in our skin color—her golden complexion juxtaposed by my dark, tan skin. She's so little against me, so dainty, that I want to fold her against me and protect her from any and all harm.

But instead of doing any of that, I release her and take a step back, clearing my throat uncomfortably.

"Come. This is my parents' house." I stalk toward the front door, curling my hands into fists to rein in the innate impulse I have to help Blair up the stone stairs.

Don't make this fucking weird, Tai, I internally reprimand myself. I swear my wolf rolls his eyes at me, that little shit.

"Is Sarai here?" Once again, Blair adopts that light, casual tone, but I can hear the undercurrent of anxiety in her words.

I shake my head, and her shoulders deflate as if a heavy rain washed away all of the tension. "Just my mother and younger siblings," I reveal.

"Your…mother?"

Biting down on my smirk at her sudden unease, I push open the heavy door and step inside the cottage.

"Momma! I'm home!" I call as soon as I enter.

Unsurprisingly, my mother's at the stove, her blonde hair coiffed into a bun at the top of her head.

"Oh, baby boy!" My mother throws a hand over her mouth as she turns toward me, and I'm grateful to see that the majority of her bruises have healed. That means that my father hasn't been able to lay a hand on her in the last few days. Probably too preoccupied with this damn war.

My mother engulfs me in her arms, and I greedily inhale her floral perfume as I hug her back. She barely comes up to my chest, but somehow, the strength she exudes makes her seem even larger than her five-foot frame. Larger than me, and certainly larger than Sarai.

"And you must be Blair!" My mother releases me and turns toward Blair with tears in her eyes.

"Blair, this is my mother, Enola," I introduce, feeling a surge of primitive satisfaction at seeing two of the most important women in my life together. "And these are…" I put two fingers into my mouth and whistle. Less than a second later, two small children barrel down the staircase, practically running me over as they attempt to wrap their tiny arms around my legs. "Luna and Dyson. My younger siblings. They're twins."

"Hello, Enola. Luna. Dyson," Blair greets, smiling softly at each of them in turn. I notice that her gaze fixates on my mother the longest, a tiny crease materializing between her brows. Can she see the bruises decorating my mother's tan skin? The pain emanating from her eyes?

A part of me feels a deep sense of shame—shame that I haven't been able to protect my mother. Shame that my mate has witnessed such a failure. Shame that I'm putting both women in danger just by being near them.

"It's a pleasure to meet you, Blair," my mother gushes, clutching her chest as more tears cascade down her cheeks. "I heard—"

She doesn't get to finish her sentence when the door to the cottage careens off the wall and five men stumble inside. Their malicious smiles cut at something already bleeding and raw inside of my chest, and before I can second guess myself, I shift almost imperceptibly to block Blair, my mother, and my siblings from their taunting gazes.

"Well, well, well." My father's voice scratches at my brain, leaving behind deep, bloody gorges. "Look what the cat dragged in."

15

BLAIR

DAY 1

The similarities between Mason and Tai's mom are almost uncanny. If I had any doubts in my mind that the two men were related, they dissipated into smoke the second I set eyes upon the petite woman.

Unlike Tai and even Sarai, Enola doesn't have naturally dark skin and black hair. Her complexion is light, almost golden, and blonde locks are piled high into a bun on her head, drawing attention to her elfin features.

Everything about her—from her floral dress to the apron tied around her waist—screams unassuming and submissive, but the hard edge in her gaze makes me believe the exact opposite.

This woman is a fighter, a survivor, and I can't help but wonder what horrors she endured at the hands of Sarai.

And, if my theory is correct, at the hands of Grim.

Enola places a palm to her chest as tears stream down her sunken cheeks. "It's a pleasure to meet you, Blair." Her voice is soft, almost a whisper, but it conjures up feelings of love and safety. I instantly feel at ease as she turns her kind gaze my way. "I heard—"

Her words cut off abruptly as the front door is pushed open and five rowdy men stumble inside, pushing and shoving one another with dark grins on their faces. I immediately push Enola and the children behind me, prepared to face off against the intruders if I have to.

The four younger ones bear a strong resemblance to Tai, so I figure they must be his brothers.

And the one at the front of the pack...

I've seen Sarai only a few times before, the most recent one being at the summit when the packs played a twisted tug-of-war game with me, but I've never been this close to him.

If Enola has an aura that makes you want to give her a hug, Sarai's makes you want to run in the opposite direction. Which is damn ironic, considering his name quite literally means princess in Hebrew.

Tai releases a growl and moves so he's standing in front of me, his mother, and his siblings. His back muscles tense, rippling as he flexes, and drawing attention to the black, swirling lines tattooed on his neck.

"Sarai," he bites out, his eyes spewing something almost elemental in fury.

Sarai gives his son a dismissive sneer, his upper lip peeling back from his teeth, before directing his sharp-eyed gaze to me over Tai's shoulder.

There's no denying that this man is an alpha. The power he wields is staggering, emitting from his pores in tangible waves I feel all the way to my bones. But it's a dark, malicious type of power—almost sticky in nature—and I have the distinct impression I'm staring into the eyes of pure evil.

He wants me to bow, wants me to beg, but I'm an alpha of my own making, one that has been forged in blood and pain and misery. Those trials broke Blair Windsor but rebuilt her immediately after with a spine of steel and a resilience capable of conquering any storm.

He can try to get me to yield all he wants, but I'm just as strong, if not stronger, than he'll ever be.

And I won't bow to any man.

As I hold his stare, I can see a muscle in his jaw twitch imperceptibly when I don't give him the reaction he apparently desires. I simply gaze back unflinchingly, allowing him to see the multitude of emotions flashing like fireworks in my eyes, none of them good.

All I know is that I *can't* look away first. If I do, then that means I'm submitting to him, that I see myself as lesser.

Which is something I'll never, ever be. Not again. My childhood was destroyed because of a man like him taking what he wanted, regardless of the consequences. I grew claws and fangs because of that encounter, and I've learned how to effectively wield them as powerful weapons.

His eyes are abysses, as cold and empty as black holes. One of us will have to look away first. One of us will have to yield. One of us—

In the next second, a broad back is in front of me, impacting my line of vision once more.

Tai.

I initially want to bite off his head for ending this staring contest before my wits return to me and I realize he probably just saved my life. The last thing I want to do is inadvertently challenge an alpha in his own territory, especially if the rumors are true and Sarai doesn't fight fair.

Wolf rules dictate that shifters fight one on one, but Sarai has been known to break them on more than one occasion.

Which is probably why Tai has never been able to unseat him as alpha.

The pieces of that puzzle finally begin to click into place as I glance from Tai, to his shaken mother, and then over his shoulder at a smiling Sarai.

I've always wondered why Tai never fought to become alpha, especially when he's so much stronger, but I've never been able to receive a direct answer from my sources. I'd wrongly assumed Tai was just as power hungry as his father, but I don't believe that for a second anymore.

He cares about people, people like his mother and younger siblings, and he'll do anything to protect them—including relinquishing his claim to the proverbial throne.

"She really is a hot piece of ass," one of Tai's brothers sneers, shifting slightly so he can give me a salacious once-over. Now this guy? He's no alpha like his father and brother. I think he's barely an omega. I immediately dismiss him as irrelevant.

"Have you fucked her yet?" another brother quips. This one has pitch-black hair pulled back into a low ponytail.

"Tell me, baby wolf." A third brother swaggers forward with his hands shoved into his jeans pockets. He has a nasty scar that curls down his cheek and touches his upper lip. "Is your pussy covered in cobwebs, or has it been used so often, it's the size of my fist?"

I find I can't hold my tongue a second longer. "Why don't you come over here and find out?" I practically purr, my hand wrapping around the hilt of my dagger. I push past Tai to meet the asshole's glare head on. "Now, is that a toothpick in your pocket, or are you just happy to see me?"

"Enough!" Tai takes a lumbering step in front of me once more and folds his massive arms over his chest. I can't see the expression on his face, but it must be a sight to behold because his brothers halt in mid-step and Sarai's smile broadens.

"Your brothers have genuine questions, son," the bastard says in a singsong voice. "Unless you want us to take the little bitten wolf for a test drive..."

"Watch what will happen to you if you come near me, *principessa*," I bite out, and Sarai's bushy brows raise, his eyes burning with banked flames.

"What the fuck did you just call me?" Sarai's voice remains low and amused, but there's no denying the undercurrent of danger behind every syllable.

"Do you want me to repeat myself?" I snarl before I can stop myself.

Fuck, I really can't keep my cool around these assholes, now can I?

"You've seen her." Tai pushes at Sarai's chest before spinning in a half circle to bare his teeth at his brothers. "Now we're leaving."

Sarai almost looks like he's going to protest before he squeezes his mouth shut and forces a smile. It's pained, though, and resembles a grimace more than anything else.

"Of course. Wouldn't want to get in the way of your courtship, son." He places a hand on Tai's shoulder and squeezes. Tai's large—easily one of the biggest men I've ever seen—but surprisingly, Sarai is larger. There's not an ounce of body fat on his muscular, intimidating frame. He leans his head close to whisper in Tai's ear, but I can hear every single word as if he screamed them. "But just know you can't escape me, son. Because I'll *always* get what I want."

Tᴀɪ ᴛᴇʟʟs ᴍᴇ ᴛʜᴀᴛ ᴡᴇ ᴀʀᴇɴ'ᴛ sᴛᴀʏɪɴɢ ʜᴇʀᴇ, ᴀ ꜰᴀᴄᴛ that fills me with immense relief.

"I have an apartment ten minutes away from my momma's cottage. It's not on Totemic land, so my father doesn't know about it," he says as we head to the car, both of us keenly aware of the eyes burning holes in my scalp.

And I can't help but think…

How easy would it be to spin around and stick my knife in Sarai's throat? Surely all of our problems will be solved then. He would never see it coming, never expect it. I can't imagine his smile would be so smug with blood showering from his neck as he gasped for breath.

The big bad wolf taken down by scum like me.

The visual makes me smile before I remember the four *stronzi* who always seem to surround him. Omega, Ponytail, Scar, and Dumbass. Tai's brothers.

I can kill Sarai easily enough, but I have no doubt all four of them will kill me in retaliation. Hell, maybe even Tai will. I don't know the Totemic prince well enough yet to judge. Besides, once I cut off one monster's head, two will just grow in his place.

The princes may not be alphas, but I have a feeling that only makes them more dangerous. I can see in their eyes that they're desperate for power and respect, and they'll do whatever they can to claim them for their own. They won't abide by any rules or societal norms in their quest for power. That makes them unpredictable. And I'd rather have a threat I know than one I don't expect.

But fuck, I want to kill Sarai so bad, it's like a need burning inside of me.

Keep smiling, bastardo. *By the time I'm done with you, the walls are going to be painted red in your blood.*

I turn my back to him as I get into the car—one of the highest signs of disrespect a shifter can give another shifter. Basically, I'm telling him that I don't see him as a threat, that I'm not scared of him, that I don't need to be on guard when I'm in his presence. That's not true in the slightest, but if his growl of indignation is any indication, it pisses him off.

As we finally pull the car onto the pebbled street, I'm grateful to see Sarai—the pretty, pretty princess —and the rest of Tai's brothers moving *away* from Enola's cottage. Now that we're no longer there to taunt and ogle, it seems they have better things to do with their lives.

Thank fuck for that because I know the bruises darkening Enola's neck and arms didn't come from a nasty fall. And if I had to witness those pieces of shit hurt her, I would've lost my fucking mind.

Tai and I are both silent as we drive away from the tribal lands and toward a desolate section of town. I tap my fingers repeatedly against the window as Tai stares moodily ahead.

Finally, when the silence grows and stretches between us like a taut rubber band, he bites out, "You shouldn't push him like that."

I spin my head toward him in surprise. "Push whom? *Sarai?*"

His teeth lock together as he tightens his hands on the steering wheel. "Not safe," he grunts out.

I debate my next words very, very carefully, wondering if my theory is correct, if he truly is my mate like Vincent and Mason. I don't feel a bond connecting my soul to his, but then again, I didn't feel one toward Mason or Vincent until they were balls deep inside of me and their teeth were in my neck. Still, I have to tread carefully until I know for sure whether Tai is friend or foe.

"Sarai is a piece of shit," I say at last, focusing intently on the side of his face.

His eyes flash and darken with fury, and at first, I think that anger is directed at my words. But then he speaks.

"I want to kill him," he growls. "I want him to bleed for all of the sins he's committed."

I search his expression for anything that hints he's deceiving me, but I only see sincerity shimmering in his dark eyes.

"Good," I say at long last, reclining back in my seat and turning to stare out the window. We'd just pulled in front of a large apartment complex, the red and brown brick walls covered in a layer of ivory and the grass overgrown with weeds out front. "Then we're on the same page."

We don't speak again as Tai stops the car, races around the front, and opens the passenger door for me. I'll never admit to anyone the way my heart gallops in my chest at the chivalrous gesture.

"Your stuff is already upstairs," Tai mumbles, staring down at his feet and refusing to meet my gaze. It's something he does a lot, I've come to realize, and I can't help but find his timidity alluring. As we move toward the front entrance of the complex, he once again runs forward to open the door for me. "I know it's not much…"

"Tai," I say, deciding to be blunt, "I'm grateful we don't have to stay with your family, despite how beautiful your community is." When a crease appears between his eyes, I continue. "I have a feeling that your father or one of your brothers would've tried to attack me if we had stayed there. Or they would've done God knows what." I shudder just thinking about it, my mind conjuring up images of Grim's predatory smile and wandering hands. Fuck him. "So this place is an oasis, even if there is mold on the walls."

Tai ducks his head and runs a hand over his scalp. "Never would've let them hurt you," he rumbles.

I give him a smile—all cutting edges and sharp knives. "I wouldn't have either."

Tai leads me toward an elevator, up to the top floor, and then to an apartment at the end of the hall.

He seems almost nervous, his eyes constantly flickering in my direction, as he shoves his key into the lock and pushes the door open.

I don't know what I expect the apartment of a bachelor to look like, but this isn't it.

Everything is clean and scrubbed so meticulously, I swear I can see my reflection in the floorboards. To the immediate left of the entryway is a walk-in kitchen, with smooth marble counters colored gray and black. Matching appliances decorate the small kitchen, giving the entire apartment a modern flair. Directly in front of the bar, and adjacent to the living room, is a small table with four black chairs positioned around it. From there, the wooden floors transition into soft white carpeting that leads into the living room. Black leather couches rest in a semi-circle in front of a flat screen television.

To the immediate right of the doorway is a hallway that I suspect leads to the bedrooms and bathrooms. A balcony is positioned just outside of the living room, giving view to the street below.

"I prepared your room," Tai says gruffly, leading me down the hallway I noted earlier and toward a room at the end.

Once again, he hesitates, his large shoulders practically touching his ears.

Is he…?

Is he giving himself a mental pep talk? I swear I can see his lips moving, but no words come out.

Whatever he does, it seems to work, and he

pushes the door open with a dramatic flourish, gesturing for me to enter.

My breath hitches as I step inside, surveying the room with wide eyes.

"Tai, this is incredible."

"Grayson told me pink was your favorite color," he confesses softly, seemingly uncomfortable. "I tried to make it feel as homey as possible."

Undefinable emotions flood me as I look around the tiny room.

The walls have been painted a light pink, the same shade as my bedspread. Darker curtains provide a gorgeous contrast to a room that might've been considered girlish and childish. The smooth mahogany dresser and matching desk complete the decor.

"This is...I...I don't know what to say."

"I did this for you." Tai shuffles from foot to foot before nodding toward my suitcases on my bed. "And I had your clothing delivered. Um...if you need anything...just holler. My room is down the hall. Food is in...um...the fridge. If you like food." He scratches absently at the back of his neck, and I bite down on the smile that wants to make an appearance. Is this really the same cocky man who swaggered into the bitten wolves' camp, flirted incessantly with me, and then demanded I show up to the summit? I can't quite correlate this nervous man to that confident one.

I like it.

Tai opens his mouth, closes it, opens it a second time, before snapping it shut. Then, without another word, he steps out of the room and slams my door.

Men are very, very strange creatures.

16

BLAIR

DAY 5

I don't talk to Tai for the next few days.

Granted, I see him everywhere, but I don't actually speak to the strange, gruff man. He's a constant presence I feel as keenly as my own limb —but he doesn't engage me in any conversation. And because of that, I don't speak to him either. We seemed to have developed an unspoken truce as to how we can exist in relative peace in his tiny apartment.

I can feel his eyes on me whenever I rifle through his fridge, grabbing food at random. And I can feel that burning, penetrating gaze when I sit at the bar and dig in. I can feel that stare when I move into the living room and watch some shitty television show, all the while my mind swirls with worry. Worry for Papa Grayson and the other bitten wolves. Worry for Vincent and Valentina. Worry for Mason and Brett.

I've been in constant communication with all of them, but that does very little to alleviate the anxiety burning a hole in my stomach.

Whenever I leave the apartment—which isn't often, mind you—Tai follows me like an overbearing shadow. He doesn't say a single word as he remains at my side, his hands tucked into the pockets of his leather jacket and his dark sunglasses obscuring his eyes from view. I want to be mad at him, furious even, but I can't deny the sense of comfort and security his presence evokes in me.

On the fifth day, I can't handle it. I'm literally about to scream from his lack of communication. If this is his attempt to woo me, then he's going about it the completely wrong way.

"You know," I begin casually from where I sit at the bar, licking yogurt from my spoon. I don't turn around to face him, but I can feel his eyes on my back. It's not a predatory sensation or even a primitive one. It almost feels…natural, like the caress of the sun on a hot summer day. It's like my body craves the satisfaction of knowing his eyes are on me. "You can say more than two words to me. I don't bite."

He mumbles something I can't quite hear, and I finally spin around on the bar stool to face him fully, crossing my legs so my leather skirt rides up. His eyes drop to the sliver of skin revealed on my upper thigh before he swallows and immediately turns back to the television, flipping channels at random.

"I do talk to you," he grunts out, his eyes intense on the screen.

"Three words a day does not constitute talking." I roll my eyes as I jump off the stool and move into the living room. "If we're going to do this thing—"

"What thing?" he interrupts, ripping his gaze from the television to meet my stare. "The one where you're virtually a prisoner in my home and are forced to spend time with me? That thing?" He looks so damned peeved about my predicament that I have to bite down on my smile.

"This isn't a case of Stockholm syndrome, Tai. Believe it or not, I actually want to get to know you." *Especially if you're my fated mate.* I don't say those words out loud. "Come on. What happened to the flirty, confident shifter I met sixty days ago?"

"The day my people attempted to slaughter

yours?" he deadpans, not removing his gaze from the screen. "What do you even want from me, Blair? I know you despise me."

A surge of indignation courses through me. "I never said that," I counter immediately.

"You didn't have to," he grunts out. "I can see it written all over your face."

"Then you're horrible at reading faces." I move to sit beside him on the smooth leather couch, running my hands over the cold surface. "I hate your father," I confess bluntly. "Not you."

"Some people have trouble differentiating between father and son," he points out, the muscles in his shoulders tensing almost imperceptibly.

"I'm not most people." I bite down on my lip before directing my gaze toward the show that has captured his attention. A laugh bubbles out of me before I can contain it. "Come on. You can't tell me you're really into..." I squint to read the title visible on the lower left corner of the screen. "...*Paw Patrol.*"

A blush paints his cheeks when he realizes what he has absently switched to, and he turns off the TV with a scowl.

"I'm going to my room." He rises gracefully to his feet, all six foot five of solid muscle, and immediately turns toward his bedroom.

"You cut your hair," I blurt out, my eyes dropping to his ass before I can stop myself and then rising to focus on his buzzed scalp. He stills, one foot raised as if he was in mid-step when my comment startled him.

"Excuse me?" He doesn't turn around to face me, but I know I've captured his complete attention.

"When I last saw you a couple months ago, you had that long strip of black hair at the top of your head." Despite the fact that his back is to me, I still feel the need to show him what I mean. One of my hands moves to my own waves and traces the pattern his hair had been in. "It was a fauxhawk, correct?"

"What the fuck are you doing, Blair?" He spins around to face me and crosses his huge arms over his chest, his lips twisted into a scowl. Instead of answering, I allow my eyes to travel over him, noting all the similarities between this Tai and the one from before. He still wears all black, and his T-shirt molds to the impressive muscles of his chest and forearms. Whenever he goes outside, he slips on a leather jacket despite the heat, and I swear I practically drool at the sight. His dark hair is now buzzed short, but before, it was cut close to his scalp on the sides with a longer, wavy strip directly on top. The only thing that hasn't changed is the color of his eyes—a shade of brown lighter than Vincent's and flecked with gold. As I watch, those eyes narrow and his lips compress into an unyielding line. "Are you... Are you checking me out?"

Once again, I don't answer, simply folding my arms over my chest and cocking one eyebrow in a silent challenge. He growls, nothing but a hiss of breath, before stomping toward me and towering over my small form. I can see the intent in his eyes—he wants me to feel small and weak, but I'm not an omega. And this alpha is about to use her claws.

"All right." His tongue snakes out to lick his lower lip. "How about a game?"

My damn, traitorous mind immediately conjures up images of the two of us in bed together, his powerful body thrusting into mine.

"What type of game?" My voice is nothing but a breath of air.

His smile turns sharper, revealing perfectly straight teeth, and I feel my heart pound erratically in my chest.

"You'll see," he growls.

"This...This is not what I had in mind," I say, glancing from Tai's face to the game board and then back to Tai's face.

He smirks at me as he shakes the dice in his closed fist.

"What type of game did you have in mind, little wolf?" he taunts as he drops the dice, revealing two sixes. He grabs his top hat and moves it around the Monopoly board, his smirk growing when it lands on the still unsold Boardwalk. "I'll buy that, thank you very much."

With a scowl, I accept his money and place it in the bank before handing him his property. He already owns Park Place, so with that damn property, he just made a monopoly.

"Nothing in particular," I say in answer to his previous question, making sure to keep my voice light and airy. I know it irritates him, especially when I toss a smile in as well. "I like all games. Monopoly. Life. Checkers. Chess. Charades. I'm the best at games."

I roll the dice as well, biting down on the curse word that wants to escape when I land directly on his just bought property.

"That will be..." He glances down at his card.

"One hundred dollars, because I own every property in this group."

"That will be one hundred dollars," I mock in a low, masculine voice under my breath, handing over the bill. "Anyway, as I was saying..."

"You were expressing your love of games," Tai fills in for me, offering me a teasing smile. I half want to punch that smile off his face and half want to kiss him senseless. I kind of hate my emotions right about now.

"I just love games that are hard," I say, placing an extra emphasis on the word 'hard.' "The harder the better is my motto." Releasing a breathy moan, that even to my ears is entirely too sexual, I sit back in the chair.

Stronzo.

I watch in satisfaction as he swallows roughly, his hand tightening around the poor, abused dice. What did they ever do to him to get such poor treatment?

"My favorite thing in the world is opening up a brand new game," I continue, adopting a perfectly innocent expression. "There's nothing better than going to town on it, am I right?"

"Okay, enough!" He drops the dice onto the board with a growl. "At this point, you're just saying random shit in an attempt to—" He cuts himself off abruptly, casting an almost surreptitious glance at his cock.

"I don't know what you're talking about, *un lupo grosso e cattivo.*"

"What did you just call me?" His brows furrow together.

"Whatever do you mean?" I blink my lashes at him as his scowl deepens.

"Don't go saying sexy shit in Italian. You know what that does to me."

"No. Please enlighten me," I say with a saccharine sweet grin.

"You drive me insane," he grunts out, running a hand over his head.

"I'm going to drive you even more insane when I take your money," I taunt, nodding toward the board.

He releases a derisive snort. "As if. I believe I'm in the lead, little wolf."

"Are not."

"Are too."

"Are not."

"Are—" The ringing of my cell phone interrupts his protest, and he immediately settles back in his chair with a tiny growl. Considering the fact that he looks like a petulant kid throwing a tantrum—complete with pouty lips—I can't help but chuckle.

"Hello?" I say into the phone, keeping my gaze on Tai. He narrows his eyes, but I simply stick my tongue out at him in response. Lust darkens his features almost instantly as he fixates on my lips. I can feel his body heat, and my own temperature seems to rise just by being in his proximity.

"Blair?" Papa Gray's voice is a bucket of cold, icy water being dumped over my head. I sit up straighter, startled by the alarm in his tone.

"What happened?" I'm on my feet before I have even finished speaking, stalking toward my bedroom. Tai follows behind me as I duck under the bed and grab out one of the knives I hid there. "Where are you?"

"Blair, we were attacked. You need to get home. Now."

17

BLAIR

DAY 5

"What the fuck happened?" I demand before I'm even fully out of the car. The camp that has been my home for the better part of my childhood still looks exactly as I remember it. I don't know what I expected—maybe all of the buildings reduced to ash and smoke—but everything appears unscathed.

The trailer park is hidden deep in the woods, tall oaks interspersed with maple trees creating a protective barrier around the encampment. Campers and tents are scattered throughout, all surrounding a large log building that serves as our base of operation, as well as our community center and school.

It's there we go, Tai silently following behind me once more.

I don't know why I even allowed him to come with me, but after my phone call with Papa Gray, I took one look into Tai's brown and black gaze and knew that he would quite literally tie me up if I tried to go alone. And I didn't have the mental capacity to argue with him.

My packmates will be pissed I brought the enemy into their territory, but hopefully, they'll understand that Tai is here to help.

The first person I see when I enter the immense structure is Johnson, a bloody gash marring his haggard face as he leans against the wall. He glances up, his narrowed-eyed glare immediately falling onto Tai.

"What the fuck is he doing here?" he growls out as I rush to him.

Waving away his worries, I survey the wicked-looking gash on his forehead, concern pinching my brow. "What the fuck happened? Where's Papa Gray?" Johnson doesn't immediately answer, his eyes shifting to Tai and heating with an elemental fury, but I reclaim his attention once more. "Tai's here to help," I assure him. "Now tell me what happened."

"We were attacked." The wobbly voice is familiar, and a second later, Papa Gray ventures out of the nearest room, leaning heavily on his cane. I rush to him immediately, inspecting the old man for any injuries. Besides a bruise decorating his left cheek, he appears relatively unharmed.

"Who was it?" Tai bites out, and I glance over my shoulder at him in surprise. His hands are balled into tight fists, and his teeth are bared. Anger hardens every line of his body as he glares at something over my head.

"The Bloody Skulls," Papa Gray answers, his voice crisp and almost curt. He levels Tai with a distrustful glare before turning his attention onto me. He raises one of his gray eyebrows, and I can see the silent question in that eloquent gesture.

Can we trust him?

I want to be indecisive and admit that I don't know if I can trust Tai or not.

But the truth is…I *can* trust him. I can, and I do. It's impossible for any man to fake the rage that Tai does whenever he speaks of his father or brothers.

To anyone else, the expression that darkens his eyes might've been terrifying, but I don't feel even a sliver of fear with Tai. I don't know how to explain it with words, but I know innately that his ire will never be directed at me. At least, not at the level he seems to loathe his family members. It's a gut feeling, something that tightens up my insides, and trying to go against it would be like wading opposite a strong current in the ocean.

Is it the mate bond between us? The irrevocable feeling of safety and security that I also feel with Vincent and Mason?

I shake my head to clear those thoughts and allow Papa Gray and Johnson to lead me into a conference room. It's already full of bitten wolves, and my eyes immediately land on Martha where she sits at the head of the table, a tiny wolf cub curled up into a ball on her lap.

"Martha. Jacob," I greet, running forward to engulf them in my arms.

The older woman sniffs before releasing me and shooing me away. "None of that, girly. I'm fine. My kid's fine. We're all fine."

Despite her words, I find my gaze traveling over each wolf present, ensuring with my own two eyes that they're truly okay. I stop when my stare lands on Tai, standing awkwardly in the entryway, a scowl marring his plush lips and his large arms folded.

Turning away from him, I focus on Papa Gray once more.

"What happened?" I demand, pacing. "Tell me everything."

"There's not much to tell, child." The old bitten wolf runs a hand through his gray hair as he all but collapses into the nearest chair. Johnson rests a reassuring hand on his shoulder and gives it a soft squeeze. "They came here, roughed us up a little bit, and then destroyed our latest delivery of food."

"That's it?" My brows furrow together. While destroying our food is an inconvenience, it isn't life-threatening or something that will incapacitate us for long.

So what is their goal? Why did they do this?

"And everyone's okay?" I ask, needing that reassurance more than anything. I think I'll lose my damn mind if I lost one of them—my found family, forged in sweat and tears instead of blood.

"My hiney hurts from when I tripped over a garbage can," Martha laments, shifting uncomfortably on the wooden chair. "But I'll survive."

"Besides a few cuts and bruises, we're all alive, and that's what matters," Papa Gray tells me sincerely.

"Grim wouldn't do something like this if he

didn't have an ulterior motive," Tai pipes up from where he still stands in the doorway. He frowns when everyone swivels in their chairs to stare at him, seemingly uncomfortable with their attention.

"What the fuck is the Totemic's precious prince doing here?" one of the wolves, Mattias, snaps, flashing his fangs.

"Blair!" Martha hisses, the reprimand clear to hear in her voice.

Johnson and Papa Gray don't say a word against me, but they also don't defend me either, their faces hewn from stone.

"Stop it," I hiss at my packmates and friends. "I trust him."

Tai raises his brows at my confession, surprise coloring his features, as Tony slams his fist down onto the table.

"You trust a totemic wolf?" His voice is laced with haughty disbelief and incredulity.

"He hasn't given me a reason not to," I huff, not elaborating further. I'm not going to defend my choices to these people, family or not. I'm the most powerful shifter here, and I won't allow my decisions to be challenged a second longer.

"All right, boy," Papa Gray turns his glare onto Tai, "explain yourself."

Tai's scowl deepens, emphasizing the masculine lines and angles of his face, as he pushes himself off the wall and stalks farther into the room. The men and women present all tense, and I notice Martha protectively cover Jacob with her body. If Tai notices that defensive gesture too and is offended, he doesn't let it show, keeping a scowl firmly plastered into place.

"If there's one thing I learned from Sarai and Grim from all the years I've known them, it's that they never do anything without a big purpose. Every move they make is decided meticulously to benefit their pawns on the gameboard. Even Blair is nothing but a cog in their fucked up machine." He turns an apologetic glance my way, but I wave off whatever he wants to say. I already know I'm nothing but a piece for them to use in this game of chess.

"And you think this attack is a cog in the machine?" Johnson interjects, frowning.

"How can destroying our food benefit them?" Papa Gray adds. "If they knew anything about us, they would know that a setback like that wouldn't hinder us."

"A distraction," Tai says without thought. "That's what this is."

"A distraction." My mouth curls into a grimace.

"What are they trying to accomplish by distracting us?"

Tai seems to think about it for a long moment, his fingers tapping against his jeans, before his eyes widen in his face and horror emerges in his dark eyes.

"Those men I saw around the perimeter…the ones in the suits and ties…they're Davenport's men, aren't they?" There's not a hint of accusation in his words, but I still feel myself struggling to come up with an excuse for their presence.

"I…" I trail off helplessly as he nods once, my silence answer enough.

"No doubt, the second they arrived at the camp, the team contacted Vincent. And if my theories are correct…" Tai turns to stare at me for a long moment, his expression unreadable, before focusing on the room as a whole. "…then Vincent would deploy more of his security to the camp to protect you guys. Is that correct?" He directs the question at Papa Gray, who nods once, his jaw clenched beneath his whiskered beard.

"We sent them away as soon as the BS members left," he confesses.

Which is understandable. It's hard to obliterate centuries of wariness and distrust in a span of seconds. Though the Davenports have been immensely helpful the last fifty days, providing food, clothes, and security for my people, Papa Gray still struggles to trust them completely.

"So what you're saying..." I trail off as understanding dawns on me. A cold chill that has nothing to do with the air conditioning skates down my spine. My lungs struggle to replenish their air supply.

"I don't think the bitten wolves were the target," Tai finishes for me, his eyes sympathetic despite his hardened mouth.

Without another word, I turn on my heel and race outside. My heart pounds so loudly, it drowns out every other sound, including Tai's footsteps just behind me. All I can hear is the repetitive *thump-thump-thump* of a heart that isn't working properly and the sluicing of blood in my ears.

I grab my phone out, Vincent's number already pulled up, and press it to my ear.

"Come on. Come on. Come on." My words are a prayer, a mantra, a warning, and a threat. If something happened to him...

If something happened because of me...

The phone rings and rings and rings before his

voicemail picks up. Cursing, I try again, biting on my nail as I struggle to remember to breathe.

"Blair," Tai says gently, placing a huge hand on my shoulder.

"He has to be okay, right?" I release a strained, semi-hysterical laugh. "He's Vincent fucking Davenport. He's okay, isn't he?"

Voicemail.

I try calling ten times before dialing Mason's number instead.

Ring. Ring. Ring.

Voicemail.

"No. No. No. No." I shake my head rapidly from side to side as a rock the size of Texas settles in my gut. Acid crawls up my throat as I struggle to beat down the mounting panic. "Come on, Mase. Pick up. Please pick up."

Tai keeps his hand on my shoulder, a surprisingly reassuring gesture, as I call both men again and again. I try Valentina and Brett as well, but I'm always sent to voicemail.

Panic threatens to eat me alive, and my gut lurches with fear. I lose myself in the rage that cascades through me, the full brunt of it pouring out of me in a wave.

If Grim or Sarai hurt my men, my brother, or Valentina, I'll—

"Shit." Tai releases me suddenly and growls, the noise emphasizing the pure, venomous rage he harbors.

My dagger is in my hand in seconds as I spin toward the new arrival, my head spinning rapidly.

But it's not Sarai or Grim I see staggering out of the woods.

Her hair is wildly disheveled, clumps of dried blood and twigs sticking to the inky strands. Her pencil skirt is torn up the side, revealing a leg covered in dirt, and her white blouse has been completely destroyed, her bare breasts on full display.

Tai turns away instantly, his shoulders stiff, as I run forward to meet my trembling friend.

"Valentina!" My voice croaks with alarm as I take off my own shirt and hand it to her. She eyes the material for a long moment without saying a single word. I wonder if she's in shock, and my heart races even faster at the thought. "What happened?"

After a long, long moment, she slides off her destroyed shirt and shrugs into mine. It's a size too big, but at least it covers her.

She wraps an arm around her stomach as she shakes.

"It's Vincent," she whimpers as I draw her into my arms. She settles her head underneath my chin as a sob is wrenched from her throat. "They got him."

18

BLAIR

NIGHT 7

I twist my head to stare at Valentina's sleeping face, safe in Tai's secret apartment.

Her features are slack, and without that combative, glacial glint in her eyes, she almost looks like a completely different person. Violet shadows line the skin underneath both of her eyes, something that hasn't gone away even with the sleep she gets. Worry for her brother is evident in the taut lines between her brows.

Worry I feel as well.

The last two days, I've done everything in my power to make sure Vincent and Mason were okay. I stole Tai's bike—a fact he wasn't happy with—and drove to first Vincent's mansion and then Mason's apartment. I searched desperately for any clues I could find that would help me find them, but my search proved to be futile. If anything, seeing the state of their living quarters only amplified my unease and fear.

Vincent's beautiful foyer had been completely destroyed, the stone statues in the entryway demolished and lying in pieces on the marble flooring. Mason's apartment wasn't much better, though I'm not sure how it looked before I broke into it. For all I know, the biker always leaves his clothing on the floor and dirty dishes in the sink. I mean, it's not as if I saw him in his natural habitat when I stayed with him. The apartment we lived in wasn't even technically his, but one that he frequents.

I even check the bar and the sleazy apartment above it.

Nothing.

Not even a trace that they've ever been there.

Anxiety begins to break through the numb barrier I attempted to build around myself. It claws at my insides, leaving me bloody and wounded.

The only saving grace is that I know they're still alive. Don't ask me how, but I can feel it in my very soul that their hearts are still beating, their lungs are still taking in air, their eyes are still seeing. But I have no idea the state that they're in.

Are they hurt?

Bleeding out?

Dying?

I would know that, wouldn't I?

But there is one thing I can do to help find them, consequences be damned.

Sarai and Grim have officially declared war after attacking my people and taking my men. Now, it's time they pay in blood.

Slipping out of bed, I move on silent feet toward my bedroom door. I fell asleep still dressed in my black leathers, something Valentina commented on but didn't question, and kept my favorite dagger on my nightstand.

Fear for my men washes over me in a torrent, painful in its intensity, but I shove it away.

I need to be calm if I'm going to do this. I can't break apart. Not now. Not until I get all the information I can.

The door squeaks softly when I try to shut it, and I wince, holding my body perfectly still. I listen intently, wondering if the noise will wake Valentina, but besides a quiet murmur, she remains fast asleep.

A relieved breath escapes me as I venture down

the hallway, past Tai's bedroom, and toward the front door of the apartment. I work hard to moderate my breathing—in and out. In and out. In and out. In—

A large shadow steps in front of me, barring my entrance to the door, and my breath hitches, becoming caught in my throat. Tai's angular features are illuminated by the silvery moonlight cascading through the open window. His brows are drawn low over glowering eyes as he glares at me. I can't help but notice that he's still dressed for the day in a form-fitting T-shirt and black jeans.

"What do you think you're doing?" he rumbles, his arm muscles flexing.

"Shhh." I place a single finger to my lips and glance behind me at Valentina's closed bedroom door. "Keep it down."

"You're looking for Vincent and Mason again, aren't you?" Though he phrases it as a question, I can tell he already believes he knows the answer.

I purse my lips. "I'm getting information," I say at last, shouldering past him. His large hand lands on my shoulder as he spins me around to face him. In a second, I'm on my tiptoes with my knife pressed to his jugular. He freezes instantly, those dark eyes lowering to the blade before flickering to my face. "Don't touch me, Tai. And don't stop me."

"I'm not going to stop you, little wolf," he growls, taking a step closer and forcing my blade further into his neck. A trickle of blood slides down his throat, but he doesn't seem to care.

"You don't want to be there for what I'm going to do." It's as much of a warning as I can give him. Because despite the potential mate bond between us, I'm not going to let him stop me. I refuse to.

My heart batters my ribs with a frightening speed as I hold his dark gaze, refusing to lower my blade.

With half his face in shadows, he seems even harsher than usual. More dangerous. He's a predator lying in wait, just waiting to pounce on the unsuspecting prey. The downward tilt to his lips juxtaposes the lust burning in his eyes the longer he stares at me.

"Which one of my brothers are you going to torture, Blair?" His voice is a husky whisper, and it rumbles through me like a thousand watts of electricity.

"What?" I breathe, my pulse skittering.

"Which one of my brothers are you going to

torture?" He speaks each word slowly, and I feel my irritation toward him grow by the second.

"Fuck off, Tai. Go to bed."

"Because if you're going to make my family bleed, little wolf," he purrs, taking another step closer. More blood cascades down the column of his throat as he bares his teeth at me. "Then I want to be there with you."

THE APARTMENT'S SMALLER THAN TAI'S, LOCATED only five minutes from Enola's cottage.

Immediately once we enter the stairwell, the stench of sweat, piss, and mold barrages my senses. My nose wrinkles in disgust as I glance from the stained carpeting to the mildew and water stains decorating the cream-colored walls. At least, they might have been painted cream at one point. They're covered in so many stains that it's impossible to know for certain. I just pray that the brown I see smeared across a large portion of the wall is chocolate and not what I'm thinking it is.

"Your brother lives here?" I crinkle my nose as Tai scoffs.

"Jonah's dumber than a box of rocks. My father keeps him around for his muscles only."

Jonah…

He must mean Omega.

I follow Tai toward a door at the very end of the hall.

"Now, we can do this the subtle way or the explosive way," I begin, removing a pair of gloves from my back pocket and sliding them on. "Which one do you prefer?"

His smile is as sharp as a knife and as wicked as sin itself. "You know I'm all for explosives, little wolf," he purrs, and I grin back at him.

And then, without warning, I kick the door to Jonah's apartment open with all my might. It falls to the ground, tiny pieces of wood skittering in every direction, and I step over it with a scowl.

Like Tai told me, the apartment is a studio. The kitchen, living room, and bedroom all merge into open space with no doors. It's the bed I turn to first, my smile growing as Omega jerks upright, his teeth bared and a fierce growl escaping him. A woman sits up on his other side, her blonde hair teased and her face covered in makeup. She jumps from the bed with a cry of alarm, completely naked and covered in hickeys, and trips over a sheet on the floor.

"Get out of here if you want to live," I hiss at her, not daring to pull my attention away from the asshole struggling to untangle himself from his sheets.

The woman glances helplessly between her clothes on the floor and the door before eventually deciding to run out of the apartment completely naked. Tai steps aside to let her pass before stalking forward and grabbing his brother's arm. The pathetic excuse for a wolf releases a nervous whimper as his wide eyes volley between me and his brother.

Not as brave and cocky without his father there as a buffer, now is he?

"What the fuck is this Tai?" Omega hisses, attempting to puff out his chest. Oh, please. Is that supposed to scare me away? He looks like a preschooler trying to impress his crush, not an intimidating, badass wolf shifter.

I step forward, drawing his attention to me. "Don't talk to him," I say firmly, cocking my head to the side as Tai drags his brother to his feet before me. I notice that he's completely naked, his erect cock hitting his stomach, and I can't help but think that he's unimpressive in every way imaginable.

"Don't even acknowledge him. Tonight, you're dealing with me."

"And put some damn clothes on. I don't want her to see your fucking cock," Tai growls, shoving him toward the pile of clothes at the foot of his bed. Omega hesitates, glancing at me as if seeking permission, and I gesticulate with my knife for him to do so.

Once Omega has a pair of pants on, I point with my knife toward a chair in his dining room.

"Tai, be a dear and place him there," I instruct, flashing him a sweet smile.

A bead of sweat materializes on Omega's forehead and rolls into his eyes.

"What the fuck are you doing, man?" he whispers furiously to Tai as my mate deposits him in the seat I indicated. "You can't do this. I'm your brother. I'm your—"

Tai lowers his lips so it's directly next to Omega's ear. When he speaks next, his words are a sharp hiss, one that seems to rattle through him. "You're *nothing* to me." He brandishes the rope he brought from home like a weapon before forcing Omega's hands behind his back and tying them together.

"Please. Don't do this. Why the fuck are you doing this?" He turns vitriol-filled eyes in my direction. "Listen here, you little bitch—" A pained howl escapes him as Tai punches him in the face.

"Don't call her a bitch," he seethes.

"Thank you, Tai." I press up onto my tiptoes to plant a kiss on his cheek, all the while keeping my gaze on Omega. I want him to see that he won't receive any help from me or his brother. His blood is ours to spill, and if he expects either of us to show him mercy, he's sorely mistaken.

Pulling away from Tai, I move to grab my own seat and sit opposite from Omega. I balance the dagger on my knee as a reminder as I lean forward with a cheerful expression.

"I just have some questions for you, Jonah." I say his name with a rictus twist to my lips, and he gulps, his tan face draining of all color.

"I don't know anything."

"You see…I don't believe that." I allow my fingers to caress the blade of my dagger, the moonlight sprinkling in from the open window bathing it in a silvery glow. "Did you know that it takes only thirty-three seconds to cut off a man's finger using this particular blade?" I ask casually, wrapping my hand around the hilt and holding it up for him to see.

He begins to sob, big, slobbery tears that turn his

entire face beet-red. Snot drips from his nose as well.

"Please. Please don't do this. Tai, please!"

"I told you." I lean forward, and he cowers, a strangled noise escaping him. "You don't talk to him; you talk to me." Without diverting my attention away from this despicable, slimy man, I say, "Tai, you can leave if you don't want to see this."

"No," he bites out, moving to stand beside me with his arms crossed over his chest. The expression on his face even scares me a little. "I've been waiting for this moment for too damn long to be sidelined."

I bite down on my lip to hide my smile as appreciation and respect for Tai bubbles up inside of me.

"Very well." Without waiting for either man to catch his bearings, I lunge forward and stab my knife into Omega's thigh. Blood immediately wells, seeping through the material of his jeans, as he howls and screams to the universe.

But if he really thought someone would hear him and save him, he was poorly mistaken. I'm sure the other residents heard his screams, but in this part of town, no one will step in or call the cops. They're too scared of their own shadows to do anything but cower under their blankets.

"Oh god. Please. Please help me!" he cries, and I

lean forward, pressing my lips directly to his ear. My other hand tangles in his dark hair, pulling just tight enough to get him to cry out a second time.

"No God, you disgusting piece of shit. Only me." I slowly lower my free hand to the blade in his thigh and give it a twist, relishing in his pained screams. "You're going to tell me what I need to know. And afterward, you're going to beg for me to kill you."

19

BLAIR

NIGHT 7

I wipe a bead of sweat from my forehead as I lean heavily on the shovel.

The only light is from the crescent moon high above, illuminating the woods in shades of pastel white and gold. The forest seems eerie at this time of night, almost malevolent, and I can't help but think of the trees as malicious monsters just waiting to drag me down into hell.

After all, hell is where I most definitely belong.

My eyes drop to Omega's dead body, his mottled face barely recognizable. His eyes have been swollen shut, so at least I don't have to stare into his vacant orbs as I bury him.

I should feel grief, sadness, or even guilt for the life I just took, but all I can muster up is an intense feeling of satisfaction. It's an insidious type of feeling —one I know I shouldn't feel yet do all the same. It seeps into my bloodstream like a corrosive acid, shooting pain throughout my body.

But fuck, I'm relieved the bastard's dead.

Tai stands on the other side of the hole we're digging, his muscles tensing as he slams the shovel into the dirt.

"Tai, you don't have to do this," I say softly, wiping at my forehead once more. He glances up at me, his eyes unreadable, but doesn't speak as he scoops away another layer of dirt. "Tai, seriously."

"Blair." He moves to mimic my position, one of his arms slung casually over the top of the shovel as he crosses his legs at his ankles. "Do you think I'm upset that he's dead?"

"Aren't you?" I ask seriously, cocking an eyebrow. "He's your brother."

Tai's face could've been hewn from stone with how readable it currently is. All I can do is stare into his dark brown eyes, flecked with gold, until I fear the ground is crumbling beneath me, pulling me into a pitch-black abyss. After a long, long moment, he drops the shovel to the ground and shrugs off his leather jacket.

"Um..." I bite down on my lower lip when he grabs the back of his shirt near the neckline and pulls it over his head. "I don't know what you think you're doing, but sex on the grave of the man I just killed isn't something I'm into."

He gives me a droll look as he stands before me completely shirtless. My eyes greedily travel over his muscular, tan torso and the black tattoos rippling across his skin like water. He's so beautiful, so hand-some, that my breath literally catches in my throat.

I know what I just said, and I stand by it, but he's seriously making me regret my whole, "Don't have sex near dead bodies" rule.

"You see this?" Tai questions, pointing toward one of his intricate tattoos. I take a step closer, the moonlight my only guide, and peer at the expanse of skin.

"Yes?" I question tentatively, reaching a hand out as if to touch it. At the last second, I pause, my hand hovering just above his skin. He gently grabs my wrist and guides my fingers to the tattoo—and to the scar puckering underneath it. As wolf shifters, one of the only things that can scar us permanently is a silver blade. What the fuck happened to him to have so many scars?

"I got this scar when I was twelve years old," Tai confesses, his voice devoid of any emotion whatsoever. "I heard my mother screaming for help and ran downstairs to see my father smacking her around. When she accidentally bumped into Jonah, he punched her in the face, laughing as she fell. He was eighteen at the time. I stepped in front of her, trying my best to defend her from the monsters made of my blood, but my father simply laughed and called me a runt. He held me down as Jonah cut me up, smiling the entire time."

"Tai..." My heart breaks for him, for the pain he endured, and I want more than anything to take him in my arms. Rage coils inside of me like a hungry beast as I drop my gaze onto Omega's—Jonah's—dead body. Before I can stop myself, I spit on his corpse, taking moderate satisfaction from that gross act.

"So no, I'm not sad he's dead." Tai's tone is acerbic, almost bitter, and his eyes spew nothing but hate. "I'm not going to grieve for him or mourn him or think about him any more than I have to. To be completely honest, I probably won't spare him a single thought after today. I don't know if that makes me callous or not." He shrugs his broad shoulders before bending down to grab the shovel once more. "He's nothing to me. Always has been and always will be. I'm happy the bastard's dead and that he can't hurt you, my mother, or my younger siblings ever again."

"Or you," I interject, pulling his gaze away from the hole and back onto me. "He can't hurt you again either."

His shoulders tense as he begins to dig once more. "I don't matter."

"Why the fuck would you say that?" I can't quite keep the incredulity out of my tone. When he doesn't answer, I feel myself grow angrier. Bitter, even. "Seriously, Tai. Why would you say that? Do you really think so little of yourself?"

For reasons I choose not to look at too carefully, that prospect bothers me. A lot. It churns in my gut like acid, burning a hole through my stomach lining.

"It's not that…" He frowns as he finishes digging the hole, standing back to survey his work. "It's just…"

"You spent your entire life looking after others, so you're not used to looking after yourself. Is that it?" I quirk an eyebrow, daring him to disagree, and his frown sharpens, unveiling lines on his face. They somehow make him look years older than his actual age. It's as if the entire world is resting on his shoulders and he has given up carrying the weight, allowing it to shove him into the ground.

"You speak as if you know what I'm talking about," he points out as he moves around the hole and to my side. Together, we roll the body into the dirt, where Mother Nature herself will devour his rotting corpse. Well, maybe not. Maybe Omega is so toxic, so evil, that not even the earth herself will be able to stomach him.

I grab my shovel and begin the tedious work of burying this fucker. "You don't think I do?" I ask seriously, my muscles aching from the strenuous activity. "Tai, you have to keep in mind that for my entire life, it's been just me protecting everyone else. Don't get me wrong. I love my job and the responsibility it entails...but it's a pretty big burden to carry alone. And in the span of months, I discovered there are people who care about me. Brett, Valentina, Vincent, Mason..." My throat closes as I speak the last two names.

Talking to Omega was a waste of my goddamn time. Not only had he pissed all over the floor, but he also had no information about the whereabouts of my mates. He was too low on the totem pole to be trusted with that. I don't regret killing him, but I do regret not pushing him for information. Someone, somewhere knows what happened to Vincent and Mason. And I'll be damned if I don't do everything in my power to figure it out.

"You really care about them, don't you?" Tai says softly from beside me as we work in tandem to fill in the hole.

"Who?" My heart pounds unevenly in my chest when I realize what I unintentionally confessed to. But I'm almost positive Tai knows how much the two men mean to me. Maybe not all of it, but enough to make him wary.

"Don't play dumb with me," he whispers. "Because I'm not an idiot. For one, I know that Brett is your brother." I open my mouth to demand how he discovered that, but he waves me off with one hand. "I've been following you for a while, Blair. I think I'll be able to not only see the resemblance, but hear the way you speak to one another. Keep in mind, I was there when you said goodbye." He throws me an amused grin as my cheeks pink. Yup. Maybe I hadn't been exactly subtle, but it's not like my relationship with Brett is a huge secret.

"So you also saw the way I behaved with Mason then, right?" I ask, my voice just as soft as his. It's almost a whisper in the breeze, the night air blowing it away within seconds.

"I can see the way Mason and Vincent both look at you," he confesses. "I have eyes, you know. I'm not a complete idiot."

"Mason and Vincent…us…It's complicated," I finish at last, wincing.

Tai's voice is gruff when he speaks next. "I'm not afraid of a little competition." He clears his throat. "I care about you, Blair. A lot. And I know it's soon, and you probably hate me, and—"

"I don't hate you," I interrupt immediately. When he glances at me, his eyes shadowed, I hurry to continue, "I don't know you that well yet, but I can promise you that I don't hate you. I even think—" I cut myself off abruptly before I can say the words hovering on the tip of my tongue.

I think you might even be my mate.

That will be a surefire way to scare him off, of that I have no doubt. And the last thing I want is for him to go running to the hills, especially with how new this relationship is. How fragile.

"You know…" Tai's white teeth glimmer as he flashes a smile. "I never really thought my first date with you would be killing my brother and then burying his body."

"You think this is a date?" Girly flutters erupt in my stomach as goosebumps pebble on my arms.

"Isn't it?" He shovels more dirt into the hole before patting it in. "All I need to do is buy you dinner afterward."

"Murder and dinner? You really know how to spoil a woman."

Oh, be still my beating heart.

"Only the best for you," he says gruffly, and my eyes latch on to the curl of his plush upper lip. What would he do if I leaned forward and kissed him right now? If I ran my hand down his bare chest and cupped his—

My god, Blair. Slow the fuck down. You're burying his dead brother, for fuck's sake. A brother, might I add, that you murdered.

"I don't know if this is our first date," I confess, using the back of my shovel to smooth down the dirt. We're far enough away from any civilization that no one will find the body. Still, we can't be too careful. We're going to need to plant twigs and leaves on the fresh dirt in order to conceal it a little better.

"What would you consider our first date?" he questions, leaning on his shovel.

"Monopoly," I answer immediately. "A game you cheated at."

He places a hand over his chest, affronted. "How did I cheat, little wolf? It's not my fault I'm so much better at it than you."

"Oh, please. You can't be better at monopoly than another person. It's all about luck."

"Not luck." He waggles his eyebrows salaciously. "Skill. And, baby, I have it in bucket loads."

I make a face at him. "You stole all of my money."

"You gave me all of your money," he contradicts, his lips twisting. "And of course, I happily took it."

"We'll have to do a rematch," I say. "And this time, I'll kick your ass."

"We'll see, little wolf. We'll see." He clicks his tongue before grabbing the shovel from me and swinging them over his shoulder. With both his hands full, he nods toward his discarded shirt and jacket, and I pick them up immediately. "And, Blair?" His use of my full name stops me in mid-step, and I quirk an eyebrow curiously at him.

"Yeah?"

A muscle in his jaw twitches, barely visible through the canopy of trees disrupting the moonlight.

"I'll do what I can to find Vincent and Mason, okay? I promise you, I'll help you find them."

A tangled knot of yarn gets caught in my throat, one that makes swallowing impossible.

"Thank you, Tai." I want to wrap my arms around him, hold him to me, but instead, I simply offer him a timid smile. "That means the world to me."

He grunts, dipping his chin once in acknowledgement, before stalking back toward where we parked the car.

As I watch his retreating back, I can't help but feel that I'm losing him. I can't tell you how I know that, only that I do. It's like he wants to distance himself from me, like he's worried that if he allows me in, I'll hurt him.

The thought rips me apart, but what can I possibly do?

How can I tell this man that I think he's my fated mate?

And that he has to share me with two of the men he hates most of all?

20

BLAIR

DAY 15

The search for Vincent and Mason proves to be fruitless. I return to the Davenport manor with Valentina and Tai but can't find anything that will help me locate the where-abouts of Vincent.

According to Val, over a dozen lycan wolves arrived at the mansion about ten days ago. Annabelle had, fortunately, been in Paris at the time of the attack, but both twins had been home. Vincent had thrown himself at a wolf hell-bent on attacking Val, sacrificing himself to allow his sister to escape. He screamed at her to find me, but since she didn't trust the totemic wolves, the only place she could think to go was the bitten camp. It was just sheer luck she had stumbled upon me.

Worry for my mates consumes me as I use my sources to uncover anything and everything I can. So far, I haven't been able to get a spy in the Bloody Skulls' clubhouse, a fact that I'm cursing now. I call Mason and Brett repeatedly, but both of their calls go straight to voicemail. And after the fiftieth call, their phones stop ringing all together.

"You're going to ruin the carpeting if you keep up your pacing," Valentina deadpans from where she sits on the leather couch in Tai's living room. When we went back to the Davenport mansion to search for clues and reconnect with the staff, Val packed a small suitcase of clothes. I'd been letting her wear my own clothes—tight jeans and T-shirts—but I can tell she's much more comfortable in her pencil skirt and blouse. It's her battle armor, a way for her to hide from the world while putting up an apathetic front. She straightens her dark hair, applies ruby-red lipstick, and suddenly, she's a completely different person.

The Valentina who arrived at the bitten camp days ago was scared and shivering, her clothing destroyed, her dignity in shatters, and her family in ruin.

This Valentina is poised and confident. Cocky and suave. She always has her phone in her hands, utilizing her own sources the same as I do.

"Vincent wouldn't dare leave you," Valentina continues without looking up from her screen. "You know that. And as much as I hate to admit it, Mason wouldn't either."

I swallow heavily and move to stand directly behind the couch, resting one hand on the top of it. "So you're aware…?"

"That Mason's your mate as well?" She finally glances up from her phone and cocks a perfectly manicured black brow. "And that Tai completes the dynamic trio? Or would it be a quad? But either way, yes, I'm aware."

My mouth opens, shuts, and then opens again as I gape at her, suddenly at a loss for words. She crosses one leg over the other and flashes me a cocky smirk.

"I'm a Davenport, princess," she taunts, her smile broadening. "I know everything that goes on here. I knew you were Vincent's mate from the moment you shot at us in the warehouse. I've never seen him so smitten with a woman before…especially one that, for all intents and purposes, he was supposed to hate. And I knew Mason was your mate the second I saw the two of you together at the art gallery and came to the conclusion that the Tin Man actually has a heart."

I scratch absently at the back of my neck before bringing my hand to my forehead and dragging it down my cheek.

"Everything about this is so…complicated," I confess. "I mean, it's rare to have multiple mates—impossible, even—but that's not the issue."

"The issue is that they're all sworn enemies with only one thing in common," Valentina finishes for me. "You."

"I care about them all a lot," I say, surprising myself with the enormity of my emotions for these men. "And that terrifies me."

"I can imagine." Valentina gives me a gentle smile. "You went from having no one to having multiple someones. And not only that, but you found your brother. And did I hear that Vincent got in contact with your grandma?"

"This is all happening so fast, Val." I move to sit beside her on the couch, resting my legs underneath me and twisting sideways. It suddenly occurs to me how different we truly are. She's a lot like Vincent in that respect, her gaze as glacial as her acerbic words. She's elegant and sophisticated, her dress always immaculately straightened and free of wrinkles and her hair styled to perfection. And then there's me, with my disheveled ponytail, ripped jeans, and a crop-top that shows my toned stomach. Yet despite our differences, I've come to think of her as a sister. "I'm not used to having people care about me. I'm not used to having a family."

"I know, sweetie." She blows out a heavy breath, and for a brief second, her eyes darken with pain I can't quite encapsulate with words. "I sometimes feel the exact same way."

I want to press her for more information, especially when her eyes shadow even further. She has a brother who adores her and a mother who loves her more than anything, yet her life is still empty. Still characterized by pain and suffering.

Pain and suffering at the hands of her father? Someone else?

Before I can ask one of the many questions resting on the tip of my tongue, the door to the apartment opens and Tai steps inside.

Valentina and I both immediately jump to our feet as the totemic wolf makes a beeline toward the fridge. He bends down, giving me a perfect view of his sculpted ass, before grabbing two beers. He moves around the counter to hand me one before flashing a sheepish smile in Valentina's direction.

"Errr…do you want one?" he grunts out, embarrassed. He always seems to forget that she's in the room, like I'm the only girl he ever sees. It's flattering because Valentina is drop-dead gorgeous, enough to make any straight man drool. But it's almost as if Tai doesn't notice her ethereal, elegant beauty and only ever sees me.

Butterflies erupt in my stomach at the thought.

Valentina smirks before casting me an amused look. "No, I'm fine. Thank you though."

"So…" I press, focusing on the topic at hand as I stare at Tai.

He runs a hand over his short hair and heaves out a breath before uncapping his drink and chugging it down. "Couldn't find any information about Vincent or Mason. I bothered all of my sources in the tribe. I even asked Paco, who my father trusts, but he hasn't been able to come up with any information besides what Valentina told us."

"Fuck," I curse, ripping at a strand of brown hair that has tumbled loose of my pony. "Fuck. Fuck. Fuck."

"You're doing it again," Valentina says with a pointed look at my feet pacing the carpeting.

"I'm not doing anything," I protest as I wear a hole in the white flooring.

"You're spiraling." She gives me a droll look and folds her arms over her chest.

"I am not!" I whirl around to face Tai. "Am I spiraling?"

His eyes widen in his face, and he makes a move as if he's preparing to spin on his heel and run in the opposite direction. Considering the fact that behind him is nothing but a creamy white wall, he's choosing death by head injury over confronting me. Such a sweetheart.

"Tai," I growl, advancing a step. He glances helplessly at the wall once more, as if he's seriously considering the merits of getting a face full of plaster to escape me.

"You're not spiraling?" He words it as a question, his voice going adorably high-pitched in his panic.

"Whipped..." Valentina sings under her breath.

"Look me in the eye and repeat after me," I instruct Tai, and he winces, slowly lifting his golden-flecked gaze to mine. "Blair," I begin.

"Blair," he repeats, still grimacing as if he just ate a sour lemon.

"Is not."

"Isnot." His words rush together.

"Spiraling," I finish.

"Smallorp," he mumbles, turning away.

"Couldn't hear you. Could you repeat yourself a little louder?"

"Spellaring." Another mesh of words.

A rapid knock-knock on the front door interrupts me. All three of us freeze, turning toward it in alarm.

As one, we move.

I step protectively in front of Valentina while Tai stalks to the door, his back muscles rippling in agitation.

"Hide," he hisses out through clenched teeth, his hand closing on the knob.

"No way in hell," I protest, pulling my knife free and holding it at the ready. "But Val can—"

"Stand right here and help my best friend kick ass?" she finishes for me with a quirk of her brow. "Yes. Yes, I can."

Stubborn. So fucking stubborn. It must be in the Davenport genes.

Tai releases a frustrated growl, glancing over his shoulder at me once, before ripping the door open and wrapping his hand around the intruder's throat.

"Tai!" I scream in alarm as soon as I catch sight of the figure waiting on the other end.

Brett's face is covered in bruises and gashes, one of his eyes completely swollen shut. Blood covers the front of his shirt, and when he pulls it away from his abdomen, I see it's slicked with blood.

"Oh my god!" Valentina rushes over, ignoring my attempt to hold her back. Tai releases Brett as quickly as he grabbed him and casts a quick look in both directions of the hallway, ensuring my brother came alone.

Val places a hand on Brett's biceps and stares up at him with wide, terrified eyes. I've never seen that particular expression on her face before.

Brett stares down at her just as intently before he slides his gaze to me.

Shaking myself out of my trance, I run forward and grab his other arm, helping him stumble into the living room. Tai appears behind us, supporting Brett's back as we lead him to the couch.

"What happened?" I demand as Valentina announces she's going to grab her first aid kit.

"Grim," Brett signs. His features harden and tighten as he winces slightly. Valentina returns just at that moment, a strangled sound escaping her at his obvious pain. I want to comment on her strange reaction to him, especially since I'm one hundred percent certain they have never met before, but Brett gestures for me to grab him a piece of paper and pencil. I rush into the kitchen to retrieve the items before handing them back to him. His hand shakes as he writes out the next words. "He attacked the bitten wolves who worked for the Bloody Skulls. Killed all of them. Mason helped me escape." He winces again as Val dabs at his arm, fretting like an overbearing mother.

He hesitates, tapping the pencil repeatedly against the paper, and I can see in his eyes that there's more he wants to write.

"What?" I ask desperately. "What aren't you telling me?"

"It's Vincent," he confesses, his sloppy hand-writing commandeering my complete attention. Valentina stills, and my own heart takes a running leap right off a cliff. "Grim captured him. And he's planning on executing him tonight."

21

VINCENT

DAY 15

I'm not placed in a prison cell in the underbelly of hell itself. The walls aren't constructed out of drab, gray cement, and the scent of piss and blood doesn't permeate the air. Instead, I find myself in a modestly furnished bedroom in the basement of the Bloody Skulls' Clubhouse. The peach-painted walls, cheerful white and pink furniture, and modern appliances give it a deceptively welcoming feel.

But there's nothing even remotely welcoming about this room.

My arms strain from where they're held above my head, connected to a wooden beam that runs the length of the ceiling. My dress shirt has been ripped open, and blood stains the white material, running in rivulets down my abs. Numerous cuts and lines mar my skin, each one deeper than the last. I can't see clearly through the swelling on my face. My eyes are so puffy, everything appears blurry and indistinct. My head lolls against my chest, but I don't have the strength to lift it back up.

Maybe once I get my strength back...

My mind unwillingly conjures up thoughts of Blair and Valentina. I pray that my twin has made it safely to the bitten camp and that Papa Gray was able to get ahold of Blair. I know he doesn't trust us yet, but I also know that he's a good man who will never let a young female fend for herself.

I swallow heavily, a knot of yarn taking up residence in my throat, just as a hand tangles in my dark hair and lifts my head.

"Don't think you can pass out from the pain, runt," a malicious voice sneers. I recognize him as one of the lower ranking fenrir wolves in Grim's pack. Phantom or something. His white-blond hair is cut short, brushed away from his face and showcasing his evil green eyes.

"Wouldn't dream of it," I murmur groggily as Phantom moves to his table of toys. He grabs a large hunting knife and brandishes it in front of my face. I can't help but think of my father just then and his own similar table of weapons. These two men must be cut from the same cloth.

"Such a wise mouth," he taunts, clicking his tongue in irritation.

"Your mom seems to like my mouth," I respond dryly, blinking through puffy eyes and smiling when his face turns beet-red with anger. Before I can say another word, he brings the silver blade to my stomach and begins to meticulously cut through my skin. I grit my teeth through the pain and miraculously manage to remain silent. Only life under my father's malevolent thumb could give me the pain tolerance to endure hours upon hours of torture.

"Are you going to tell me what I want to know?" Phantom demands, and I grin.

"About your mother's pussy? That's perverted."

With a bellow of pure rage, Phantom lunges at me and begins to cut at my skin once more. And cut. And cut. And cut…

"Has he talked yet?" an imperious voice demands as the door to the room opens and a familiar man steps inside. He has pitch-black hair pulled into a low ponytail, and his skin is a few shades darker than my own naturally tan complexion. I recognize him immediately, mainly because his features are eerily similar to another wolf I know and despise.

Tai's brother.

Denali, if I remember correctly.

He's a sick, twisted bastard, one that has been on my radar for years. I probably would've killed him for his crimes against women if I didn't fear his father retaliating against my family.

"Not yet," Phantom answers, turning toward the totemic shifter. Phantom looks like a fucking ghost next to Denali, his body almost translucent and revealing bright blue veins underneath his papery skin.

"Lycan scum," Denali says, moving to stand in front of me with a sneer.

"Totemic asshole," I quip immediately, my voice still hoarse from screaming. "So it's true then. You guys have made an alliance?" I glance between the BS member and then the Native American prince. Their eyes are both shadowed with anger and pure, unbridled hatred.

"Nothing will be more satisfying than ridding the world of mutts like you," Phantom sneers, but before he can say more, Denali holds up a hand, signaling him to remain silent.

"Enough." He turns back toward me. "How many lycan wolves did you send to the bitten camp?"

"Fuck you," I hiss, already preparing myself for the pain. With these wolves, there's *always* pain.

"No." Denali grins at me as he gives my body a slow perusal, moving in a circle around me. He pauses when he's at my back, his hand sliding down to my ass, still mercifully covered by a pair of black dress pants, and giving it a squeeze. All I can do is hang there suspended, helpless and terrified. "But I can fuck *you*."

"I'll fucking kill you," I rage as something akin to fear percolates in my stomach.

The asshole's hand wanders up the muscles in my back, trailing over my skin as he moves to stand in front of me once more. Slowly, keeping his eyes on me, he lowers his hand down my stomach and toward my cock.

"You're helpless, Vincent Davenport," he says with a curl of his lip. "You're my little bitch."

I retreat to a place in my mind that I know will allow me to survive. A place where the rest of the world fades away and all that remains is a numbness that surrounds me like ice. In that place, the world can't touch me. These men can't touch me.

It's the only way I'll survive this.

"I'll kill you," I whisper as his hand lowers even further, stopping inches above my waistband.

"Or…" Denali removes his hand from my stomach and takes a step away. The relief I feel is momentary, shattered into pieces by his next words. "I can have some fun with that sweet, little bitten wolf instead. Blair, is it?"

Rage darkens my vision. I'm in too much pain, too injured, to hold my instinctive reaction in. "Don't you dare touch her!"

"I wonder how her pussy would feel clamped around my cock. Tell me, Vincent, is she as tight as she looks? As wet?"

I struggle against the silver cuffs binding me to the ceiling, my rage manifesting in a wave of pure red.

"Don't you even fucking think about her! I'll—"

"What are you going to do, lycan bitch?" Denali takes a step closer, his lips pulled away from his yellowing teeth. "Kill me?"

"No," a belligerent voice says from directly behind him. "But I might."

A gun fires.

Denali freezes, his eyes widening in surprise and horror. Blood drips from the gunshot wound in his forehead as he falls forward and into me, the momentum causing my body to swing back and forth like a pendulum.

"You fucking trait—" Phantom's words are cut off by another gunshot, and I hear the audible thump of a body hitting the ground.

"Took you long enough," I murmur drowsily, just barely able to keep my eyes open as I pierce Mason with a glare.

He shrugs nonchalantly, tucking his gun into the waistband of his pants as he hurries toward me.

"I told you," he replies with a roll of his eyes. "I needed to get Grim to trust me with his plans before I freed you." He grabs a knife from the table and uses it to cut me free. I fall unceremoniously onto the floor, a grunt of pain escaping me, and Mason watches me struggle with blank eyes. "You look like shit."

"Thanks, man," I deadpan, struggling to my feet. My legs wobble, suddenly too heavy for my body, and I nearly fall over a second time. With a sigh of reluctance, Mason slings one of my arms over his shoulders and leads us toward the doorway.

"Can you shoot?" he demands, nodding toward the gun on Denali.

I give him a dry look, and with another sigh, he rests my beaten body against the wall before grabbing the gun and handing it to me. I check the bullets once before putting all of my weight on Mason and allowing him to drag me toward the door.

"What did you discover?" I ask him as we stagger forward. Mason holds his gun with his free hand, his eyes flickering from side to side, always on alert.

When I was first brought in by Grim's men, I saw Mason. The blond wolf had taunted and tortured me, all under the watchful eye of Grim. This went on for days until Grim eventually trusted Mason enough to leave him alone. It was then that Mason confessed the truth—he was regaining Grim's trust to uncover all that he could about the alliance and takeover. I agreed it was the best option, though I really hated that I had to be tortured because of it. I'll heal, but not quick enough for my liking.

"Grim has lost his damn mind," Mason bites out as we move into the hallway. Two fenrir wolves shout in alarm when they catch sight of us, but they're dead in seconds from our two bullets. Somehow, I know innately which wolf Mason will kill and which one I have to. Don't ask me how. "He attacked and killed most of the bitten wolves."

"Brett?" I query, worry for Blair's brother swarming inside of me like a nest of angry hornets.

"I got him out," Mason supplies grimly. "Sent him to Tai's apartment."

"You trust Tai?" I query, surprised. I don't trust anyone but Blair and my sister. And maybe, quite possibly Mason, though I would shoot myself before I admitted that out loud.

"I do." Mason nods once as three more wolves hurry into the hallway, guns raised.

Three shots later and they're dead, blood pooling around their corpses.

"Why?" I gasp out as pain reverberates through my body. All I want to do is see Blair and my sister, ensure with my own two eyes that they're safe and well. And then I'll sleep. Forever.

And maybe I'll kill a few people too. After all, these assholes destroyed my favorite suit.

Okay, my plan for the day. Find Blair. Sleep. Murder all of the fenrir and totemic wolves. Then sleep again.

"Grim told me that Tai and Blair killed one of Tai's brothers the other day. At least, that's what they suspect. They haven't been able to find the body. Sarai's fucking pissed, but he doesn't dare challenge Tai by himself," Mason explains, and I nod once, the barest dip of my chin.

If the reports are correct, Tai is ten times more

powerful than Sarai, yet Tai has never been able to challenge his father as alpha because Sarai likes to cheat and refuses to fight him one-on-one. And now that his army of sons is dwindling…

"We should head to Tai's apartment then," I decide as we push open the back door of the bar and step out into the bright sunlight. I squint my eyes against the blistering glare of the sun. Fuck, I don't remember it ever being this hot or bright before. Have I really been kept in the dark for so long I'm not used to feeling the sun on my face?

"Are you a vampire or a wolf?" Mason teases as he drags me toward his motorcycle. "Because I half expect you to scream 'I'm melting' any second now in a piss-poor imitation of the Wicked Witch."

"Fuck off," I mumble, eyeing the bike with barely veiled distaste.

The other man slings his leg over the sleek metal machine before glancing over his shoulder at me. "Get on."

"You want me to ride like your little bitch?" I ask, my voice as frosty as a winter wind.

"It's either that or you get left behind." Mason shrugs. "I mean, you could ride in front of me if you're feeling dizzy, but you might have to deal with my boner pressed against your ass."

"Why the fuck would you have a boner right now?" I demand as I sling my leg over the seat behind him.

"Killing people does something to my manly bits," Mason confesses with another shrug. "Good things."

"My god." I search the seat for anything to hang onto, but the only thing I can see is Mason's stomach, and there's no way I'm wrapping myself around him like a koala.

"Hold on," Mason warns as the engine purrs. Behind me, I hear the door of the bar open and shut, followed immediately by raised voices and screams. A gun fires, a bullet just barely missing my head, as Mason revs the engine. "Are you hanging on?" he asks, raising his voice to be heard over the shouts.

"I'm not going to—"

He takes off with a screech of tires, leaving the shooters behind.

And I hang on to his stomach like my damn life depends on it, squealing like the little piggy who went wee, wee, wee all the way home.

22

BLAIR

DAY 16

Executed.

The word tumbles around in my head as my heart hammers against my rib cage. Blood rushes to my ears as I work to moderate my breathing, consciously remembering to breathe in and breathe out.

Executed.

It's an evil word. Insidious, even. It just sounds so...harsh. Even the words "death" and "murder" don't evoke such an innate sense of dread and finality inside of me.

Executed.

I can barely focus on anything besides that one damning word as I change into my pajamas for the night. Valentina fell asleep hours ago, though I can tell her slumber is anything but restful. When she's not crying softly, she's tossing and turning, muttering inarticulate phrases.

Brett still rests on the sofa, though he's in significantly better shape than he had been mere hours ago. Already, the bruising on his face has subsided and his advanced shifter healing has scabbed over most of the scars and gashes.

Sleep evades me, and I find myself pacing Tai's small apartment with no destination in mind. I'm mindful to keep my footsteps silent, as to not wake the others, though I can't stop the occasional enraged snarl from escaping my lips.

After a few minutes, I find myself in front of the one door I haven't yet ventured through. I know it doesn't lead to Tai's bedroom or a bathroom, so just what is the Totemic prince hiding? I bite my lip, debating, before pushing it open and flicking on a light switch.

The room overlooks a grassy expanse of fields, a few trees scattered throughout. The windows take up the entire wall opposite the door, allowing pasty moonlight inside. A stationary bike rests between a treadmill and an elliptical. Opposite all three machines is a blue mat and a stand of weights. A punching bag dangles from the ceiling, and it's that I focus on, my pulse skittering in anticipation.

Yes.

I need to let this rage out, this anger, before it manifests in an explosion of heat I can't control. The need is almost physical, and I know it'll only be tamed by expelling some of this restless energy.

I hurry back to the bedroom I share with Valentina, slip into the connecting bathroom, and change into a pair of spandex leggings and a sports bra. I tug my hair into a high ponytail before wrapping both of my knuckles in tape. When I arrive back in Tai's makeshift gym, I don't hesitate to move directly to the punching bag.

I imagine Sarai's smug, grinning face and release a bellow of rage before I can contain it. The image of Sarai's face transforms into Grim's the day he attacked me, and I punch the bag as hard as I can, ignoring the pain reverberating through my knuckles.

I punch, and punch, and punch. Sweat beads on my forehead, dripping down my face, but I don't let up. I know the punching bag isn't truly Sarai or Grim, but for a brief moment, I can pretend.

I think of Mason and Vincent enduring God knows what, and my punches become weaker. My legs tremble underneath me, feeling like two cooked noodles, and I wrap my arm around the bag when it swings back toward me, holding it steady. I gently place my forehead against the cool material and take a deep breath. My lungs protest, screaming at me for air, and I realize I worked myself too hard.

Stupid! How can you save your mates when you can't even look after yourself? my mental voice chastises, disapproval heady in its tone.

A throat clears behind me, and I spin around in alarm, mentally scolding myself for not having heard anyone come in. I practically sag in relief when I see Tai standing in the doorway with a water bottle in his hand.

Without a word, he hands me the bottle, and I take it in surprise.

"Thank you," I whisper, my throat hoarse.

"Let me look at your hands," he demands in that gruff, domineering way of his. After I unscrew the lid of the water bottle and take a few swallows, Tai grabs it from me and rests it on the seat of the bike. He then grabs my right hand and inspects my red, bloody knuckles.

"They'll heal soon," I tell him as a growl rumbles through his massive frame. With a tenderness belying the tightness in his frame, he runs the pad of his finger over my knuckles, eliciting full body goosebumps.

"Need to be more careful," he grunts out, releasing that hand to take the other.

"I know." I can't quite hide the bitterness in my voice as self-deprecation rears its ugly head. "I can't save anyone if I'm broken."

"You're not fucking broken, Blair," he bites out, releasing my left hand at last and once again handing me the bottle of water. "You're perfect."

Butterflies take flight in my stomach, but I force myself to shove them down. I focus instead on chugging down the rest of the water before tossing it in the recycling can near the door.

"I'm just worried," I confess, swiping at a strand of sweaty hair that has escaped its binding.

"About Mason and Vincent?" There's no reproach in his tone, yet I find myself unable to meet his eyes.

"Yes."

"You care about them." Once again, I get no sense that he's judging me. It's almost as if he accepted my answer before I've even said it. And while he has apparently accepted it, I can tell that it still pains him.

"Tai…"

My words taper off when my enhanced hearing becomes aware of a door opening and closing. I tense automatically, my stomach muscles tightening, as Tai bares his teeth and spins around.

"That was the front door, wasn't it?" I whisper as I hear the sound of someone moving. Or is it multiple someones?

Fuck.

"Stay here," Tai barks, pulling the gym door open and stalking in the direction of the intruder.

I just barely hold in the urge to roll my eyes.

Silly, overprotective alpha male. As if I'll ever play damsel in distress so he can save the day. He may be a knight on a gallant steed, but I'm right there with him, breaking into castles, rescuing princesses—or princes, as the case may be—and slaying ferocious dragons.

I move on silent feet out of the gym, mentally cursing myself for not grabbing a weapon for protection when I left my bedroom. Fortunately for me—and unfortunately for whomever broke into Tai's apartment—I can use my body as a weapon. If I need to shift into a wolf and tear someone's throat out, then so be it.

"Blair." Tai's voice is rife with surprise but no alarm, and I quicken my pace, skirting the corner to enter the living room.

My eyes first land on Brett, standing beside Tai despite his injuries and prepared to defend us, before they travel over his shoulder to the two men present.

"Holy shit," I breathe, my eyes widening as I catch sight of Mason and Vincent.

The first emotion I feel is relief—an over-whelming sense of it that washes over me in a torrent, almost painful in its intensity. That relief quickly transitions into horror, followed very closely by white-hot anger.

Mason appears to be relatively unscathed, his cocky grin firmly in place as he supports Vincent.

And Vincent...

His face is swollen, covered in so many bruises I can barely see his pupils. His shirt is ripped open, revealing a myriad of bloody gashes as if someone had cut at his stomach with a knife. Repeatedly. The skin is bright red and bleeding, leading me to believe the damage had been done by a silver knife. It'll heal in time, but at a much slower pace than a normal weapon would've allowed.

"Tell me they're dead," I whisper, not moving. My legs wouldn't be able to move even if I could remember how to walk. I'm frozen to the ground. "Tell me that the people who did this to you are dead."

"Deader than dead, baby girl," Mason says, flashing me his customary smirk. "I made sure of that." With the hand not supporting Vincent, he makes a finger gun and shoots it at my head. "There is a reason they call me Bullseye, after all, and it's not because my cock never misses a hole."

"For the love of…" Vincent murmurs, drawing my attention to his mottled face.

"You love my humor. Admit it," Mason says arrogantly. "You wouldn't be hugging me so tightly earlier if you didn't."

"Hugging…?" I cock an eyebrow as Vincent groans.

"I had no choice but to be your little bitch," he mumbles.

"Little bitch?"

"It's a long story," Mason says with a dismissive wave of his hand. He then leans forward slightly to add conspiratorially, "It involves me getting a boner and Vincent wanting to rub against it."

"I'm going to shoot you in the head," Vincent deadpans, and Mason scoffs.

"You can't even stand upright without me holding your fat ass up," he taunts. For emphasis, he releases Vincent, and I watch in horror as the lycan wolf immediately begins to fall. Mason catches him just before he can hit the ground and kisses the tip of his nose. "You *loooove* me."

"Fuck off."

"So…" Mason glances in my direction, where I'm still unable to move a single step. "How about we grab some bandages and tell you what happened?"

I wake Valentina up while Tai grabs some medical supplies. Afterward, we all reconvene in the living room as Mason and Vincent tell us what transpired after the Davenport mansion was attacked.

While they talk, I fret over Vincent, applying cream to his numerous cuts before wrapping them in bandages. Valentina sits on his other side, one hand clasped in his for comfort.

She levels vitriol-filled eyes at Mason. "I can't believe you allowed him to be tortured," she hisses.

"Val…" Vincent begins placatingly, but she simply raises her hand to stop whatever protest he's going to make.

"No, Vincent. I'm not allowing you to defend him." She sniffs and sits up even straighter. On her other side, Brett looks as if he wants to comfort her, his eyes almost pained, before balling his hands into fists and scooting farther away.

Interesting.

"You're right," Mason says at last, surprising even me. "I never should've allowed it to go so far, but I had to get Grim to trust me. I needed to know his plans."

"Plans that he probably changed as soon as you betrayed him," Tai points out.

"Maybe." The blond biker shrugs once. "But there's one thing we know with absolute certainty."

"Which is?" Valentina cocks an eyebrow.

"A time and location." He rubs his hands back and forth on his jeans as he leans forward. "In just ten days, Sarai and Grim will be meeting with a representative from the Holman pack," he begins, referencing a cruel and sadistic group of wolf shifters known for their brutality against outsiders.

"Fuck." Tai runs a hand down his cheek and to his chin, resting it on the slightest stubble that has begun to grow there. "If they form an alliance…"

"I know," Mason interjects gravely. "We can maybe survive an attack from two packs. But three, especially three as ruthless as them? We'll be slaughtered."

"Ten days, correct?" I tap my fingers against my leggings rapidly as my heart judders in my chest. "We have ten days to get an army together and attack."

"I doubt they'll expect us to attack first," Tai reasons, though he doesn't sound convinced. "Especially with the Holman pack there."

"Or it could be a trap," Valentina points out. Her voice trembles ever so slightly, and I watch with a mixture of confusion and amusement as Brett brushes his pinkie finger against hers in silent comfort.

"We'll have to take that chance," I say, debating my next words. "We'll make sure everyone who fights for us understands the risks and is willing."

"Agreed," Tai, Vincent, and Mason all say in unison. They immediately glare at one another, as if annoyed they spoke at the same time.

"Fuck, I don't like this," Tai bites out, once again

running a hand over his scalp. I notice it's something he does frequently when he's agitated or anxious.

"None of us do," Valentina says. "But we don't have a choice." She glances from face to face, her eyes resting on Brett a second longer than the others. Both of them turn away from each other at once. "Let's head to bed tonight and talk about battle plans in the morning."

"Is this place secure?" Mason demands, and Tai nods once, his jaw clenching.

"As secure as any. My father and brothers don't know it even exists, so it's the best option we have." He hesitates, dipping his gaze down to Vincent beside me. "Blair, Vincent," he clears his throat, pain tightening his features, "why don't you guys take my bed?" He nods toward the second couch in the living room. "I'll sleep out here with Brett. Be the first line of defense."

"But—" I open my mouth to protest, but Mason is already on his feet, picking me up and all but tossing me over his shoulder.

"Sounds like a plan. I'm assuming you meant me as well?" He doesn't wait for Tai to respond as he begins to move down the hallway, toward where the bedrooms are.

"Mason," I growl, though my relief at seeing him

alive and well isn't allowing me to actually be mad at him. "Put me down."

"No can do, baby girl. I've been away from you for way too long, and now I need to get all of my cuddle time in."

"Mason…"

He opens doors at random until he enters the master suite, depositing me directly in the middle of the bed before collapsing onto the mattress beside me.

Vincent travels much slower than the blond fenrir wolf, his swollen, bruised eyes half-mast with fatigue. He moves to perch himself gingerly on the side of the bed. He already removed the remnants of his dress shirt when I was cleaning out his cuts, and I can tell he's desperate to remove the rest of his bloody clothes. He probably needs to shower too, but he can do that after a night of sleep.

"Here." I knee-walk to the end of the bed, jump down, and move to stand directly in front of Vincent. Slowly—careful not to exacerbate his injuries—I unbuckle his pants and shimmy them down his thighs. He painfully moves to his feet as well to help me get the material down to his ankles. As soon as he's able, he sits back down on the bed with a pained groan.

He's in only a pair of black boxer briefs that leave very little to the imagination. I can see his cock straining against the material, desperate for me, but now isn't the time for sex.

I want to take care of him.

I unlace first one dress shoe and then the other, setting them next to his now folded pants. I then slowly remove both his socks as well.

Once he's completely undressed sans his boxer briefs—the entire exchange lasting only a few minutes but taking place in complete silence—I grab his forearm and guide him onto his back.

The second his head hits the pillow, he rolls onto his side, still gripping my arm. I crawl over his muscular body and nestle myself between the two men as Mason immediately places a hand on my hip.

I feel his lips feather over my shoulder. "Love you, baby girl," he whispers, his voice drowsy with sleep.

"I love you, Blair Windsor," Vincent groggily states.

Before I can respond to either man, I hear their soft snores fill the room, surrounding me in a blanket of love and safety.

Fuck, what will I do if I lose them?

I run the pad of my finger down Vincent's cheek,

allowing my eyes to travel over his harsh, masculine features, now serene in sleep. Mason's chest expands against my back as he inhales, and I lose myself in the rhythmic sound.

They're alive. They're safe.

And as long as I have air in my lungs, they'll remain so.

"They really love you," a masculine voice whispers from the doorway. I lift my head, my eyes landing immediately on Tai's massive silhouette. Our eyes meet, and a bolt of heat slashes through me, setting me aflame. He takes a step closer, and the dim light from the bedside lamp illuminates his chiseled face. "I should go."

He doesn't move.

"You should stay," I whisper.

I can't put it into words, but I know in my heart that I want all three of them with me right now. I *need* them with me.

"I…I can't." He shakes his head and takes a step backward.

Away from me.

Away from us.

"Tai." I don't want to beg—I've never begged for anything or anyone before—but I will for him. Can't he feel this connection between us? Can't he sense how much I need him?

"I just..." His eyes drop to first Mason on one side of me and then Vincent on the other. Those brown orbs seem to focus on where each of them touches me, pulling me closer to them unconsciously in their sleep.

"It's okay," I say softly, trying to ignore the pain that unfurls in my chest. When he hesitates, seeming uncertain, I force a gentle smile. "Tai, it's okay."

Something settles in his eyes then, something I would almost describe as resolve.

Without a word, he storms out of the room, allowing the door to swing shut behind him. My heart cracks into thousands of pieces, and those pieces splinter into even smaller ones until I fear it'll never be whole again. That *I'll* never be whole again. There will always be at least one or two pieces missing.

I've just settled back in Vincent's and Mason's arms, trying to ignore the pain reverberating through my entire body, when the door reopens and shuts a second time.

I watch through half-open eyes as Tai places his pillow and blanket on the floor directly at the foot of the bed. His eyes meet mine, and in them, I can see an ocean of pain and yearning. Want and desire. Lust. He tears his gaze away, disappearing on the floor.

When I wake up the next morning, I'm alone.

But I know in my heart that what happened last night wasn't a dream. All three spent the night in Tai's room, and it makes me think…

It makes me think that there's still hope for us.

23

TAI

DAY 25

With war brewing, tensions are high.

I don't see Blair often since she travels back and forth between the bitten camp and my apartment, Vincent or Mason always with her. Never me.

Never me.

I throw myself into my work, calling Paco repeatedly to get updates on my father and remaining brothers. The last I heard, Sarai believed we had run, leaving the bitten wolves to fend for themselves. His twisted mind never would've even comprehended an alliance with Vincent Davenport and Mason.

Tomorrow, we're going to have to fight.

My stomach curdles in anticipation and dread as I pore over the map we taped to my dining room table. In the last nine days, my apartment has turned into a war room, with weapons stockpiled in the gym and maps littering every available surface. All together, we have four hundred and thirty-seven troops at our disposal. Four hundred and thirty-seven men and women with families. Kids. Siblings. Parents.

And now, their lives are in our hands.

The unease grows and grows inside of me, sprouting roots and branches that caress every available surface in my stomach. There's so much we're leaving up to chance, and I hate that more than I care to admit. People's lives are at risk, and it's my job to do everything within my power to minimize the damage done. To make sure we lose no wolves.

I can feel my throat close up as emotions bombard me, a deep-rooted fear that one of those people I'm going to lose will be my mate.

Blair.

Even her name in my head is able to calm the turbulent storm rumbling through me. A sense of peace and security cascades over me.

She's safe. Here. In the bedroom she shares with Valentina.

As the relief dissipates, I'm left with an emotion that oddly resembles guilt.

I'd be the first to admit that things have been tense between us since that night a few days ago, when she cuddled between Vincent and Mason in my bed. My entire world shifted on its axis at the sight of her with them. My wolf knew she was his fated mate—*our* fated mate—but apparently, the message hasn't been made clear to her. A part of me wanted to pull her out from between their bodies and handcuff her to me, refusing to allow her to ever set eyes upon another man again.

But the rest of me…

The rest of me just wanted her to be happy. And if that happiness came from Vincent and Mason, who was I to stop her? She was my mate, and that meant her happiness eclipsed my own. I'll willingly remain in the shadows, a silent sentry and observer, just to see that smile on her face.

Fuck, I love her.

I love her so damn much, I can barely breathe. It's like my world revolves around the sun, and that sun has the face and body of Blair Windsor.

There's no greater pain than loving someone who will never love you back.

Self-pity threatens to drown me, but I shove the pesky emotion away and focus on what's important. And right now, that's planning our attack against Grim and Sarai. I truly believe that this entire war will be over before it has even begun if we can kill those two men. Mason and I can step into our positions of power, reforming the packs in a way that will benefit us all. It's true that when one head is cut off, two more grow in its place, but this time around, those heads belong to two men who want nothing more than peace.

You should've killed Sarai when you had the chance, Tai. This entire battle could've been avoided.

I ignore the strident voice in my mind, absently scratching at the stubble lining my face.

There's a lot of things I wish I would've done differently, but all I can do now is stand on the front line, ready to fight and defend my family, my people, and my mate.

"Tai?" Her soft voice warms my skin like a breeze in mid-July. I squeeze my eyelids shut, gripping the edge of the table until my knuckles scream in protest, before reopening them and piercing Blair with a long look.

She stands on the other side of the table, her gorgeous brown and gold hair tied back into a French braid. She's dressed in fighting leathers that mold to her curvy body, emphasizing her perfect figure. My mouth waters at the sight of her before I come to the mind-numbing conclusion that she's not mine. She'll never be mine.

I lower my gaze to the map before she can see the intense yearning in my eyes.

"Have you talked to Papa Gray?" I ask gruffly, trying to focus on anything besides how much I want to peel those leathers away from her skin and kiss down her stomach. My cock is uncomfortably hard against my jeans as I wrestle with my baser impulses.

Mate, my wolf rumbles inside of my head, as if I need the reminder.

Shut up, I hiss vehemently. The surly bastard simply huffs, swishing his tail back and forth impatiently, before curling into a ball in the far corner of my mind, his ears alert despite his passive position.

"I did." She nods once. "He's leaving about twenty men behind to guard the camp alongside twenty of Vincent's. The rest are on their way to the location now."

We decided a few days ago that most of our

troops will arrive early to the stretch of forest where Sarai and Grim were supposed to meet the other pack. They'll hide a few miles away in order to not alert the others to their location. Hopefully, this will give us an advantage. We still have no way of knowing how many men Sarai and Grim will choose to bring with them.

"Good. That's good," I say, still keeping my attention fixed on the map as if I found something on it particularly interesting. "Where are the others?"

"Mason and Brett are meeting with some of their trusted contacts from within the Bloody Skulls, and Valentina and Vincent are picking up their mother from the airport." She pauses, a muscle in her jaw twitching almost imperceptibly. "Tai..." she begins helplessly, and I hear the soft patter of her footsteps as she rounds the table. I freeze, my heart racing, as her soft, delicate hand rests on my shoulder. Heat migrates from where she touches me, unfurling in my stomach like fireworks. "Do we need to talk about this?"

"Talk?" It takes every ounce of willpower to shrug her off of me and take a few steps away. Once I'm no longer breathing in her sweet, floral perfume, I feel calmer. My brain is finally able to think clearly.

"Tai, don't do this," she pleads, once again taking

a step closer. She stops suddenly, and out of my periphery, I watch her entire face twist and distort, pain flashing in her eyes. She takes an automatic step away, her gaze lowering. I know she's only respecting my wishes, granting me space, but fuck, I want her to come near me. I want her to place her hand on my shoulder again, because I can't help but feel as if that's the only connection I'll have with her.

A touch on the motherfucking shoulder. How pathetic is that?

"Just…just talk to me when you're ready. Please." She swallows heavily. "I don't want things to be like this between us before we go…" She trails off, but I know exactly what she's about to say.

Before we go to war.

Her words slash at something inside me, something already hurting and bleeding in my chest. Something that has been hurting and bleeding for a while now, if I'm being completely honest. Since I first discovered I wasn't the only man Blair has strong feelings for.

She turns on her heel, and I just know she's going to walk away from me. And this time, I fear she won't come back.

"Wait." I raise my hand as if to grab her and pull her toward me but stop myself at the last second. All

I can hear is the rapid *thump-thump-thump* of my heart in my chest. It stutters when she turns to stare at me, like a train careening off its track.

"Tai—"

"I can't stop thinking about you," I interrupt, feeling uncharacteristically small and vulnerable. The last time I felt like this, I was eight, maybe nine, and witnessed my father stab my mother in a fit of rage. I wanted to go to her, protect her, but I felt helpless. What the fuck is Blair Windsor doing to me? "I try to stop, but I just…I just *can't*. You're in my head, Blair, and I can't get you out of it."

"Tai—" she begins again, but I once again cut her off.

"I know Vincent and Mason are your mates." My words are a rush of air, practically meshing together. I watch Blair's face drain of all color as she inhales sharply. "I can see the way they look at you and the way you look at them. I told you…I'm not stupid. But that doesn't change the fact that I think about you all of the goddamn time. It doesn't change the fact that I think you might be my mate as well."

I can barely breathe after I say the final sentence, staring at her with my damn heart in my eyes. All of my hopes and dreams for the future…they all hinge on her response. Does she feel this mating bond between us too? Does she know she's my mate? Does she even believe me?

I never thought I would share my mate with other men, especially men I used to despise, and to be completely honest, I still don't want to. At all.

But I'll do just about anything to have Blair. To love her. To cherish her. To take on the world and everyone in it with her by my side.

When Blair remains silent, her eyes wide in her beautiful, heart-shaped face, a sliver of self-consciousness and pain embeds itself in my heart like a splinter I can't remove. I duck my head back down, absently scratching at my buzzed head, and begin the painstaking task of marking the route we need to take tomorrow.

"I'm gonna go to my room," I grunt out, a tiny piece of myself dying with her silence.

Why the fuck did you say that to her, Tai? I chastise myself. *You scared her away!*

Mate, my wolf growls, once again sounding fed up with me.

Maybe not, I respond, my heart leaping up my throat and becoming trapped there. Maybe I was wrong. Maybe I pushed her too fast. Maybe she doesn't care about me the way she cares for the—

Blair's soft hand touches my cheek, tilting my

face down toward hers. And then, before I can catch my breath, her lips are on mine.

For a moment, I simply stand there, stunned, before lust consumes me completely, and with a growl, I begin to kiss her back. It's a battle, our tongues tangling together as my hands roam over her perfect body. I cup her ass, holding her to me and grinding my erection against her, as she digs her nails into my shoulders

I break away from her lips to smile down at her, feeling like a predator seconds from devouring his prey. "Little wolf," I purr, my heart thrashing at the sight of her swollen lips, "do you really think you're in control here?"

She bares her teeth at me, the scent of her arousal permeating the air. "I know I am, big wolf." She drops her gaze to my erection, and a bark of laughter escapes me.

"Let me show you just how big I am." I desperately claim her lips once more, devouring her tiny moans and mewls of excitement. Her hands roam across my body, almost as if she wants to memorize the feel of my shoulders and abs. Licks of fire dance across my skin as I curl my arms around her, practically dipping her at the waist to deepen the kiss.

"Tai..." she moans, my name a prayer on her sultry lips.

"Wait." I pull away from her and take a single step back. Her hooded eyes drop to my cock, and I watch as she licks her lips. "What about Vincent and Mason?" I hate even saying their names when I'm seconds from sticking my cock in my girl, but I'm man enough to step back if that's what she needs.

"They know," she whispers, sashaying forward. My eyes drop to the way her hips sway enticingly, and I feel my cock give an excited jump.

"They know?"

She moves onto her tiptoes and wraps her arms around my neck, her fingers playing with the dark hairs there.

"Are you going to kiss me?" she asks, planting a chaste kiss to the corner of my lips. She continues trailing kisses across the skin of my cheek before her lips touch my earlobe. "Or am I going to have to kiss you?" she breathes.

My wolf howls with excitement at the thinly veiled challenge as I grab her legs, forcing them to lock around my waist, and reclaim her lips. She tastes like the forest—wild and free and completely untamed—but her touch is like a fire running rampant through the trees. Everywhere she touches, I burn.

I'm too drunk on her to get us to the bedroom, so when I collapse on the couch, still kissing her, she doesn't stop me.

With a fierce snarl, she attempts to switch our positions so she's on top, the momentum of her body pushing us off the couch and onto the carpeting. My body lands on top of hers, but I make sure not to apply any pressure as I bend over her.

"Submit," I growl, wrapping both of her wrists in one hand while my other palm caresses her toned stomach.

"Make me!" she hisses, bucking against me. My eyes roll into the back of my head when she inadvertently presses against my hard cock with each thrust of her hips. Or perhaps she knows exactly what she's doing to me, the little temptress.

As my mind hazes over, consumed by lust and wanton need for this woman, she rolls us over so she's on top, her shirt askew and revealing the swell of her breast. I glare at my intoxicating mate as she places both her hands on my chest, pushing me into the ground.

"Submit," she whispers as she begins to kiss down my chest, her lips feather-soft over the gray T-shirt

I'm wearing. I want her lips on my bare skin more than anything.

With a growl, I allow one of my fingers to lengthen into a claw and use it to cut down the middle of my shirt. Her eyes turn hooded, burning with a banked flame, as the material slides apart, revealing my abs.

"Fuck..." she curses as she runs her nails down my chest and stomach, stopping just above the waistband of my jeans. While she's distracted by the V of my hips, I roll us over a second time so I'm on top of her, shrugging off the rest of my shredded shirt.

"Is this where you're going to tell me that you're in charge?" she mocks, her chest heaving as a blush rises up her neck and to her cheeks. "That you're the alpha?"

"I *am* the alpha." I grin wickedly at her as I allow my gaze to rake over her prone body, ready and waiting for me. How many times have I imagined this exact moment? Probably one thousand. It's been the only thing that has kept me sane since I saw her over seventy days ago at the bitten camp.

My imagination didn't do her justice.

"Prove it," she says on a breathy exhale, her pupils dilated. She can pretend to fight me all she wants, but I know she wants this—needs this—just as much as I do. Blair and I are fire and gasoline. Together, we're explosive in the best fucking way possible. All of these days of pent-up feelings and lust, all of these emotions we both struggle to articulate, they've finally reached their boiling point.

Quickly, I place one large palm between her back and the carpeting and then flip her onto her stomach. She releases a startled noise as this new position puts her ass up in the air.

"Tai…" she warns, but there's a breathy quality to her voice that I've never heard before. It makes my cock jerk to attention.

"Yes, little wolf?" I tease as I use my nails to cut through the material of her leathers. She's wearing only a tiny pair of black panties that leaves very little to the imagination. My fingers toy with the material as she moans low in her throat. "Do you know how much I want you? Need you? Did you know how badly I wanted you when I thought I couldn't have you?" I demand as I smooth one of my palms over her ass cheek.

"I…I didn't," she confesses, breathless.

"I don't know if I believe that." I tug at her panties, smiling in satisfaction when they rip for me. From this angle, I can see only a little bit of her pussy, but I can tell that she's wet and ready for me. "I think you liked driving me crazy. Teasing me."

"Fuck you," she hisses, but her words lack any heat.

"Maybe." My cock tightens as I once again smooth my hand over her perfect ass. "Or maybe not. I guess we'll have to see, won't we?" Before she can say a single word in response, I slap down on her ass. Hard. A surprised gasp escapes her as I stare intently at the perfect, red handprint on her right cheek.

"Tai!" she squeals as I soothe away the sting.

"Yes, little wolf?" I duck my head to kiss the spot I just spanked, and her entire body shudders, trembling with exhilaration. "Tell me you want me. Tell me I'm not just imagining this."

"I want this," she all but cries out. "I want this so, so much. I want *you*."

"Good girl," I rumble, spanking her ass again. She screams, the noise quickly transitioning to a moan of pleasure when I stick a single finger inside her pussy and begin to circle her clit. "I'm going to take my time with your sweet body, do you understand me?" When she doesn't answer, I remove my hand from her cunt and slap her ass a third time. "Do you understand me?"

"Yes," she whimpers.

"Good." I remove my hands from her body and move to my feet. She scrambles upright as well, that spark of defiance I noted earlier still in her bright blue gaze. Good. This game is always more fun with a partner that fights back.

"What the fuck are you doing, Tai?" she growls out, naked from the waist down.

I move casually to the couch and sit on it, sprawling my arms out on either side with an indolent grin.

"I want you to strip for me," I say, and she raises her eyebrows.

"What?" She crosses her arms over her chest, unintentionally—or perhaps completely intentionally—pushing up her breasts. "You're not in charge here, Tai. I do what I want to do, when I want to do it."

I quirk an eyebrow at her, amused. And so fucking in love with her, I fear I might start writing motherfucking sonnets. "So you don't want to get naked for me?"

"Oh, I definitely do," she purrs, dropping to her knees before me. Her hands travel up my legs and to my thighs until they're mere inches from my throbbing cock. "But there's something I want to do even more."

And who am I to say no? When a gorgeous girl you're in love with is on her knees in front of you, her large blue eyes peering into your very soul, you do whatever the fuck she asks of you.

A rumble reverberates through my chest as she removes my belt and tosses it aside. I lift my hips to help her get my pants and boxers down, my cock springing free immediately. I know I'm massive compared to most men. How can I not be, when my entire body is made up of pure muscle?

But instead of looking scared, Blair's eyes glimmer with excitement and lust. She wets her lips again—the move driving me goddamn crazy—before bringing her lips to the head of my cock.

"Oh...fuck!" I curse, my balls clenching. I'm honestly afraid I'm going to blow my load in mere seconds if she keeps this up. She licks around the head of my cock like it's her own personal lollipop before hollowing her cheeks and taking it completely in her mouth. I'm big—almost too big for her—so she uses a hand to wrap around the part of my dick her mouth can't quite reach. "You look so sexy sucking my cock. So goddamn sexy."

Her mouth suctions around my throbbing member as her hand leaves my base to fondle my balls. I hiss out a breath through clenched teeth, my hips jerking.

"Fuck, baby," I growl, wanting to wrap her gorgeous hair around my fist and guide her movements. I just know my girl will become furious if I do that though, which only amplifies my desire to do so.

I reach for her braid cascading over her shoulder and remove the hair tie, running my fingers through the silky strands so it flows free and curly around her face. She's so fucking beautiful, so perfect, that I find myself once again asking the universe how I got so lucky to have her as my mate.

Claim, my wolf demands inside my head, and immediately, I'm bombarded with an image of my teeth sinking into the skin of her throat. Marking her.

"Come here, baby." I tug at her hair until my cock slides free of her swollen lips, brushing against her cheek. She stares at me through heavily-lidded eyes, almost as if she's as drunk on me as I am on her.

"Can't hold your load, big guy?" she teases, biting down on that plush lower lip of hers. Fuck.

I lean forward, overcome by an irresistible urge,

and replace her teeth with my own, tugging until she gasps out in pain.

"I can hold my goddamn load," I growl against her mouth as I move my hands to her leather shirt. Grinning wickedly, I rip at the fabric, allowing her perfect tits to spring free. A low groan catches in my throat when I realize she's been walking around the apartment without a goddamn bra all day. "Fuck, little wolf. *Fuck*."

"I figured since my brother and Valentina were going to be gone, there was no reason to cover the girls," she says cockily, pushing out her breasts. And she has every damn right to be cocky. Her tits… They're fucking magnificent. Not even my imagination is able to conjure up such a perfect pair. Her dusky red nipples are pointed, ready for my mouth. They're just begging to be sucked and kissed.

I duck my head, swirling my tongue around her right nipple as she moans and grips my head, holding me to her. I allow the tiny nub to slide through my teeth before giving the same attention to the left breast. I kiss her dark areola before licking a sensuous pathway around her nipple. When she moans again, I flick my eyes upward toward her face, relishing in the lust splayed across her gorgeous features, before taking her breast in my mouth and sucking.

"Tai," she breathes, gripping my cheeks and forcing my face away from her tit. "I want to ride you."

"Sweetheart…" I nip at her neck, eliciting a sharp gasp from her lips. "I'm not a bottom."

Her fingernails dig into my shoulders as she moves to straddle my lap, my cock pressing against her slick entrance but not quite entering.

"Want to bet?" she whispers as she begins to slide down. Before my cock can enter her, though, I growl sharply and throw her onto the ground. She gasps, surprise coloring her features, as I land on top of her and thrust inside her with one fatal thrust of my hips. "Tai!" she screams as I begin to ram into her like a man possessed.

She does this to me.

Destroys me.

Obliterates me.

And somehow, tapes me back together.

Her fingers claw at my shoulders, tiny gasps of pleasure escaping her. Right then and there, we're not Tai and Blair. We're not mates or humans or even wolf shifters. We're just two vessels of pleasure, our bodies moving in tandem. It's a fight, a dance, a battle, a war more dangerous than any we're going to face.

She grips my shoulders, using her enhanced strength to push me onto my back, my cock never leaving her pussy. Now on top, she begins to ride me, her breasts bouncing in a way that has me gasping. I rest my hands on her hips, helping her slide on and off my cock, before pushing her backward. The momentum forces my cock out of her for only a second before I grab both her legs, place them over my shoulder, and then thrust back inside of her. This new position has my cock brushing against the sensitive bundle of nerves with every gyrate of my hips.

She screams, her eyes rolling into the back of her head, as she comes. Her nails dig into the skin of my ass, making my own orgasm sharpen and heighten. It's a foray of lightning and thunder, ecstasy and elation, as my balls tighten and my hips judder. I come as hard as water breaking free of a dam.

"Fuck!" I roar, moving my lips to Blair's neck.

And then, I bite down.

Hard.

Her essence flows through me—everything spicy and sugary that is Blair Windsor—and I drown in the now familiar sensation that is her.

Us.

Mates.

I can feel my cock swell inside of her, becoming trapped by her pussy walls. I continue to pepper kisses against her sweaty skin as a silver bond materializes between us, bright and vibrant and so full of life. It's the one real thing I have, and I'm determined more than ever to hold on to it with all of my might and never let it go.

"Oh my god," Blair breathes as her pussy squeezes around my engorged cock.

I slowly drop her legs from my shoulders, allowing them to nestle comfortably on either side of my massive frame, before leaning down to plant another tender kiss to her lips. Holding myself on my elbows, I peer down at her beautiful, angelic face. With her hair cascading around her head, her eyes bright and half-mast with lust, and her lips swollen from our kisses, she's the most beautiful thing I've ever seen. Painters everywhere would rush at the chance to have Blair Windsor as their muse.

And she's mine.

"You're really my mate," I whisper, wanting desperately to stroke the silver bond between us. Right now, it's new and tenuous, but I just know it's going to grow and strengthen over time.

This incredible, fantastic, badass woman is my mate.

My mate.

My mate.

Exhilaration courses through me, and I can't stop the giddy smile from unfurling on my lips.

"And you're really mine," she whispers breathily, her eyes darting to my lips. Her pussy clamps around my cock again, and a groan of pain leaves me. I begin to move my hips once more, desperate to alleviate some of the tension. My balls are so heavy, I just know I'll be able to come a second time. And a third time. And a fourth time.

Fuck, this girl is making me insatiable.

"How long does this last?" I ask as I kiss a pathway down her jaw and to the hollow of her throat.

"With Vincent, it lasted about a half hour. Same with Mason," she gasps out as I suckle on her smooth skin.

At one point, hearing their names and knowing that they've been inside of her would've made me crazy with jealousy. And in a sense, I'm still jealous. I don't know if I'll ever be willing to engage in a fucking foursome with the two of them, but I'm happy she has them in her life. She's a force of nature, a firecracker, and if there's anyone who deserves all of the love and happiness in the world, it's Blair. And while I might not want to participate in an orgy with those two assholes, the thought of watching them with her has my cock swelling even further inside of her tight channel.

Where has this peace and contentment come from?

Is it because I've finally claimed Blair as my own? Is it because I know in my heart and soul that she'll never choose between us? That she cares about us all equally?

The knowledge that she belongs to me—just as much as she belongs to Vincent and Mason—fills me with a sense of serenity that has been missing the last few days.

Mate, my wolf rumbles.

Mate.

I don't know how long we remain in each other's embrace, but it's enough for us to have a repeat performance. And this time, I allow Blair to top me.

I can't say I mind it too much.

By the time my cock finally returns to normal and I reluctantly slide it out of her, her eyes are shut, a wistful smile pulling up her lips.

"What are you thinking about?" I ask, planting a

kiss on her bare shoulder. She twists in my arms to smile at me.

"How happy I am," she confesses. "Tai, I—"

Her phone takes that moment to ring, its shrill noise causing both of us to jump and disrupting the tranquil bubble we have found ourselves in. My brows furrow as Blair crawls toward where she left it on the couch.

We instructed everybody to only call if there's an emergency in order to keep the line open. So if someone's calling…

I immediately move to grab my jeans as Blair puts the phone to her ear.

"Hello?" A crease appears between her brows as she listens to whomever is on the other end of the line. She's silent for a moment, her lips pursed, before her eyes widen in horror and she gasps. "Holy shit!"

"What?" I demand, zipping up my jeans.

Blair hangs up the phone and desperately searches the ground for usable clothes. Considering the fact that they've all been shredded or ripped, she won't find any here.

"That was Vincent," she says, her voice trembling. "Sarai and Grim have just attacked."

"What the fuck happened?" I demand. We've

assumed they wouldn't be dumb enough to attack without backup from the Holman pack. Our entire plan hinged on being able to attack them before they attacked us.

"The Davenport mansion has been destroyed," Blair says in an oddly detached voice. I recognize what she's doing—desensitizing herself from the situation in order to remain level-headed. If she gives in to her emotions, to the feelings no doubt running rampant through her, she risks making a mistake.

And today, one mistake might be fatal.

"So it has started," I say, already moving to my bedroom to get dressed and grab weapons.

"Apparently it has," she responds softly.

Today, everything will end.

And all I can do is pray that we've chosen the winning side.

Because if we lose? Well…

My eyes flicker to Blair as she disappears inside of her bedroom.

We can't fucking lose.

24

BLAIR

DAY 25

We arrive at the warehouse Vincent has paid—in cash—for us to use. It's an unassuming building, the windows caked in grime, but it's perfect to hide large quantities of people and weapons. It's located a few miles off the highway, in a relatively abandoned stretch of warehouses, and since it's not a location Vincent has ever been to before, Grim and Sarai will have no reason to suspect we're staying here.

Every spare inch of space is teeming with wolf shifters. Most are bitten wolves and lycans, like Davenport and Valentina, but there are even a few totemic shifters and fenrirs. I recognize Paco, one of

Tai's closest friends, deep in conversation with Papa Gray, Johnson, and Mason. Vincent and Valentina stand a little bit away, talking to their own wolf shifters and instructing them on where to go and what to do.

Now that our plan has been shot to hell, all of the troops have been instructed to meet here and discuss what to do next. We're not going to be able to wait until tomorrow anymore, not with Grim and Sarai on the move.

But fuck. I hate this. I hate this so damn much. Before, we had a plan, but now, we're running in blind and just praying we survive the onslaught of bullets.

Tai and I sidle up to the main group just as Johnson snaps out, "I vote we keep to the same plan. Ambush them during their meeting with the Holeman pack tomorrow night."

"And risk making enemies out of them as well?" Mason shakes his head slowly. "No. Not now. Not after they attacked us first. Not when they're *still* attacking us. How many lives will we lose between now and then? How many more innocent people will die if we choose to wait?"

"Do we know where they're going next?" I question, moving to stand directly beside Mason. He immediately places an arm around my shoulders and gives my temple a soft kiss. Papa Gray's eyes slide to us in surprise before shifting surreptitiously in Tai's direction. I shake my head subtly, promising to explain this entire situation at a later time, and he nods once. And though I doubt he understands the full truth—that I'm mates with all three men—he knows enough to grin knowingly before immediately smoothing out his expression, focusing on the conversation at hand.

"One of my men was able to place a tracker on their car," Vincent announces as he joins our makeshift huddle. "He'll have a location in just a second."

"So we need to attack now," Tai reiterates, scrubbing a hand over his scalp. He then turns toward Vincent completely, his eyes flashing with sympathy. "I'm sorry, man. About your house."

Vincent's jaw clenches. "They fucking bombed it. Killed everyone inside."

"How many lives?" I ask in horror.

He squeezes his eyelids shut, almost as if he wishes to shut out his pain, before snapping them open and focusing on my face. "Twenty-seven."

Anger—dark and sinister—fills me. Twenty-seven innocent people were killed because of this motherfucking war. Twenty-seven innocent people who probably had no idea there was a war in the first place. I know Vincent employs lycans, but I also know from my time with him that there are humans on the staff as well. Humans with families, friends, and futures.

And now, they're dead.

My mind unwillingly conjures up images of the tiny human girl who had a crush on Vincent. I don't know why she's the first face I see, maybe because she stood out to me, but the thought of a life so young being taken from this world leaves an acidic, sour taste in my mouth.

"And your mother?" I ask, thinking of the sweet woman I met when I stayed at the Davenport manor.

"We put her in a hotel for the night," Valentina interjects, moving to stand beside Brett. I notice that, for the first time since I met her, she's wearing leggings and a T-shirt. With a gun in a holster on her right thigh and a dagger in a sheath on her other side, she looks dangerous and fierce, not a hint of the ice queen to be seen. "She wanted to be here with us, but Vincent refused."

"I still think you should've stayed with her," Vincent grits out with a pointed look at his twin sister. She scoffs, turning her attention to her perfectly manicured nails, and I notice Brett nod in agreement with Vincent.

"I'm not a princess, brother. I can look after myself," she retorts with an eye roll. "Besides, I've been training with Blair. You're letting her fight, aren't you?"

I suddenly find myself the sole focus of three intense stares.

Tai looks seconds from throwing me over his shoulder and carrying me away, the newly formed mating bond exacerbating his natural, possessive tendencies. Mason simply grins at me, trusting me to look after myself, while Vincent's face remains impassive.

"I have the distinct impression that I can't tell Blair to do anything she doesn't want to. Am I right?" Vincent cocks a perfectly trimmed brow at me.

"Damn right." I refocus on the group, meeting all of their stares individually before stopping on Papa Grayson. "This is going to be dangerous. You guys understand that, right? Are all the men and women here today willing to fight?"

"Of course, child," Papa Gray says, sounding offended. He's a damn good man, and I know he'll never force anyone to fight in this war if they didn't want to. "This is their home, their family, that they're defending. For once, we're not leaving the burden on you alone." His ancient eyes, wise beyond his years, ensnare mine. He offers me a wobbly smile, one that speaks of the years of love and trust that have developed between us. This man has become more than just a friend to me—he's my father.

"They want to destroy us for who we are," Johnson adds, his face uncharacteristically grave and solemn. "But this time, we'll fight back."

An overwhelming amount of respect and love flows through me. A knot materializes in my chest, and it tightens as I stare at the faces of my family.

Vincent and Valentina, the rich mafia twins with stone-cold exteriors but who, in the short time I've known them, exhibited more love and compassion than anyone I've ever met.

Tai, the stoic, grumbling alpha who has quickly become my fierce protector and confidant. I know I can ask him to help me bury a body and he'll do it without question.

Mason, the man who never fails to make me laugh. The man who is more than just a lover to me, but a friend. A best friend.

Papa Gray and Johnson, the two men who have looked after me since I was a young pup. They took me in, fed and clothed me, and have never stopped loving me, even now that I'm an adult.

And finally, Brett, the brother I thought I lost. We've only just found each other, and already, the thought of losing him sends a cold chill skittering down my spine, almost like a snake constructed entirely of ice.

"We won't let this stand," I tell them, swallowing down the emotions that threaten to bubble over and scald us all. "For as long as I can remember, we've been seen as lesser than other wolves. No more."

"No more," the others echo, exchanging grim looks.

"Vincent!" My heart flutters in my chest as we spin toward the young lycan wolf hurrying toward us. I recognize him as Christopher, a promising student from MIT and a known hacker. He came up numerous times as a threat when I researched the Davenports months before, mainly because the things he can do with a computer are terrifying. But my research also showed that he's loyal to Vincent, which makes him loyal to me now as well. "We got a ping on their location."

"Where are the bastards heading?" Vincent demands.

Christopher swallows, true fear flashing in his gaze. "The bitten camp."

MY PAWS BEAT AGAINST THE FOREST FLOOR AS I RUN, run, run. I can feel my heart racing in my chest, reaching a crescendo, but I don't slow down.

I *can't* slow down.

I pause when I reach the edge of the trees, where the maples and oaks become sparser, giving way to cottages, cabins, and trailer homes. I duck down behind a bush, my furry stomach resting against the loose twigs, as I survey my surroundings.

Lying directly near the outskirts of the trees are over a dozen men, all dead. Vincent's men, if their lycan smell is any indication. Shot in the forehead.

Large black vans rest stationary around the brick building that serves as our community center. Two totemic wolves—Tai's remaining brothers—stand guard outside, each holding an automatic assault rifle.

I don't see any of the bitten wolves, and horror plagues me, trapping my heart in an impenetrable iron vise and squeezing tightly.

I can't be too late. I can't be.

Shifting back into my human form, completely naked, I grab the walkie talkie I'd carried in my mouth when I ran through the forest.

"Vincent, come in," I say softly, narrowing my eyes at the enemy wolf shifters in *my* fucking home.

"Blair?" His voice is high-pitched with alarm. None of my mates liked the prospect of me venturing to the bitten camp by myself, but they eventually caved when I reminded them it's the best course of action. I'm faster than them, stronger too, and I know this area better than anyone. I know which leaves crackle the loudest, which pathways take me through the densest thicket of trees, which sections of the forest are shrouded in darkness.

"I count..." I do another sweep of the camp, making sure I have my numbers correct before answering. "Seventeen men. Probably more inside. Seven totemic wolves and ten fenrir."

"Fuck, okay. Do they see you?" he demands, once again unable to completely hide his panic. How could I have ever thought of Vincent as cold and icy? He's pure passion—white-hot and blistering.

"No, they haven't. Is everyone in position?" I ask.

Static sounds over the radio, followed immediately by Papa Gray's gruff voice. "We have about twenty men near the front entrance."

"Thirty men coming from the east," Mason adds.

"Thirty from the west," pipes in Tai.

"And the rest of us are near the back, just waiting for your cue," Vincent finishes.

The two brothers—Scar and Dumbass—meander slowly toward each other, matching grins on their faces. I watch as Scar lowers his gun, allowing it to hang from the strap wrapped around his shoulders, and reaches into his pocket to grab a package of cigarettes and a lighter. He places a cigarette between his lips and cups it as he attempts to light the end. Dumbass says something to him, dropping his own gun, and Scar hands him a cigarette as well.

Those two are going to be our biggest problem to deal with. The other wolves are omegas, but these are betas. No match for me, but they could put up a struggle for some of our other fighters.

But now that they're distracted…

"Now," I say into the radio before dropping it into the bramble. Without pause, I shift into my ginormous wolf form.

Shifted, I'm roughly the size of a small horse. My fur is a dusky shade of brown highlighted by gold, just like my hair. I'm larger than most bitten wolves, and faster too. Papa Gray says it's because I'm an alpha, because I innately have a way of commanding

—and demanding—fear and respect from anyone who sets eyes upon me. I don't know if I believe him, but it's nice to believe that my natural domineering personality has given me an edge.

My legs carry me forward, out of the forest and toward the unsuspecting wolves still milling around. Out of my periphery, I can see Vincent run out as well, his gun raised as he fires off two quick shots at the closest wolves.

And then all hell breaks loose.

I lunge at the closest wolf shifter, my mouth opened wide in preparation. He turns toward me in alarm, a cry of fright escaping him, but the noise is cut off as I tear out his throat with my teeth.

The sound of gunfire fills the air, and terror momentarily blinds me. What if one of those bullets hits my mates? Brett? Valentina?

With newfound strength and determination, I race in the direction of the biggest threat—Scar and Dumbass.

By tonight, the camp is going to run red with blood.

I just pray none of that blood belongs to the members of my family.

25

BLAIR

DAY 25

My paws land on Dumbass's chest, forcing him to the ground.

A snarl of rage escapes him as he struggles to regain control of his rifle. I lower my head and snap at his hand, forcing him to release his weapon or risk losing his fingers completely.

"You dumb bitch," he seethes, his face turning beet-red with anger.

I growl, preparing to lean forward and snap his neck, when something heavy lands on my back. I whine, my whole body tensing, as the fourth brother, Scar, puts his entire weight on me and clings for dear life. I attempt to buck him off of me, but he simply laughs and holds on tighter. Dumbass uses my momentary lapse of concentration to punch at my snout, the pain of his fist reverberating through my entire body.

I roll onto my back, my chest heaving, as the two men tower above me, matching, menacing expressions on their faces. I hate how much they look like Tai, how similar their facial features are. Staring up into their pitch-black eyes, devoid of any warmth or compassion, I can almost imagine how Tai would look if he didn't have his mother and younger siblings. If he allowed Sarai to distort and mold him into the monster his brothers were. I truly believe that Tai's goodness proves how strong he is. Instead of giving in to the inevitable peer pressure and temptation, instead of allowing himself to embrace the darkness percolating in his stomach, he fought back. Became stronger. Better. Smarter.

And I love him for it even more.

"What do we have here?" Dumbass snarks, flashing me a dumbass grin on his dumbass face. "The little bitten wolf."

Scar simply smirks at me, the movement pulling at the scar zigzagging through his lip, before kicking me in the side. I hold in the whine that wants to escape, curling in on myself. There are two of them. One of me.

I don't like these odds.

For them.

I pretend to be weak and docile. Defeated. I even lower my eyes and begin to cry softly as the two idiotic *stronzos* circle my wolf form.

"What do we do with her?" Dumbass questions, his tone best described as haughty. He believes he won, which couldn't be further from the truth. Never underestimate your prey.

"Sarai and Grim will want to ask her questions," Scar answers, and he leans down as if he means to grab my tail and physically drag me inside the brick building.

Idiot.

The second he bends at the waist, I shoot forward, twisting my entire body so my teeth are aimed at his face. He only has a second to scream out in alarm before my massive jaws lock around his neck and twist. A moment later, his head rolls away from his body, blood pooling underneath his corpse in an ocean of deep burgundy.

Dumbass's mouth drops open, unbridled fear flashing in his eyes, before he turns toward me with malice etched across every line of his face. "You little bitch!" he rages, preparing to jump at me. I remain low, my tail wagging back and forth in preparation, but before he can reach me, a huge, hulking figure wraps his tan hands around his neck and twists it once. Dumbass joins his brother on the ground, dead.

I shift back into my human form to meet Tai's pitch-black gaze. At the moment, the pupil has completely swallowed the iris so not even a speck of brown or gold remains. He's consumed by his wolf, by his anger, and I can feel it radiating from him in almost palpable waves. His body trembles as he cocks his head to the side, staring down at the brother he just killed with his bare hands. I don't know what I expect to see in his expression—guilt, horror, shock, or even pain—but instead, there's only grim satisfaction reflecting back at me.

He knows his brother was evil—understands it, even—and he didn't hesitate to do what he needed to do. I doubt he felt any love for the man who tortured him and his mother for years.

"Sarai and Grim inside?" His voice is more wolf than man, the barest rumble of air.

"Yes." I nod once, directing my attention to the rest of the camp.

Most of our enemies appear to have been taken

care of. I see numerous bodies littering the ground and even more in handcuffs. More must've joined the fight, because I count up to sixty enemy wolves. My eyes snag on Mason, who stands off to the side, a cocky smile on his face as he watches me. When he meets my gaze, he saunters forward, tossing me an oversized T-shirt he packed with him.

"How long have you been standing there?" I query, shrugging the shirt on. The material comes to just below my knees, and one sniff confirms it belongs to Tai, the biggest of all my mates.

"Long enough to watch you kick ass, baby girl," Mason confesses, his eyes glimmering with pride.

"And you weren't going to help?" Tai demands.

Mason shrugs his shoulders. "She had it handled."

Love and respect for my mate surges through me, and it takes every ounce of restraint not to throw myself in his arms. Instead, I inspect the wolves gathering around me.

"Any injuries or deaths?" I direct at Papa Gray, who uses his cane to wobble up the stone steps. Vincent stands beside him, his gun held at the ready.

"A few injuries, but nothing life threatening," he announces, and relief courses through me, causing me to practically sag forward.

"Perfect." I turn toward Vincent next. "Keep

about fifty of your men out here. Have them surround the camp. The last thing we need are any surprises."

He nods once, turning his back to the ground to speak into his radio.

"Mason," I direct my next words at the grinning blond biker, "take your men and have them go through the back entrance. If my theory is correct, Grim and Sarai are using the bitten wolves as hostages. The last thing we want to do is spook them and have them start killing." My throat closes up at just the concept, and pure fear rushes through me. I force myself to push it away and keep a steady head. The last thing I can afford to do is give in to the emotions running rampant through me and become sloppy. "I have a feeling more enemy wolves are inside. I trust you to take care of them discreetly."

After all, there's a reason he's known around town as Bullseye.

"Aye, aye, boss woman," Mason says, saluting me. He whistles sharply, garnering the attention of the lycans loyal to us, before heading in the direction I indicated.

"Everyone else," I raise my voice to be heard, "remain out here. We don't know what Grim and Sarai have planned for us. We do know for certain that they haven't gotten into contact with the Holeman pack, so we shouldn't expect a surprise visit from them. However, Grim and Sarai are slippery bastards, and I wouldn't put it past them to have more shit planned." The wolves nod once before dispersing to protect the perimeter. I finally turn my attention to Vincent, Tai, Papa Gray, Johnson, Brett, Valentina, and Paco. "All of us are going to go inside." I swallow thickly. "But it's going to be dangerous. If anyone wants to stay outside and be—"

"Oh, for fuck's sake." Valentina flips her silky braid over her shoulder and moves to shoulder past me. "Let's get going."

Vincent growls and all but forces his sister behind him. He moves to do the same thing to me, but I slip inside the community center before he's able to touch me. He mumbles something about strong, independent women before following to the right of me, Tai taking up the left.

We move quietly as a group, the only sound the thump of Papa Gray's cane against the smooth white flooring. I wanted desperately to beg the old man to stay behind, but these wolves are his people, his family, and the last thing he'll ever do is leave them to fend for themselves.

Fuck. What are Sarai and Grim doing?

The thought of them hurting any of the bitten wolves has bile surging up my throat. I'll skin them alive if they lay even a hand on my friends. I'll gut them like pigs and string them from the rafters, allowing their blood to cascade into metal buckets. I'll—

Muffled shouting reverberates from one of the conference rooms, and it's there I turn, my heart racing a mile a minute.

Tai places a hand on my shoulder, stopping me, and I whirl around to glare at him. If he expects me to sit on the sidelines, then he truly doesn't know me at all.

Instead of begging me to stay behind, he hands me a loaded gun with a nod of solidarity, and my heart swells. I can tell he's wrestling with his wolf, his instincts screaming at him to protect me, but he trusts me well enough to know what I can do. And what I can do is kick major ass.

I accept the gun gratefully, flashing him a timid smile, before directing that smile at Vincent as well. I want to tell them that I love them, that my world has become brighter since they've been in it, but not only is that a fucking cliché, but it's also not the time.

You'll tell them when you make it out of this mess,

Blair, I tell myself firmly. *And then you'll never let them go.*

Ever.

Turning away from them—and praying that this isn't the last time I see them—I begin to move toward the conference room. My gut lurches with fear, but I ignore the insidious emotion as I stop at the door, glancing over my shoulder once to ensure everyone is in position.

And then, I push open the door and rush inside, my gun drawn.

Horror immediately engulfs me when I step into the room, and my hands shake slightly, my mind unwilling to accept what my eyes are seeing.

More than a dozen bodies lie dead in the center of the room, all of them bitten wolves. Papa Gray releases a strangled cry behind me, and Johnson bellows in pure rage.

Standing against the far wall are Grim and Sarai. The former has his arm banded around Martha, one of my closest friends in the pack. The latter has a gun trained on the head of her young son, Jacob. Both have snot dripping down their faces as they cry. In the far corner of the room, more of the children sit huddled together, sobbing hysterically as they stare at the bodies of their dead parents.

No. No. No. No. No.

"Let them go," I bite out, terror ensnaring my heart.

"Pretty little bitten wolf," Grim sings as he caresses the side of Martha's face. She grimaces in disgust, attempting to turn her face away, but he simply grabs her chin and digs his fingers into her pasty skin. Despite his attention directed at Martha, I know his words are meant for me. Less than a second later, he turns hate-filled eyes in my direction. "I didn't expect you to get an army together. And I definitely didn't expect you to turn my own son against me."

I'm suddenly grateful Mason isn't with us right at this moment. Grim is obviously unhinged, and I have no doubt that the presence of his son will send him spiraling straight off that cliff...dragging Martha with him.

"It's over," I tell them, taking a hesitant step closer. Tai makes a move as if to reach for me, but I hold up a single hand, beseeching him wordlessly to trust me. "You lost."

"Bitten wolves are scum," Grim hisses, tightening his arm around Martha. She whimpers in pain, but that noise only seems to spur him on. "So are lycan."

I take another step closer. "We're all just shifters,

Grim. Now let them go, and we can end this peacefully."

Grim releases a deranged laugh. "Did you know that a pack made up of bitten and lycan wolves killed my late wife?" he demands, his eyes abnormally wide in his face. I half wonder if he's on drugs or some other mood-altering substance.

"Is that why you hate us so much?" I question as the final pieces of the puzzle click into place. I always wondered what made Grim harbor such intense loathing for us—especially since we all share similar characteristics as shifters—and now, that question has been answered.

"Oh, enough of this." Sarai moves the gun from Jacob's head and aims it at Grim's. The sound of a gun firing echoes through the air as Martha and Jacob both scream. A second later, Grim falls to the ground, a single bullet hole in the side of his head, rivulets of red intermingling with his pale blond hair.

Martha begins to cry in earnest, desperately attempting to untangle her body from the dead man, but Sarai doesn't even spare her a glance as he places the gun snugly against Jacob's temple once more.

"I really hate evil monologues, don't you?" he says drolly, his eyes unblinking as he meets my stare.

In Grim, I saw an all-consuming hatred and loathing. Passion. Fire.

But in Sarai...

I see nothing at all. His eyes remind me of those on a puppet, lifeless, unseeing, and apathetic.

"Father, why are you doing this?" Tai demands, moving to stand beside me.

"What do you want me to say, son?" Sarai throws his head back in cruel laughter, the noise scratching at my skin. "Do you want me to give you a reason for my actions? A way for you to understand? Because I'll be completely honest...I have no reasons. Some people do evil acts for justice or vengeance. And there are others who do them simply because they want to." He tilts his head to the side, and vomit swirls in my stomach at the stone-cold realization...

Sarai is a psychopath.

A real, honest-to-God psychopath who doesn't give a shit about anyone or anything. I doubt he even cares that his own sons have just been slaughtered. As I stare into his glacial eyes, I see not a flicker of anything remotely human.

He won't hesitate to kill Jacob if it means making a point.

"To be completely honest," Sarai continues, "I'm impressed." He levels that icy gaze onto me. "We thought this massacre would be easy. Who would've thought the little bitten wolf would have an entire army at her beck and call? You must have a magical pussy if you're able to charm all three princes." Another bark of dry laughter escapes him as he momentarily removes the gun from Jacob to gesticulate wildly. Before I can get my hopes up, he places it once more against his scalp.

"Let my son go!" Martha begs, hysterical, but Sarai ignores her, focusing on me.

"We could've been good together, you and I," he tells me, and I swear I vomit a little in my mouth. "Think about how incredible our children could've been."

Yup. Definitely vomit.

"Never going to happen, *stronzo*," I hiss out.

"Father, just let the kid go. You don't need him," Tai growls, venturing another step closer.

"You must think I'm an idiot, son." Sarai rolls his eyes, seemingly unconcerned by the fact that he has half a dozen guns aimed at his face. "You see, I'm the villain in your eyes. The bad guy. And as the bad guy, I don't give a shit if this little runt," he shakes Jacob for emphasis, "lives or dies. But unfortunately, you guys do." He smiles sharply, revealing razor-sharp teeth. It's the smile of a mad man, not a hint of genuine amusement visible in it. "Here's what's going to happen. I'm going to leave this room *and* this camp with young Joshua here," he begins, and I don't bother to correct him.

Martha begins to sob harder, and out of my periphery, I watch Papa Gray move flush against the far wall, his cane discarded.

"You're not leaving here alive, Sarai," Tai whispers, giving up all pretenses that he actually considers this evil man his father.

"Then the boy dies." Sarai shrugs as if it doesn't matter either way, clicking off the safety.

"No!" Martha screams, struggling to her feet.

But before she can do something stupid, Papa Gray rushes forward, tackling Sarai to the ground. Jacob falls, collapsing beside his mom in a fit of tears, as Papa Gray and Sarai struggle.

The gun goes off.

My entire world seems to freeze as I watch Papa Gray's eyes widen in shock. I'm running forward before I'm even consciously aware that I'm moving, Tai, Vincent, and the others a step behind me. Johnson screams out Grayson's name, his voice laced with pain, as the man who has been my father, my friend, my companion collapses on the ground.

"No. No. No." I slide forward on my hands and

knees until I'm directly beside him, clasping his hand tightly in mine. Tears roll down my cheeks as I stare into Papa Gray's pale, whiskered face. Blood forms in the corner of his mouth, and he coughs.

"You did good, kiddo," Papa Gray whispers, his voice hoarse with pain. More blood cascades down his chin as he stares up at me through glossy eyes.

"Stay with us, Grayson!" Johnson demands, moving to kneel on Papa Gray's other side. "Stay with us!"

I'm dimly aware of a struggle behind me, but I can't focus on that. I trust my mates and friends to handle Sarai.

"I'm proud of you both," Papa Gray whispers, blinking rapidly. "And I love you both so much."

"You're going to be okay," I reassure him, running my free hand through his tangled gray hair. "You're going to be okay."

But I know I'm speaking to a ghost. Papa Gray's lifeless eyes stare vacantly in my direction, not a glimpse of the ornery, combative man I've come to know and love.

Papa Gray is dead, and I just know I'll never be the same.

MASON

DAY 25

I stand on the highest hill near the outskirts of the bitten camp, Tai on one side of me and Vincent on the other. At my feet, his body broken beyond repair, is my father.

He's always been a twisted man, fucked up and sadistic, but I truly believe that at one point, he loved me. At least, as much as a psychopath like him could ever love another person. I have vague memories of him bringing me to a park to play catch, but I half wonder if I imagined the entire encounter. Maybe it was some other pack member who took me? Maybe I'm so desperate to have one good memory of my father, that my brain is playing tricks on me? Either way, the love my father bestowed upon me was a sadistic type of love, but it's the only parental love I've ever known.

I wonder if that's why it's so hard when a parent lets you down. You want to believe in them so badly, you want to trust them and believe they care about you, that when they do something that contradicts the mold you put them in, it destroys you irreparably.

I don't regret that my father's dead, but I do regret that I hadn't been there to save him. It's not my job to look after my father, but I can't help but wonder if things could've been different if I'd just…

I don't know.

Done something.

But I can't think about that. Not right now. Not when I have hundreds of eyes on my face, a handful of them wearing the familiar cuts of the Bloody Skulls.

The president is dead. And now, I'm stepping into his place.

Tai clears his throat beside me, forcing all eyes onto him, as he pushes Sarai forward. The man is gagged and tied up, blood dripping from a wound on his head, yet his eyes crinkle with a smile. If there was ever a man fucked up beyond repair, I truly believe that man to be Sarai. There's something not quite right about the Totemic alpha. Something deranged and insidious that lives inside of him, clawing against his skin, desperate to get out.

"Today, everything ends!" Tai bellows, his strident voice carrying over the masses as effectively as if he were using a microphone. Shocked murmurs ripple through the crowd, but one icy glare from Vincent has them shutting up immediately. "No more hatred. No more killing. No more fighting."

Vincent takes a step forward, looking as immaculate as ever in his black, three-piece suit. I would've believed the pampered prince hadn't even joined the battle if I hadn't been fighting right alongside him. There's not a single hair out of place. Asshole. I'm actually a little jealous, considering I still have blood splattered across my face and my hair looks like I put my finger in an electrical socket.

"The three of us have taken control of our packs," he adds, and though he hasn't raised his voice like Tai, I have no doubt that everyone heard him.

"And we have declared a truce. Our three packs and the bitten wolves," I say, my mind drifting to

Blair. When we left her, she'd been sobbing over Grayson's corpse, the horrid sound rattling around in my brain and leaving me scarred. Her brother had promised to look after her until we could return. Fuck, I hated leaving her like that, but what could I do? What words of comfort could I offer someone who lost her father all over again?

We may not be able to bring Grayson back to life, but we can achieve his life-long goal—peace amongst the packs.

"We know this won't be easy," Tai continues, surveying the crowd of wolves with flinty eyes.

"But hatred and bigotry are learned skills, not ones you're born with," interjects Vincent.

"And while both of those emotions have been ingrained inside of us from a young age, we're here to tell you that we won't tolerate them a second longer," I finish.

For the first time since I met Vincent and Tai, we're in harmony. We have three different voices, but we speak as one. And I can't help but wonder if this is what fate intended for us all along, if loving Blair was necessary to end the incessant fighting that has been going on for centuries.

Maybe the universe decided that enough was enough. Maybe they threw that perfect bitten wolf in our pathway, knowing it'll be impossible to resist her. I can't imagine the three of us would be shoulder to shoulder, side by side, speaking of peace and harmony if it wasn't for her.

I was being honest before—hatred and bigotry have been ingrained inside of me from a young age. I've been taught to despise the totemics, lycans, and bitten wolves. But somehow, these men have become my brothers, and that bitten wolf? She's become my whole damn world.

Fate is a fickle bitch, isn't she?

"You can't be serious!" an incredulous voice interjects, and I recognize him as Hawk, a member of the Bloody Skulls who has always been loyal to my father. "You can't really expect us to have peace with our enemies?"

"I can, and I will," I snap back. "And if you have a problem with that, you can either leave the pack or face the consequences."

More murmuring erupts among the crowd, and I gauge their expressions carefully, searching for any wolves who might cause us problems. The majority are men and women from our own army, so I see nothing but hope on their faces. But there are a few…

I make a note of everyone who looks upset by

our proclamation, everyone who snarls or growls or glares. I'll talk to Vincent and Tai and make sure we keep an eye on them in the days to come. In order for this transition to go smoothly, we can't have vocal discontent. We need to be a harmonious whole if we're going to make effective change.

"Grim is dead!" I continue, nodding toward my father's corpse. Something tightens in my stomach, something akin to pain, but I shove the pesky emotion away. I hate my father with everything that I am, everything that's inside of me, but he's the only blood relative I have. *Had.*

Though I'm speaking to all the wolves, my words are intended to those of my own pack. "And as your new president, trust that I'll lead you guys on the path to greatness. Trust that I'm doing what's best for our club."

More grumbles and noises of dissent echo throughout the clearing, but I notice that there's less this time around.

"My father has done unspeakable acts," Tai interjects, his eyes shadowed with pain. "Some of which you know about. Most of which you don't. And for his crimes…" His hand shifts into keen claws, though his face remains expressionless. "He will be put to death."

Sarai begins to laugh through his gag, his eyes sparking with mirth, but Tai isn't perturbed as he lowers his hand to Sarai's throat and slices, creating a macabre smile of blood. Someone screams in the crowd, but everyone else remains silent.

Watching.

Waiting.

Trusting us to do what is right for our packs.

Sarai falls to the ground beside my father, dead.

"Change is coming!" Tai declares, reaching a blood-soaked hand out to me. I don't hesitate to clasp it in my own before extending my other hand to Vincent. He takes it immediately, and the three of us stand on the hill, unified for the first time in our existence.

And all because of one tiny slip of a bitten wolf who has turned our entire world on its axis.

The road to peace won't be easy—I imagine we'll face challenges every day from wolves who wish to unseat us and push the packs into chaos—but the battle will be worth it. I've spent my life refusing to even consider peace because I didn't think it would be possible.

But now that it's within my grasp, I'm more determined than ever to hold on with all my might and never let it go. I want this world to be a safe place for my mate to live in.

And if anyone has a problem with that, then they can fuck right the hell off.

27

BLAIR

DAY 30

The funeral takes place five days later, in a cemetery bitten wolves have been using for years. The grounds are overgrown, sprinkled with knee-high weeds, and the gravestones are beginning to crumble with age, but I know this is where Papa Gray would want to be.

Buried alongside his late wife and daughter.

It's a simple ceremony, and I choose to sit beside Johnson, our hands tangled together as we both grieve the man we loved and lost.

"He cared about you, kid," Johnson tells me as we stare down at Papa Gray's freshly dug grave. It's strange to think about a man as lively and exuberant as Papa Gray buried beneath six feet of earth. It just seems so cliché. Why should his story have to end with him in a coffin below ground? How the fuck is that fair? "A lot."

Emotions bombard me, and tears sting my eyes, though I stubbornly refuse to let them fall. Funerals are supposed to be a time of remembrance, not pain. At least, that's what Papa Gray always told me. "I know he cared about you as well," I whisper. After his wife died, I know Grayson didn't believe he'd find true love again, but he did. In Johnson. Their romance was short-lived, but in the time they spent together, I've seen more life in Grayson's eyes than ever before.

"I'm going to miss him so much," Johnson chokes out, turning toward me. I wrap my arms around him and lend him some of my strength. I don't know if I'll have enough for myself afterward, but it'll be worth it to alleviate some of the pain I can sense coursing through him.

I make my rounds, comforting all of the bitten wolves as best as I can. Now that Papa Gray is dead, they seemed to have deferred to me as the new alpha. I don't know how I feel about that change in status—especially since I know I'll never be able to replace the man we lost—but for now, I do what I can to help while we reassemble our pack from the shambles the war left it in. Tomorrow, we'll have more funerals for the other bitten wolves that Sarai and Grim slaughtered.

Besides them, we lost only two other wolves, both lycans who worked for the Davenports. A man named Hunter and a woman named Ali. Vincent promised me he organized funeral arrangements for both shifters and sent a hefty sum of money to their families. I don't know if that gesture will replace what the families lost, but it's a start.

"How are you doing, baby girl?" Mason's arms encircle me from behind, and I breathe in his leather and pine scent.

"About as well as you'd expect," I respond, twisting in his arms. He places his chin on my hair and squeezes me tighter, breathing me in just as I do him. "And how are you doing?"

"Me?" Alarm laces his tone as he pulls away to stare into my eyes.

"You lost your dad, Mason," I say gently, and he opens his mouth as if to assure me he's fine, but I cut him off, "Don't put on a brave face for me. I know you. And I know you're not one hundred percent okay."

He looks as if he still wants to protest, his mouth

opening and closing, before he sighs and runs a hand through his shaggy blond hair. The smile carved into his mouth is grim and weary, the crack in his mask visible for the entire world to see. "You're right, baby girl. I'm not all right, and I'm not sure if I ever will be. My dad was an evil bastard, I know that, but he…" He trails off again, his lips tightening into a thin line.

"But he was still your dad," I finish for him, my heart lurching at his obvious pain. I hated Grim with all the fires of hell itself, but I can't even begin to understand what Mason must be going through.

"He was the only family I had left," he whispers, his voice hitching.

I want to tell him my theory, but before I can get a single word out, someone taps me on my shoulder.

"Blair," Vincent's cool voice brushes over me, "there's someone I want you to meet."

I spin around, allowing Mason to keep his arms around my waist, to see Vincent standing beside Brett, Tai, and Valentina. And beside the three of them…

My heart races as I face the woman I haven't seen in person since I was a young kid. Her photographs don't do her justice.

She exhibits an ethereal, ageless beauty, one I can

only hope to have myself when I get older. Her dark hair, peppered in streaks of gray, is twisted into a chignon that emphasizes her sharp features. She wears a flowing black dress that covers most of her body, but she moves with a gracefulness and elegance that belies her age.

"Blair. Is that you my *dolcezza?*" Her voice wobbles slightly as she takes a tentative step closer, her hands extended as if she wants to reach for me. When I don't immediately run to her, she breaches the distance between us and places her hands on my cheeks. This close, I can spot the telltale sign of her age. Brown spots dot her hands, and wrinkles mar her face.

Mason releases me, moving to stand with the other men, and I venture closer.

"Nonna?" I whisper.

Brett takes a step until he's at my side, placing a reassuring hand on my shoulder and forcing my attention to his face. He begins to sign, and Mason once again translates for me.

"I thought today would be a good day for you to have more family around," he confesses.

"You got into contact with our grandma?" My throat closes as a tsunami of emotions rushes over me.

"I'm so sorry for your loss, my sweet child," Nonna says as she drops her hands from my cheeks. Her eyes gloss-over with tears as she sniffles. "And I'm so sorry I haven't been there for you." She turns to face Brett as well, placing one hand on his arm. "For either of you."

A sob tumbles out of me, and I don't even bother to contain it.

"You're here now."

And then we're hugging, all three of us. I know in my heart that Nonna won't replace the bond I had with Papa Gray, that his absence will always be felt as keenly as a knife in the gut, but I know I'll heal. I have my family, my mates, and my best friend by my side.

The process will be slow and painful, and I doubt I'll ever be repaired perfectly, but at least the emptiness in my chest is no longer as prevalent. There's a piece of me that's missing, a piece of me that will always be missing, but it won't consume me. I won't drown in the pain.

I don't know for certain how my story is going to end, but I have a feeling I'll survive whatever the world throws my way.

THE DECISION

28

BLAIR

I shift in Vincent's strong arms, attempting to get more comfortable, as Mason places a hand on my thigh to stop me from wiggling. I give him a glare over my shoulder, but he simply flashes me an impish smirk and nips at my nose.

"Sore, baby girl?" he questions, waggling his eyebrows suggestively.

I hit his arm. "Stop trying to suggest that we did anything but sleep last night," I hiss. Genuine laughter escapes him as he trails his fingers up and down my legs.

"You *were* exhausted, little wolf," Tai murmurs from where he has pulled a chair up to the side of the bed. He's already dressed for the day, his hair wet from his shower. His eyes smolder with their usual intensity as he peers at me.

I blow out a breath and shift in my men's embrace, thinking through everything that is going to happen today.

It's been fifteen days since the battle at the bitten camp. Ten days since Papa Gray's funeral.

And now...

Now I had to make a decision.

"You ready for today?" Vincent plants a tender kiss on my bare shoulder as I stretch in bed, blinking rapidly to clear the fatigue from my eyes.

"No," I confess, thinking through what I'm going to say when we meet for the summit. The wolves will want a decision, and they'll get one.

By the end of today, I'll have to choose which of the three men I want to spend the rest of my life with.

And just pray that everyone accepts the final decision.

I CURL MY LONG, VOLUMINOUS HAIR AND PIN HALF OF it up, allowing the rest of my curls to tumble down my back. I wear a dress for the occasion, the pink number cinching at my waist before swooping outward in a stylish skirt. The sweetheart neckline reveals a generous amount of cleavage, and I draw attention to my breasts with a heart-shaped pendant I'd gotten as a gift from Papa Gray a few years ago on my birthday.

I swallow down my emotions as I think about the old man who became a father to me. Squeezing the pendant tightly, I conjure up an image of his face before death claimed him. Alive. Smiling. Happy. I half want to kill Sarai all over again to enact my revenge, but I know that won't bring Papa Gray back. Sarai's gone, and his evil will never tarnish the world again. Tai is now the alpha of the Totemic Tribe, and he has more goodness in his pinkie finger than Sarai did in his entire body.

The world is being renewed, and I'm so fucking grateful that my mates and I are standing at the frontline for it.

As I step out of the bathroom, Vincent, Mason, and Tai are waiting for me in the foyer of Tai's apartment. All three of them pause to stare at me, their eyes bugging out of their head in a way that might've been comical if I hadn't had the exact same reaction to them.

They look sexy as hell in their suits, each one

somehow maintaining their personality despite the fancy wear.

Vincent looks as if he was born in a suit, his hair meticulously parted away from his arresting, tan face. There's not a wrinkle to be seen on his suit coat or pants, and the white shirt underneath is crisp, conforming to his muscular physique. His tie, surprisingly, matches the pink of my dress, and I wonder if he knew what I was going to wear or if he guessed, considering the fact that my favorite color is pink.

Mason, on the contrary, looks as if he stepped straight off of a fashion shoot and has haphazardly begun removing his clothes. His suit coat is askew, a few of the buttons undone, and his undershirt hangs slightly open, revealing a sliver of fair skin. His tie is loose around his neck, adding to the appeal, and his blond hair is wildly disheveled. He looks uncomfortable in his suit, fidgeting constantly, and I know he only wore it to impress me.

And Tai...

I've never seen the Totemic alpha out of his standard black tee and jeans, so to see him dressed up is a treat in itself. Unlike Mason and Vincent, he only has on a gray suit coat that constricts against his muscular arms. The black T-shirt he wears underneath looks at odds with the coat but only adds to the allure. He wears clean black jeans that showcase his toned legs, each the size of tree trunks, and I can't help but imagine climbing him like one.

Fuck, I want to rip the clothes off of all three of them.

"Don't give me those eyes, baby girl," Mason purrs, his eyes dipping down my body. He groans low in his throat, obviously liking what he's seeing, before lifting his gaze back to mine. "We don't have time."

"If we're quick…"

"Fuck, Blair," Vincent moans, clearing his throat and fixing his tie. I can see the evidence of his arousal straining against his pants. "Stop it."

I turn pleading eyes onto Tai, pushing out my bottom lip in a pout. "Tai."

"Nope," he says simply, stalking out the door.

I watch him go in amusement before turning back toward my other two mates. "Maybe the three of us can—"

"Blair!" Tai bellows from out in the hallway, and my grin widens. "Get your ass out here before I spank it."

"So bossy," Mason mouths to me, and then he winks. "I like it."

THE SUMMIT TAKES PLACE AT THE SAME HOTEL WE visited over ninety days ago. We enter the same golden room from the first meeting—burnished, red-gold walls, brown-gold carpeting, golden chandeliers—and my eyes drop to the table full of pack allies.

Valentina sits beside Brett, looking as immaculate as ever in a burgundy dress that hugs her curves. She stands when we enter, moving breezily toward me to air kiss both of my cheeks.

"You look lovely, Blair," she whispers sincerely, before stepping away to allow Brett to take her place.

He kisses my cheek as well, all the while glaring over my shoulder at the three men surrounding me.

I allow my gaze to drift back to the table, where the remaining representatives are settled. Paco sits beside a pale-faced Enola, her blonde hair frizzy and unkempt. I can't imagine what she's going through at the moment, losing four of her sons and her husband. They were evil, sadistic bastards, but a mother's love knows no bounds.

Johnson stands against the far wall, and he nods when he catches sight of me. His face is haggard and pale, deep lines emphasizing the strain of the last few days, but he's standing. Breathing. Alive. And I just know he'll get through this—we all will.

Martha waves to me as I enter, looking surprisingly cheerful and chipper despite the hell she endured. I'm not surprised. If there's one woman who can bounce back from anything, it's her. Her enthusiasm for life and optimism is both endearing and nauseating, if I'm being completely honest.

Mason moves to take a seat beside Brett, while Vincent claims the chair next to Valentina. Tai sits opposite them both, beside Paco, while Johnson claims the chair near the end of the table.

There's only one chair left.

At the head of the table.

I don't immediately sit down as I allow my eyes to travel over all of the wolves present—a new generation, willing to fight for change.

"We're here today because I'm supposed to make an important decision," I begin, refusing to waste any of our time with small talk and pleasantries. "At the end of the ninety days, I've been tasked to choose one man from the three packs I wish to spend the rest of my life with. A man who I wish to marry." I settle my gaze first on Vincent, his once cold gaze now full of warmth and life like winter transitioning into spring. I then turn toward Mason, who simply smiles and winks at me. Finally, I rest my eyes on Tai, who nods at me in solidarity, providing me strength and comfort.

"And..." I continue, taking a deep breath and bracing myself for their responses. "I'm choosing... well..." I release a strangled laugh, absently fiddling with the ends of my hair. "I'm not choosing."

No one speaks at my proclamation, though I hurry on before I can get a read of their reactions.

"I can't choose between the three of them, so I won't. They're my mates, and I'm theirs. And this might be unconventional, but I choose all of them."

I feel like I pulled a pin out of a grenade and then threw it into the room. Silence reigns as I focus on the back of the chair I'm standing behind. I wait with bated breath for their reactions, wondering how they're going to respond. My men already knew my decision—choosing between the three of them would be impossible—but the others...

A loud whoop has my head snapping up, and I turn wide eyes onto Valentina as she cups her mouth and begins to holler.

"Get it, girl."

"Oh, Blair!" Enola cries, jumping from her seat

and rushing toward me to give me a hug. "I'm so happy for you."

"You better treat that girl well, you hear me," Johnson snaps sternly, with pointed looks at Vincent, Mason, and Tai.

An overwhelming amount of love fills me then with the realization that the other wolves not only accept my decision, but approve of it. Before I realize what's happening, I'm surrounded by my pack, my family, with words of congratulations and hopes for the future. And when Mason, Tai, and Vincent pull me into a three-way embrace, I melt against them eagerly.

"And you were worried," Mason drawls. "So does this mean we get to have an orgy now?"

"Oh shut up," I say, but I'm smiling.

I have a feeling I'm going to be smiling a lot the rest of my life.

AFTER THE CONGRATULATIONS, WE GET DOWN TO business, discussing the peace treaty in detail. Over time, we would like to merge all of the packs together, but we know that won't happen overnight. For now, we'll each run our own packs separately, forging friendships and relationships until we're able to coexist in relative harmony. As expected, we've had a few protests, but none of them have gotten violent and all of them have been stopped before they could truly begin.

It's going to be a long, strenuous battle, but I just know everything will be worth it in the end.

When the summit commences for the night, deciding to meet up again tomorrow, I remain behind, along with Enola, Tai, Mason, and Vincent.

Tai sits beside his mother, one hand on her shoulder in silent comfort. She keeps her gaze focused on her clasped hands, her body trembling with every passing second. I can feel Mason and Vincent giving me inquiring stares, but I don't take my attention off of the frail but fierce woman.

"Enola? There's something you want to tell us, isn't there?" I say softly, and her head snaps up, her eyes instantly locking on Mason before she turns away.

"Blair, what is this about?" Tai rumbles, glancing between his mother and me curiously.

"Enola?" I press. I don't want to force her into anything, but I also don't think her silence and secrecy is fair to Mason or Tai. I want them to know the truth, and I think she does too.

Enola lifts her chin once more, and though her lips are wobbly, there's a fierce glint in her eyes that amplifies my respect for her.

"Twenty-four years ago," Enola begins in a soft voice, "I went with Sarai to a summit meeting."

A crease appears between Tai's eyes, but he doesn't interrupt his mother, allowing her to articulate her thoughts.

"He was at the beginning stages of an alliance with Grim at the time." She snorts, the noise laced with self-deprecation, and slowly shakes her head. "Sarai was…optimistic. He wanted power more than anything, and he saw a friendship with Grim as a way of getting more of it. Sarai had just taken over the pack from his father, but unlike your grandpa," she gives Tai a pointed stare, "Sarai was pure evil. He didn't have the best interests of the pack at heart, only his own. He was cruel and conniving…but a part of me loved him. A part of me still loves him, even after everything he's done." She sniffles, bringing her sleeve up to wipe at her face, and Tai wraps a comforting arm around her shoulders. "I don't know how it happened exactly—if Grim decided to just take what Sarai had or if I was part of some sick deal Sarai made—but on the third night of the summit, Grim snuck into my room."

"Fuck," Tai curses, his face draining of all color.

Mason goes still beside me.

"I won't give you guys all of the gory details," Enola says, attempting to laugh it off with a dismissive wave of her hand. But you can't laugh off that type of pain. "Shortly after that encounter, I discovered I was pregnant."

"No," Mason whispers, shock coloring his tone. "Fuck no. No, this can't be happening."

"I begged Sarai not to tell Grim, but he thought it would be a way to strengthen their alliance," Enola confesses tearfully. "So when my beautiful baby boy was born—"

"No," Mason interjects.

"—Grim came for him. I wasn't even allowed to say goodbye." Enola's gasping for breath now, tears cascading down her swollen, red cheeks.

Vincent places a hand on Mason's shoulder and gives it a squeeze.

"This can't...you can't..." Mason's head snaps in Tai's direction, his face still abnormally pale. "Did you know about this?"

"No," Tai responds, his voice devoid of any emotion. I can tell it's his way of dealing with the shock of his mother's words, the realization that he has a brother he never knew about. A brother he shares a mate with. He's trying to compartmentalize his pain, if only to comfort his mother. "I didn't."

"I wanted to tell you so badly," Enola sobs. "I wanted to meet you more than anything, but Grim wouldn't allow me to. And I just wanted to keep you—"

"I can't..." Mason swallows heavily, standing abruptly and pushing over his chair. "I can't deal with this right now."

"Mason," I begin, but he shuts me up with a quick kiss.

"I'll be in my room," he says, not sparing Enola a second glance as he races into the hallway.

Fat tears drip down Enola's cheeks as she stares helplessly after him. Tai's hand slowly drops from her shoulders, almost as if his strength has waned with each word she spoke until he's incapable of lifting his arm.

"Give him time," I tell Enola seriously. "He went from believing he has no family...to discovering he has a mom and three siblings." I offer her a wobbly smile. "But he deserved to know the truth. They both did." I twist my head to include Tai in that last statement as well, and he swallows.

"Thank you," Enola whispers. "For looking after my boys."

"Always," I reply without thought.

And I always will, even if they don't want me to.

"We'll talk to him, Mom," Tai whispers, giving her shoulders another squeeze. He seems to have regained some semblance of control, though his eyes are still frantic. I can't imagine what he must be feeling—first discovering that his mom had been raped and then learning that he has a younger brother.

Enola squeezes Tai's hand. "It's all right if he's not ready to know me," she whispers. "But maybe in time..."

"Right now, Mason needs some time to think. He'll come to you when he's ready," I tell her, knowing with absolute certainty that Mason will come to her. Right now, he's confused and probably a little scared, but he's also desperate to know his mother. It'll take time, but I can feel in my heart that Enola made the right decision in telling him the truth. Their relationship might be strained and laden with explosives, but at least they'll have one.

But for now, I need to comfort my mate.

BLAIR

"Mason," I say, entering the hotel suite we've been assigned. Tai and Vincent follow along behind me, both completely silent. I know I need to comfort Tai as well—after all, his world also imploded in a span of seconds—but I recognize that Mason needs me more right now. This strange, unconventional relationship will only work with balance.

"I don't want to talk about it, Blair." Mason's hands are balled into fists by his sides, and his chest heaves. Before we entered the room, he must've had a pretty intense battle with the coffee table, for it's currently in shatters against the opposite wall.

"Then don't talk about it," I say calmly, moving to stand behind him. I don't touch him right away, allowing him to come to me if he desires to, and for a brief moment, he simply stands there, his back muscles taut.

And then he turns around and throws himself into my arms. The forward momentum sends me staggering back, and I probably would've fallen if Vincent hadn't materialized behind me, keeping me upright.

"I thought I had no one," Mason whispers against my neck, and I feel something wet touch my skin.

Tears, I realize blankly.

"Oh, Mason…" I smooth my hand down his back as his entire body seems to tremble with some strong emotion. I don't know what words I can say to comfort him, but I do know that words are pointless when someone you love is in pain. "Tell me what to do to make this better."

"I don't know if I can be around her." Mason pulls back slightly to meet my eyes, his own glazed with unshed tears. "And I *know* it's not her fault. I know my fucked up father…" He swallows, a muscle in his jaw ticking and commandeering my attention. "But it's just…a lot."

"Do you want a relationship with your mother, Mason?" I ask bluntly. When his face drains of color, I add, "You don't have to decide now, but the ball is in your court. If you want a relationship with her, you need to speak up. But you can wait. We have time."

A wry grin pulls up Mason's lips as he settles his hands on my waist. "Look at you using sport metaphors. You know that turns me on, baby girl," he purrs, a flash of his signature humor returning to his despondent gaze.

"Everything turns you on," I retort, but secretly, I'm happy to have him smiling again.

"That's true," Vincent responds drolly, and Tai and I both turn to stare at him.

"How do you know what turns Mason on?" I query, quirking an eyebrow. "Is there something I need to know about?"

I'm totally teasing, but it's fun watching the aloof Vincent squirm.

"He wrote about it in his diary," Vincent states without pause, his expression entirely impassive.

"Hey! Why ya reading Betty?" Mason demands, aghast.

"You named your diary Betty?" I raise an eyebrow, and he shrugs sheepishly.

"What else am I supposed to name that nasty girl?"

Tai clears his throat, drawing all of our attention

to him. He stands slightly behind Mason, his arms hanging by his sides as if he doesn't quite know what to do with them.

"I guess this means that we're…you know…" He gestures helplessly between the two of them, and Mason reluctantly releases me to face him fully.

"Brothers?" He arches a blond brow as he gives Tai a cursory once-over. "I don't see it."

"Oh come on!" I move to stand on the other side of Mason and glance between the two of them. "You guys have the exact same faces!"

Tai stares at me hard. "How long have you known?"

"I didn't. Not for sure. I mean, I suspected…"

"Brothers." Mason whistles softly, running a hand through his blond hair. "Wow. Don't go thinking I'm gonna, like, braid your hair or something."

Tai's eyes warm marginally, and a fierce sense of love and awe shoots through me. These men…

They're my family.

And now, they're each other's as well.

Tai and Mason need each other. Vincent, too. They might not realize it yet, but the bonds between the three of them are just as important as the one they share with me.

"I'm sorry for all the perverted things I said to

you before I realized we were, you know, related," Mason deadpans.

Tai smirks. "You said most of those perverted things to Vincent."

"What can I say? There's something about a man in a suit that just gets to me." Mason sighs wistfully, and Vincent reaches over me to whack Mason over the head. "Ow! Rude!"

"You're not my brother." Vincent shrugs once, but his lips twitch in the beginning stages of a smile. "There's nothing stopping me from shooting you between the eyes."

"Why, Vincent!" Mason gasps in mock horror. "How dare you? I thought we shared something special! Especially when you rubbed your boner against my ass—ow!" He glares at Vincent and rubs at the back of his head where Vincent hit him a second time.

Tai shoves his hand into his jeans and rocks backward on his heels once more. "Just because we're brothers, don't go thinking you can, like, steal my underwear or some shit."

Conversation stills. All three of us stare at Tai in disbelief. Then, as one, we break into raucous laughter.

"Steal your underwear?" Mason roars, wiping

tears from his eyes. "Is that what you think brothers do?"

"What the fuck is wrong with you?" Vincent laughs.

Tai's cheeks turn crimson. "I hate you all."

"No, you don't." I sashay forward until I can rest my hands on his broad shoulders. "You loooove us," I say in a singsong voice.

He nips at my nose. "I love *you*," he counters immediately before glaring at the others. "I tolerate them."

"Hey!" Mason waves his hand in the air with a shit-eating grin on his face. "I'm your brother. You're sorta defaulted to love me."

"And I'm your brother by mating," Vincent interjects, scowling.

"Awww, Vincent, are you getting jealous you don't have a brother?" I remove my hands from Tai's shoulders to step in front of Vincent. When he continues to scowl, I press up onto my tiptoes to kiss the underside of his jaw. "I looove you," I sing.

His hands dig into my waist, his fingernails no doubt leaving crescent-moon indents. For a man who shoots people for a living, I'm honestly surprised that he has time to get manicures.

"Say that again," he breathes, and I smile broadly.

"I love you." Twisting to stare over my shoulder at the other men present, I say, "I wanted to tell you all individually, but…" I shrug sheepishly. "I love you all. So, so much. And…I guess you technically can say that we're all engaged. Is it even possible to be engaged to more than one man? I suppose we can move to a country that—"

Vincent's lips are on mine less than a millisecond later as he pushes me back against the bed.

"Oh, are we doing this?" I tease, running a finger down my cleavage. I practically salivate at the sight of all three of my men surrounding me. My loves. My mates.

Who would've thought that ninety days ago, my biggest enemies would become the three best things in my life? That together, we would stop a war and work as one to bring about peace?

"I call dibs on the vagina!" Mason calls eagerly, already shrugging out of his suit coat. Before he pulls his pants down completely, he turns to glare at Tai. "Don't look!"

"Why the fuck would I look?" my giant of a mate grumbles before moving to claim a chair near the edge of the bed. He sprawls out on it, his movements decidedly lackadaisical, and begins unbuttoning his shirt.

"Back," Vincent growls, gripping my legs and pulling me toward the edge of the bed.

"What if I want both?" Mason taunts.

"You can't have both. That's not the way it works," Vincent retorts, shrugging out of his shirt.

"I have a cock and fingers. I can have both ends if I want to."

"No."

As the two bicker, Tai slowly stands from the chair, grabs my hips, and drags me toward him.

I laugh wildly, feeling more free than I ever remember being in my life.

I have an incredible, ride-or-die best friend.

A brother.

A grandma, and potentially other relatives.

Friends. Family.

And my mates.

I've been torn to bits and ripped to shreds, but with them in my life, I somehow emerged whole.

AFTERWORD

AHHHH!!!! Can you believe it's over? I can't! It's so hard to say goodbye to characters, and Blair and her mates are no exception. But have no fear! I plan to revisit these characters and this world.

You didn't really believe this was the end, did you?

That's right! Valentina will be back with her own story and mates. She has grown to become a character I love desperately, and I feel as if she deserves a happily ever after. Blair, Vincent, Mason, and Tai will of course make appearances in her story.

Join my group Katie's Gang for updates on *Vicious Wolves*, coming hopefully in 2022!

But for now…

Scream with me. Because I've just completed another series! Woot! Woot!

ACKNOWLEDGMENTS

First, I would like to say thank you to Mila Young and C.R. Jane for putting this shared world together. You ladies rock! I would also like to give a shout-out to all of the other authors in the Kingdom of Wolves world. I've loved working with each and every one of you, and I admire your books so much!

Secondly, I would like to thank my incredible alphas. Ash, Ellen, and Kelly…you ladies are my life-savers. Thank you for your feedback and encouraging words. I doubt this book would be where it is today without your input.

And finally, I would like to thank my family! I can't even express how much I appreciate all of your support. Thank you for encouraging me from the very beginning. Love you.

ABOUT THE AUTHOR

Katie May is a reverse harem author, a KDP All-Star winner, and an USA Today Bestselling Author. She lives in West Michigan with her family, cat, and adorable puppy. When not writing, she can be found reading a good book, listening to broadway musicals, or playing games. Join Katie's Gang to stay updated on all her releases! And did you know she has a TikTok? Yeah, me neither. Follow her here! But be warned…she's an awkward noodle.

Together We Fall (Apocalyptic Reverse Harem, COMPLETED)

1. The Darkness We Crave

2. The Light We Seek

3. The Storm We Face

4. The Monsters We Hunt

Beyond the Shadows (Horror Reverse Harem, COMPLETED)

1. Gangs and Ghosts

2. Guns and Graveyards

3. Gallows and Ghouls

Paranormal Prison (Prison Reverse Harem, COMPLETED)

1. Blindly Indicted

2. Blindly Acquitted

The Damning (Fantasy Paranormal Reverse Harem)

1. Greed

Kingdom of Wolves (Shifter Reverse Harem Duet)

1. Torn to Bits

2. Ripped to Shreds

CO-WRITES

Afterworld Academy with Loxley Savage (Academy Fantasy Reverse Harem, COMPLETED)

1. Dearly Departed

2. Darkness Deceives

3. Defying Destiny

Darkest Flames with Ann Denton (Paranormal Reverse Harem, COMPLETED)

1. Demon Kissed

1.5. Demon Stalked

2. Demon Loved

3. Demon Sworn

STAND-ALONES

Toxicity (Contemporary Reverse Harem)

Not All Heroes Wear Capes (Just Dresses) (Short Comedic Reverse Harem)

Charming Devils (Bully/Revenge Reverse Harem)

Goddess of Pain (Fantasy Reverse Harem)

Demon's Joy (Holiday Reverse Harem)

9 798890 640123